Kate's Crucible
A Bleeding Kansas Novel
Elmer Fuller

Allegiance
Press

Published by Allegiance Press LLC, Overland Park, KS 66223

This is a work of fiction. Names, characters, places, business establishments, events, locales, and incidents either are the product of the author's imagination or are used fictitiously.

This book quotes a newspaper from 1855 containing a racial slur. The quotation displays the prejudices of the time but does not reflect the author's opinion.

Scripture quotations are from the King James Version.

Cover design by Diane Turpin Designs

ISBN 979-8-9989324-2-7, hardcover
ISBN 979-8-9989324-1-0, paperback
ISBN 979-8-9989324-0-3, Kindle

Library of Congress Control Number: 2025910049

Contents

Don't Miss the Free Prequel!

Download a free novelette featuring the start of Kate's adventure. *Dreams in Conflict* is available as an ebook at:
https://www.elmerfuller.com/books/dreams-in-conflict/

1

April 18, 1855, Kansas Territory

The morning sun warmed Kate's back, promising a beautiful day, as she tramped near the back of a wagon creaking along the top of a long hill on the California Trail, the last of three that had split from the main group. The treeless prairie rolled before her like gentle waves in a green ocean, and the wind hissed through the grass and rustled her dark blue skirt.

Had it only been a year since the argument with Mother? Kate smiled at the memory of the day her mother had announced a plan to send her to Boston. She had objected before sensing the opportunity set before her. Though she had attended parties to placate Mother, the move to Boston allowed Kate to pursue her dream of fighting slavery rather than Mother's dream of marrying her off to the son of a prominent family.

She would arrive in the new town of Topeka tonight or tomorrow. Their first teacher. Would the children like her as much as the two she'd tutored in Boston? She drew a deep breath and savored the earthy scent of the prairie.

"A beautiful morning."

"It certainly is." Hattie Lee strolled beside her, a short woman in a tan cotton dress and a light blue bonnet.

Kate had never asked, but Hattie could only be a year or two older, perhaps twenty? They'd met at the New England Emigrant Aid Company office in Boston when Kate joined the group. Hattie and her husband, G.W., had agreed to transport Kate's trunks for a modest fee.

G.W. tramped next to his oxen, a taciturn, broad-shouldered man in a wide-brimmed hat. Ahead of him, G.W.'s brother, Allen, drove the middle wagon, and William Goodnow plodded beside the first one in the line.

"I suppose the wind will soon rise and buffet us." It had blown a constant gale after they'd left Kansas City two days ago.

"At least it's a warm breeze," said Hattie. "This land is so different than New England."

The cloth ribbons of Kate's white bonnet fluttered, the long sides protruding past her nose like blinders on a horse. She left the cap untied to enjoy the morning air against her cheeks. A line of trees wearing the bright foliage of spring snaked through the valley on her left and traced the course of the Wakarusa River, broken in spots where timber had been felled. Distant shacks squatted in the valley like a handful of pebbles scattered by a strong arm.

Kate gestured at the valley. "I wonder how many of those settlers support a free state?"

"I think many in this area do, though I heard pro-slavery men fill a town behind us on the other side of Lawrence."

"I still find it hard to believe they stole the election less than a month ago."

Hattie shrugged. "The free-state settlers should have known they would. The Missourians did the same thing last fall and elected a pro-slavery man to Congress—so says G.W. This time they crossed the border and elected a pro-slavery legislature. Most of those elected live in Missouri."

An outrage. How could any decent man stoop so low? Kate shouldn't be surprised—no decency dwelt in pro-slavery men. Anyone who would enslave another would also cheat to preserve his power. Overcoming such evil would require women like her.

She lifted her head. "If women had been allowed to vote, it would have changed the outcome."

"I doubt it. Not many women live in the territory. I heard a thousand Missouri men came to Lawrence alone to vote. A thousand. I'm glad G.W. decided to stake a claim near the Big Blue River—farther from the border and the ruffians." Hattie shook her head as if to clear her thoughts. "Enough about politics. We should enjoy this lovely morning."

Although a talkative woman, Hattie hated conflict. She had avoided discussions of politics, suffrage, and abolition during the journey from Boston. But what else could Kate do to pass the time on the train and steamboat, play cards or drink?

Despite Hattie's lack of interest in social reform, she was a pleasant friend. Kate touched Hattie's shoulder. "I'm so happy you allowed me to travel with you. I'm indebted to you and G.W."

Her new friend blushed. "Nonsense. I'm glad we could do it. I would have been lonely after everyone else split off from the group and headed to the Osage country—just me, three men, and three wagons. I wish you would start a school near us rather than in Topeka. I'll miss you."

"I would enjoy living near you, however, the aid company agreed to pay me to teach at Topeka. I'll miss you as well."

"Your family must be proud of you, coming all this way to help the free-state cause."

Family was Hattie's favorite topic. She loved to talk about her siblings and hopes for children with G.W.

"Perhaps." Kate forced a smile. If Hattie only knew. Mother would have thundered disapproval had she heard the plan to emigrate. Father would have echoed her outrage.

The argument with Aunt Amelia had been intense enough. "Too sudden," she had said. "How can you traipse off into the wilderness on a whim?" But when her aunt realized Kate had informed her parents of her imminent departure by a letter, instead of in person, Amelia had scolded and railed. In all the months Kate had lived with her aunt, she had never displayed such anger. At least Kate had informed Mother and Father of her plan. A letter was the only way to avoid their interference.

"We might arrive at the ferry by nightfall. Are you excited?" Hattie's face brightened like a child's on Christmas morning.

"Yes. I look forward to the end of travel, even if I must sleep in a tent."

A gust lifted the bonnet from Kate's head and blew it past the wagon into knee-high grass beyond the trail. She should have tied it sooner. She gathered her blue skirt and ran to grab the headpiece. The wind whipped past her, and the bonnet opened like a full sail, skimming over the grass until it caught against rocks in a bare patch several yards away.

She ran forward and stopped near the headpiece, now marred with dust. A faint buzz sounded from the rocks. Strange. Did grasshoppers arrive this early in Kansas?

The wind stirred and threatened to lift the bonnet again. She bent to snatch it, and a long brown shape shot from the rocks toward her. Pain lanced the edge of her hand, as sharp as the stab of a hatpin. She jumped back and thrust her arm away. A snake dropped from her hand and coiled itself. She screamed.

Her heart raced as she twisted toward the wagon and stumbled over her skirt. She grabbed the fabric in her left hand and ran toward Hattie, her right hand thrust in front of her.

Hattie caught her, her eyebrows puckered. "What is it? What happened?"

"A ... a snake ... bit me." Blood oozed from two wounds between Kate's wrist and little finger. She shivered.

Hattie gasped, clutched Kate's hand, and stared at the bloody spots. "What kind of snake? Was it a rattlesnake? Tell me it was a black snake or bull snake."

"I thought ... I heard ... a grasshopper." She panted for breath as nausea flooded her stomach. She should have tied her bonnet. She should have recognized the snake's rattle.

"A snake bit Kate!"

At Hattie's yell, G.W. and the two men driving the other wagons ran toward them, G.W. carrying a shovel.

"I should have ..." Kate swayed, and her vision narrowed.

Hattie slipped an arm around her. "Help me get her back to our wagon."

Kate leaned against Hattie, and they shuffled toward the trail.

Allen, driver of the middle wagon, supported her injured arm with a firm grip at the elbow. His clean-shaven face stared at her. "Does it hurt?"

Strange. The pain had ceased. "No, it feels numb."

She tried to wiggle her fingers, but swelling stiffened them. Allen and Hattie exchanged a solemn glance.

They eased her to the ground near the back of the Lee's wagon. Hattie sat beside her, an arm across her shoulders.

G.W. ran up and tossed her bonnet into her lap. "It was a rattlesnake. I killed it."

William, a stocky man with a dark beard, planted his hands on his hips. "Too bad Dr. Hunting led the other group to Osage. He could do the amputation."

"What?" Saliva flooded Kate's mouth, and she shook her head. Had she heard him correctly?

"Best thing for rattlesnake bites. If the poison don't kill ya, it kills the muscle, and infection sets in. People usually die one way or t'other. Best to lose a limb early before the poison spreads too far and takes ya."

Cut off her entire arm? Was the bite that serious? How could she live with another defect—so much worse than a marked face?

"Does anyone know what rattlesnake weed looks like?" Allen scanned their faces. "I heard the Indians use it to make a remedy."

Everyone shook their heads.

Sweat stung Kate's eyes. "No, not my arm." She squeezed her eyes closed. "Dear God, please help me. I don't want to die or lose my arm."

Hattie embraced her as tears streamed down Kate's cheeks.

G.W. knelt and faced her, his forehead wrinkled over brown eyes and beard. "We should take her back to Lawrence. The aid company agent lives on this side of town atop the ridge. He's a doctor. He'll know what to do."

Kate sucked in a deep breath. "Dr. Robinson?"

G.W. nodded.

"I know him. Take me there." He would know how to spare her arm.

William shook his head. "The poison'll spread while we take her."

"I read you should tie off the limb and drain the poison." G.W. tossed the shovel aside. "I'll do that and take her back to Dr. Robinson. Does anyone have a cupping glass?"

No one did. Kate's stomach twisted a moment before she lurched to the side and vomited onto G.W.'s brown boots. The back of her throat burned, and a vile taste filled her mouth. Had the poison already spread?

G.W. drew his Bowie knife and slashed the cloth ties from her bonnet, then tied the strips together and cinched them above her elbow. She winced at the pain. At least the numbness and swelling had not reached that far, though her fingers were as tight as fat sausages, and puffiness had passed her wrist.

He gripped her hand and placed the tip of his knife on one puncture wound. She clenched her teeth and held her breath as he sliced two slits to the edge of her hand, one from each wound. He squeezed and milked blood from the gashes. A stream spattered her dress before Hattie wrapped a handkerchief across her swollen palm.

Her strength ebbed, and she slumped backward. Hattie's face faded away.

"Kate, please wake up." A voice drifted through the darkness.

Mother?

"Don't do this to me."

No, not Mother. Hattie.

She struggled to open her eyes. Sunlight glared against her squint. Her head lay in the crook of Hattie's arm. Vague impressions, not quite thoughts, resisted her concentration—as if an overstuffed pillow crammed the inside of her head.

"Oh, thank God you're awake." Her friend's tear-streaked face hovered above her.

Kate rolled a dry tongue against her teeth. A rancid taste filled her mouth. She shook her head as her memory cleared. A snake had bitten her. A deadly rattler.

"I must have fainted."

"Yes, you fainted. Nothing more." Hattie chewed her lower lip. Did her friend believe she fainted or that the poison caused her to fall? Had the venom reached her mind?

"William, help me with the plow." G.W.'s voice sounded like a headmaster ordering students to class. Grunts and scrapes followed.

Kate lifted her head and winced against a surge of lightheadedness. The men lowered a plow from the wagon and dropped it beside four wooden crates. "What's happening?"

"They're unloading the wagon." Hattie's smile failed to reach her eyes. "G.W. and I will take you to Lawrence."

William and Allen lowered a barrel to the ground and rolled it next to the plow.

"That's right. I remember." She licked her lips. "Hattie, what about your things? You can't leave them here."

"William and Allen will wait with our goods until we return."

Kate's stomach lurched, and she rolled away from her friend as strong heaves wracked her body. When they stopped, she flopped onto her back and trembled. "I'm cold."

"Be sure you leave a blanket out to cover her." Hattie's call brought a grunt from G.W.

He climbed out of the wagon and marched to Hattie, who scrambled to her feet. "Sorry, Kate, we need to hurry." G.W. bent and scooped her off the ground.

Her vision spun, so she rested her head against his scratchy wool shirt and cradled her right hand against her chest.

Allen stood next to the plow and barrel. "I hope the doctor makes you feel better soon."

William stood beside him, his lips tight and his hat held in front of him like he mourned at a graveside.

Hattie scrambled into the wagon, and G.W. lowered Kate onto the edge of the tailgate. "Can you make it from here?"

"Yes." Kate used her uninjured hand to crawl onto a pallet of blankets and collapsed, her head on a feather pillow. Nausea twisted her stomach.

G.W. shut the tailgate as Hattie spread a blanket over her and sat. "You rest now."

The wagon lurched forward. Kate's stomach tightened, but had nothing more to spill on the blankets. The wagon creaked, and its canvas cover swayed above her. G.W. hollered, and the wagon pitched, rattled, and bounced over the trail.

"Might be rough, but trotting the oxen will get us to Dr. Robinson's sooner. You rest easy." Hattie gazed out the back of the wagon. "I wish your family were here."

Kate closed her eyes. If Mother were here, what would she say? Would she shake her head and pronounce her daughter a fool to emigrate?

Kate panted for breath as if she ran with the oxen. How could she think such a hurtful thing about Mother? Tears flooded her eyes. "I wish they were here too. Hattie, I'm glad you're with me."

How could she have been so heartless? She'd left for Kansas without saying goodbye, without hugging Mother or Father. Instead, she'd written a letter to avoid their disapproval and interference in her plan. How unworthy of their devotion to her, their only child. What must they think?

Aunt Amelia had been right. Her parents deserved more respect. As did Amelia, who had never asked for compensation while providing a home in Boston, even though Kate had lived with her for several months. Amelia had accompanied her to parties and supported her dream of working for abolition. They'd even stood together to protest the return of Anthony Burns to slavery. Why had she ignored Amelia's advice? How could she ever repay her kindness?

A cold sweat stung her eyes, and she shivered despite the blanket. Would she ever see her family again? Had she failed in her dream to teach school and attract families to Kansas?

What about the Forbes family? The experience of tutoring their children, Richard and Phoebe, had given her the confidence to teach in Kansas. Their parents, staunch abolitionists, had funded much of the expense when she'd revealed her thoughts about emigration to Kansas. She had set out to strike a blow against slavery—her dream to improve society—but after three days in the territory, she lay dying of snakebite. She had failed the Forbes family. Her parents. Amelia.

Grandpa Williams' white-bearded face hovered in her mind. How disappointed he must be, looking down from heaven at his only grandchild. How foolish she had been. She should have tied her bonnet. Should have recognized the sound of a rattlesnake. Should have stayed in Boston.

But if she had, what would she have said to Arthur? She enjoyed their long discussions of books, his brown eyes focused on her. He had also escorted her to a lecture on abolition. Was that only three months ago? But her friendship with Arthur had progressed far enough. She needed to focus on her goals instead of the pleasure of his company. What would he say about her failure? Why did she care?

The wagon swayed and jostled her. How long before they reached the doctor's home? She drew quick breaths, but they seemed empty of air. She panted a prayer.

"Stay with me, Kate." Hattie's cool hand stroked the side of her face.

2

Five months earlier, Boston

Arthur Eliot faced the Forbes' parlor fireplace, where gingerbread stars and red ribbon bows decorated the mantel. Flames crackled and cast flickers of light that mingled with the glow of lamps. A murmur of conversation rose from the men, women, and children filling the room—a colorful collection of evening gowns and dark suits. He stood in the corner farthest from the entry and closest to the refreshments in the adjoining dining room. A man and woman standing by the table laughed at his dark-haired friend's comment. Frederic always teased and joked at parties. Unlike Arthur, gatherings filled his friend with energy.

Frederic nodded and stepped around the couple, carrying two porcelain cups. His dark coat fit perfectly over a red plaid vest. A smile lit his smooth cheeks as he handed a cup to Arthur. "I am eternally grateful you traded your duties on the ward and joined me tonight. The Forbes host a wonderful fete."

"Yes, they do, though I was content to curl up with a good novel by a warm fire."

"Nonsense." Frederic slapped Arthur's shoulder. "You need to expand your social life. A year has passed since Dahlia."

Arthur drew a deep breath. "Yes. A long year." His sense of loss had eased. Had her hold on his heart crumbled? Did he want it to crumble?

"A break in your routine will serve you well." Frederic turned toward the entry doorway. "I wonder which young lady will grace us tonight with her presence."

Arthur sipped a rich, creamy eggnog, though spiced too strongly for his taste. Frederic also lifted his cup, eyes scanning the entry hall. Why had his friend not married or at least announced an engagement? Most women admired his handsome appearance and delighted in his wit. He claimed studies occupied his attention, but the man never missed the chance to enjoy the flirtatious attention of any pretty woman.

"Do you see Miss Putnam?" Frederic nodded at a buxom blonde in a pink gown, talking to two young men near the door to the hall. Three strands of pearls circled her neck.

"She is hard to miss." The gazes of many men turned toward her laugh. With such a blemish-free face, a bright smile, and a neckline scooped well below her shoulders, every man appreciated her presence. Jealousy must also strike every woman.

"You should go and speak to her." Frederic nudged him with an elbow.

"I have spoken to her before."

"Don't you want to reacquaint yourself?"

"No, I find her boring. Perhaps you should entertain her."

"I may do so before the evening ends. However, I can't believe you find a woman so beautiful a bore."

"She does not share my interests."

Lucinda Putnam obsessed over the social hierarchy of Boston society. She gossiped about other prominent families—what furniture they owned, the gowns and styles women wore, rumors of courtship and unfaithfulness. Though educated well, she wasted the instruction. She only used it to opine about her peers with perfect grammar and a large vocabulary. She was nothing like Dahlia.

Miss Putnam and her two admirers crossed the room to a vacant chair. With elegant grace, she sat and draped her gown about her feet.

"Ah, more arrivals."

Frederic lifted his cup as if toasting the two women who had entered the hall. They shrugged out of their winter coats, removed their hats, and handed them to the maid. The Forbes' son and daughter scampered to one, and each clasped a hand.

Frederic drew a deep breath. "I have seen these women before. The one has a very memorable face, though unpleasant."

Arthur snorted a soft breath. Frederic often expressed impolite judgments, but his charm almost always smoothed them aside. At least the women stood far enough away that they missed his comment.

"Yes, I have met them as well."

"I know the older one, Miss Amelia Williams. They are not sisters, though they look very much alike—except for the birthmark on the younger one."

Both women stood a head taller than the maid, each with brown hair gathered behind her neck. Amelia's dark green gown sported long, flaring sleeves.

Frederic turned and studied Arthur's face. "You talked to the younger woman last summer after I dragged you to her aunt's party, didn't you?"

"Yes, Kate Collins is her name."

He had discussed *Uncle Tom's Cabin* with her. She possessed an enthusiasm for the book much like his. Much like Dahlia's. But the discussion on women's suffrage had raised memories of his loss, and he had bolted away from her like a rude child.

Mrs. Forbes approached the two women and chatted with both before guiding her children away from Kate. Amelia scanned the parlor, and her gaze met his. She took Kate's hand and moved toward him. His throat tightened. Would a conversation with Kate again stir memories of Dahlia?

"A pleasure to see you again, Miss Williams." Frederic bowed.

Arthur echoed a polite greeting.

Amelia smiled at Frederic. "Mr. Coffin, a few months have passed since we spoke. How wonderful to see you and your friend. Mr. Eliot, correct?"

Of course, she knew his name. They had met several times, though none since the summer. Did she mention his name to remind Kate?

"I hope you both remember my niece, Miss Kate Collins." Amelia pulled the younger woman forward a step. Her dark blue skirt rustled against her aunt's.

"Of course," Frederic said, "how could I forget? May I bring you some eggnog?"

"How kind of you." Amelia smiled widely and Kate nodded, lips tight, as Frederic excused himself and joined the people near the punch bowl.

A white lace panel draped across the fabric of Kate's dress from shoulder to shoulder, forming a scooped neckline, though more modest than Lucinda Putnam's.

Amelia broke the silence. "Mr. Eliot, you have not attended many parties in the last few months, at least in my circle of friends."

"No, I have avoided them." Arthur shrugged his shoulder. "My studies make it difficult."

"I thought you had completed college," she said.

"I did, but decided to study medicine. I joined Dr. Jackson as an apprentice in the summer and started my first course of lectures at Harvard College last month."

"A noble profession." She nodded in salute.

"Miss Collins." Arthur nodded at Kate. "I note the Forbes children greeted you with enthusiasm."

"Yes, I teach them five days each week." Kate flashed a polite smile.

Judging by the children's welcome, Kate had won their hearts. She must be an excellent tutor.

"I recall your love of literature," Arthur said. "I hope you share it with them as well."

Her smile widened, and she nodded. "Thank you. The work allows me to remain in Boston and support abolition."

"Ladies." Frederic stepped into their circle and offered cups of eggnog to each woman, who murmured a thank you.

As they sipped, Frederic's gaze drifted to Kate's upper lip. The red and purple mark resembled a bruise, except that a distinct line traced a jagged outer edge. Cosmetics might cover it, but the amount needed would raise doubts about Kate's virtue.

Amelia scanned the faces in the dining room. "Oh, I see the Tuttles. I must speak with them. Gentlemen, I will take my leave. Please continue to converse with my niece." She smiled and walked away.

Kate watched her leave with a straight mouth. Did she feel abandoned?

"Did I miss any news or gossip during my journey to the punch bowl?" Frederic appeared as relaxed as if he gazed at a sunset on a summer evening.

"I informed Miss Collins about my studies to become a physician."

Frederic squared his shoulders. "Miss Collins, you stand in the presence of two men destined to become Boston's finest doctors."

"Two?" Kate's eyebrows lifted. "Both of you study medicine?"

"Yes," Frederic said. "We are almost halfway through our first course of lectures at Harvard College. We also attend to patients at the Massachusetts General Hospital—supervised, of course."

She pursed her lips into a prim smile and nodded. "Of course."

"Just a year and a half, and I will become Dr. Coffin." Frederic grinned. "A bit droll, don't you think?"

Kate chuckled. "I see you enjoy the irony."

"An astute observation, Miss Collins." Frederic bent in a dramatic bow, as always, the jovial entertainer.

She turned to Arthur. "What subjects do you study to become a physician?"

"We listen to sixteen weeks of lectures, including surgery, anatomy, chemistry, midwifery—"

"A most extensive curriculum." Her eyebrows raised.

"Yes. Next year we repeat the lectures."

Frederic nodded. "We even study the skin, including birthmarks like yours, Miss Collins."

Red flushed Kate's cheeks.

Arthur's chest tightened. "Frederic!" How could the man utter such a rude comment?

"I intend no insult." Frederic beamed a disarming smile at Kate. "It *is* one subject of our study. I have not been able to observe any until now. Have you consulted a physician about your case?"

A coldness spread through Arthur's middle. Did the man have no shame? How could he discuss a person's condition during a holiday party?

Kate licked her lips and lifted her head. "No, I have not consulted a doctor." Her fingertips touched the mark. "I did not choose this mark, but it does not hamper me. Are you a 'Dr. Almyr' seeking to bestow perfection on your patients?"

"I beg your pardon." The lines on Frederic's brow gathered tighter than a wicker basket.

Arthur snorted and covered his mouth. Kate's literary reference puzzled his friend. She exhibited great composure in the face of his impolite comments. Dahlia had displayed the same confidence.

"I assure you, I am no Georgianna." Kate lifted her chin and stared at his obtuse friend.

Frederic tipped his head to the side. "You have me at a loss."

"She speaks of one of Hawthorne's characters." Arthur turned to Kate. "Did you read the story in a magazine or *Mosses from an Old Manse*?"

"I read the book."

"Oh." Frederic smiled like he indulged a child. "Are you as devoted to reading as Arthur?"

"I don't know." She lifted her chin and studied Arthur's face. "How devoted is he?"

"He raves about Poe, Hawthorne, and others. He rushes to buy books as soon as they are published." Frederic shook his head as if such behavior revealed an addled mind. His friend never understood a passion for reading, preferring conversation with people to "staring at stale pages in a lonely room."

"I see." A spark lit her eyes, and her lips twitched with the birth of a smile. "You highlight the differences between each of you well. Arthur chooses to stay informed and exercise his mental capacities, but you ..." Her eyebrows arched in an unspoken question.

"Touché." Frederic raised his cup in salute. "Please excuse me. I must see if any other young ladies desire eggnog." He turned and walked toward Lucinda Putnam.

"I admire your response to my friend's impertinence." Arthur smiled. "He enjoys stirring the fire of conversation ... and a good verbal joust."

"Do you?"

"No, I would rather discuss literature. I agree with you. You are no Georgianna."

"Are you sure? I have a birthmark, though not the same as hers. Hers was smaller. Mine also thickens my lip."

"A slight effect. It does not restrict your speech ... or your smile." Why had he said that?

"Tell me, why do you think Almyr obsessed over Georgianna's birthmark?" A bemused smile lit her face. Why did that please him?

They discussed Hawthorne's story—possible reasons for Aylmer's obsession, Georgianna's compliance with his poisonous treatment, and the contrast between Aylmer's attitude toward the birthmark and his assistant's. They had moved from a deep discussion of what the birthmark symbolized to recounting the various books each owned when Kate's aunt returned. Where had the evening gone?

The women walked to the entry hall and donned their coats. Kate smiled across the room at him before they turned to the door. Warmth filled Arthur even though he stood far from the flickering fireplace or a floor vent. What a delightful conversation. Such a remarkable woman, confident and well-read.

Kate differed from Dahlia in appearance, but she was just as fascinating. He sighed. The first time he'd met Kate, his memories of Dahlia had been too fresh. Tonight, Kate's conversation had absorbed his attention without stirring pain. Had enough time passed since Dahlia's death more than a year ago? Perhaps time did heal grief. Should he call on Kate?

3

Kate sat in a chair pulled next to the front window of Amelia's library reading a book, the pages angled to catch the afternoon sunlight. She finished the chapter, closed the book, and held it to her chin, inhaling the scent of paper and ink, but she missed the earthy smell of leather. The newer, cloth-wrapped binding did not satisfy her in the same way.

Amelia sat on the library settee in the middle of the room with her head bowed over a book. Yesterday's newspaper lay folded beside her. Book spines of muted green, brown, and blue lined each shelf of the oak bookcase covering one wall of the library—poetry, biographies, and works on various scientific subjects. The shelves also held many novels, all of which Kate had read.

How wonderful that Boston had opened a free library, allowing her to borrow a new novel, *Villette*. She closed her eyes and imagined the scene of the opening chapter she had just finished. How would Lucy respond to Polly's arrival? Would adding the child's crib in Lucy's bedroom result in a troubled relationship, or would the young girl develop a kinship with Lucy? Mrs. Bretton had bowed to Polly's whims. What—

Three deep *thunks* sounded from the knocker on the house's front door.

"I wonder who seeks to visit on a cold Sunday afternoon?" Amelia inserted a bookmark into her novel and laid it on the newspapers. She stood, straightened her shirtwaist, and walked to the entry hall. Kate rose from her chair and edged toward the center of the library as Amelia swung the front door open.

"Greetings," said a male voice. One Kate should recognize, but didn't.

"Good afternoon. Please come in, Mr. Eliot."

Arthur Eliot? A cold draft brushed Kate's face. What brought him to visit on such a blustery afternoon?

Amelia ushered Arthur through the door and relieved him of his top hat and coat, hanging them on the coat tree. "Do you wish to speak to me"—she gestured at the library—"Kate, or both of us?" Her eyes sparkled like a child eyeing Christmas candy.

"Uh ... both of you." He wrapped the fingers of one hand around the opposite fist, thumbs twitching against each other. "If it is convenient, of course."

"Please, have a seat." Amelia ushered him into the parlor and glanced over her shoulder. "Kate, do join us." She flashed a grin.

Kate had enjoyed a pleasant conversation about literature with him two nights ago. He had spoken to her at length, unlike the first time they'd met when he'd bolted away when she discussed women's rights and suffrage. But nothing he had said in their recent meeting hinted at a visit. Though they spoke of their collection of books, he offered no promises to lend her any.

Arthur sat in the chair on the far side of the room. She settled onto the Victorian sofa, selecting the place farthest from him. Amelia pursed her lips and cast a disapproving glance before she sat closer to Arthur, no doubt thinking Kate should have sat closer to their guest.

"I am surprised you chose such a cold day to visit." Amelia directed a polite smile toward him.

"The wind is quite frosty, but I had the afternoon free from duties at the hospital." His gaze darted from Amelia to Kate and back. "I hope I do not intrude."

"Of course not," Amelia said. "We were each enjoying a good book. Your visit brings a welcome diversion."

"May I ask what tale has captured your interest?" Arthur gestured at Kate's lap.

She realized her book rested there but had no memory of carrying it from the library. "Oh ... yes ... this is *Villette* by Currer Bell."

"An excellent book. I believe it better than *Jane Eyre*." Arthur's smile twitched at the corners.

Why did he seem nervous? "I've just started reading it, though I enjoyed *Jane Eyre*."

Arthur leaned forward. "Did you know Charlotte Brontë wrote both books?"

"*Villette* and *Jane Eyre*?"

"Yes. Currer Bell is her pseudonym."

"It is? How do you know—"

"Mr. Eliot." Amelia tilted her head. "What is the purpose of your visit? Did you come to discuss literature?"

Arthur cleared his throat. "No. Literature is a passion of mine but not my purpose here." He clasped his hands and rested them on his knee but immediately stopped and smoothed the top of his trousers, which were already free of wrinkles. He *was* nervous. "Please do not consider me impolite, but may I inquire whether anyone is calling on Miss Collins?"

Kate sucked a breath through open lips. Why would he ask such a thing? While not rude, the question bordered on impertinence. Amelia gazed at her, lips fighting a smile.

"I beg your pardon." He coughed into his fist. "I intended to ask if anyone has accepted an invitation to call on Miss Collins."

Amelia lifted her chin. "No one has accepted an invitation at this time."

Of course, no one had accepted an invitation. They were not offered in a willy-nilly fashion. Invitations were extended to suitable men who showed interest. No one had ever shown the least bit of interest in her. One look at her lip and any flirtatious light left their eyes.

A knot formed in Kate's stomach. A man would only ask such a question if he were interested in courting the woman or asking for a friend. Was he interested in her, or was Frederic?

"Such an invitation would honor any man." Arthur squared his shoulders. "Your niece is a confident, intelligent woman."

Warmth crept across her cheeks. She sat frozen in place like a child's snowman, sipping shallow breaths between her lips.

"I agree with the esteem you express for her." Amelia pressed her lips together, but the corners of her mouth curved upward.

"Will Miss Collins' parents visit soon? I would like very much to meet them."

He *was* interested. Why else would he seek to meet her parents? Her knuckles whitened as her grip on the book tightened.

"I'm afraid they will not visit anytime soon," Amelia said. "We plan to travel to their home in Belchertown in time for—"

"But it is a family affair." Kate's voice sounded rough, a croak. "We … uh … you should wait until they visit Boston."

Amelia's eyes rounded.

Arthur leaned forward and wetted his lips. "When will they arrive?"

Kate swallowed through a thick throat. "Nothing is planned at this time. We might discuss it during our Christmas visit."

"Kate, I think your mother and father would be quite impressed with Mr. Eliot. Do you agree?" Amelia lifted her eyebrows.

Ecstasy would fill Mother if that were possible. Arthur was the exact sort of young man Mother dreamed would marry her daughter—the son of a prominent and wealthy family. Was Mother's dream becoming a reality?

The book trembled in Kate's grip, and she forced her hands to relax. Marriage was not her plan, even though Arthur was polite and attractive. His attention flattered her, but they held incompatible views of suffrage and women's rights. Would he allow her to pursue a college degree? Would he support social reform?

Arthur shifted in his chair, his gaze an unspoken question.

Amelia leaned over and placed a hand atop Kate's. "What are you thinking? Would your mother and father approve?"

"Mother would be ... quite pleased to meet Mr. Eliot ... as would Father."

Amelia patted Kate's hand and turned back to Arthur. "Mr. Eliot, when Kate came to live with me, my sister and I discussed the possibility of extending invitations to young men to call on her. She entrusted this task to me."

"She did?" Arthur's eyes widened.

"I am happy to offer you an invitation to call on my niece."

A smile spread on Arthur's face, and he exhaled. "I accept your gracious invitation." His gaze turned to Kate. "I will call on you after the first of the year. I hope you enjoy your visit to your parents."

A heaviness settled onto Kate's shoulders. What could he possibly see in her? He said it would be an honor to call on her. Did he mean those words, or was he only being chivalrous?

"Kate?" Amelia lifted her eyebrows and tipped her head toward Arthur.

Heat warmed her cheeks. "Um ... oh ... thank you." She forced her lips into a smile. "I look forward to your visit."

Arthur beamed, rose, and excused himself. She managed to acknowledge him before Amelia escorted him to the door. Kate drew a deep breath and slowly released it. What had happened?

Amelia returned in haste, skirts swishing. She plopped down next to Kate. "You must write your mother forthwith."

"Now?"

"Yes. You must be excited. Share that excitement with her."

Kate shook her head. "Do I have to write her?"

"You may not be excited ... yet. But imagine the happiness your letter will bring to your mother."

"For what? He will call on me a few times and then reject me."

Amelia frowned. "Why do you say such a thing?"

"Boston must be filled with young women thrilled at the prospect of marriage to an Eliot. He will find another woman." A beautiful woman.

One who cares nothing for suffrage. One from a fine family, fashionably educated and desirous of entertaining other wealthy people.

"Perhaps. Perhaps not." Amelia waved her hands and prompted Kate to rise. "Now, go write the letter."

Kate wandered to the small desk in the library, where she sat and extracted a sheet of paper and a steel-tipped pen. Mother would be delighted by the news. Her conviction that marriage was the only path for Kate would now increase. But college and leading social reform was her future, not Mother's dream of marriage.

Kate poised the pen over the inkwell. She had to see Arthur. To live in Boston, she had agreed with Mother to entertain anyone who would court her. And Amelia had promised to introduce her to Boston society in hopes of finding a husband as she'd told Arthur. But Boston allowed Kate to pursue her plans. Besides meeting bachelors at parties, she had met many abolitionists. Her employment tutoring the Forbes' children provided funds she saved for her goal—attending the Oread Institute. She wanted a college education, but Mother wanted her to marry. Amelia seemed to desire both for her.

She dipped the pen and wrote the date. Though Arthur promised to call on her, nothing required her to encourage his pursuit. She would enjoy his attention and discussions a few times before ending the relationship. Courtship included tests of a young man's dedication. She would raise an obstacle, feign an emotional crisis, or find another test. Stating her doubts may be all she needed. He would turn to another woman. How could he not? Who would marry a woman with a face as blemished as hers?

4

April 18, Lawrence

"Hello!" G.W.'s shout roused Kate. The wagon rattled and lurched. "Anybody home?"

A voice shouted back a reply.

"Whoa."

She felt the wagon ease to a stop, and the rustle of wind against the canvas wagon cover replaced the creaks of the bumpy ride.

"We're here." Hattie rested a hand on her shoulder.

"We have a woman ... bit by a rattlesnake." G.W.'s breathless voice passed down the side of the wagon. His sweaty face appeared above the tailgate a moment before he lowered it and stepped aside.

A large man clambered aboard and stooped to fit in the narrow space. He kneeled next to Hattie and leaned over Kate. "Where did it bite you?"

"My hand." Her words croaked from her parched throat. She pulled her arm out from under the blanket and laid it across her stomach.

He inspected her bandages and laid his large hand on her brow. "I'm Doctor Robinson."

"I know."

His brow wrinkled, and he nodded. "I believe we have met."

"Yes." She licked her dry lips. "In Boston."

"Can you help her?" Hattie peered into the doctor's bearded face.

"I will try. Bring her into the house." He backed out of the wagon.

"Kate, can you get to the back by yourself?" Hattie pulled the blanket away.

"I think I can." She sat up and scooted, feet first, toward the edge. Her vision blurred, and she swayed.

Hattie caught her before she fell backward. "G.W., I think you'll need to carry her."

She steadied Kate and helped turn her body across the wagon. G.W. slipped one arm under her knees and the other across her back. He dragged her across the blankets and lifted her. Her head throbbed as she slumped in his arms.

He carried her around the wagon toward a house. Its unpainted clapboard siding rose one story, but the second story and rafters formed a skeletal structure.

A short, dark-haired woman met them. "I'm Sara Robinson, the doctor's—" Her eyes rounded. "Oh. You're Amelia Williams' niece."

She tried to smile. "Yes, Kate Collins."

"I heard you planned to come to the territory. I never imagined we would meet like this." She scrambled up the steps and held the door against the breeze. "Put her over there."

G.W. clomped across the board floor and lowered her onto a mattress. The doctor set a cane-bottom chair next to her and laid white muslin cloth, rolls of bandages, and other items on the seat. Sara placed a cup in her trembling left hand. The sip of water cooled her throat.

The doctor hurried across the room, returned, and placed a pan of water on the floor. "Miss Collins, I need to examine your hand and arm."

She nodded as Sara took the cup from her good hand. The doctor scanned her swollen forearm, pressed tight against the white fabric of her sleeve. Dried blood spotted the cuff.

Dr. Robinson slid the tip of a pair of scissors under her sleeve. He snipped the material to the elbow and pulled it away. He unwrapped the bloody handkerchief from her palm and studied the wounds.

"The swelling has spread."

Her hand appeared twice the normal size, the skin stretched tight, a muddy red color with tinges of purple. The doctor dipped a square of muslin in water and lathered it with lye soap. With a gentle touch, he washed the wounds, but she felt nothing, no pain, no sensation of temperature. Was her hand already dead? Would he need to amputate?

She dropped her head back on the mattress. Light filtered between boards laid loosely across the joists above her. Wall studs stood exposed—no lathe or plaster. The floor did not extend between the studs. Could a rattlesnake crawl into the house through the gap? Did snakes live everywhere in Kansas?

"Interesting." Dr. Robinson peered at her palm. "One fang poked through the edge of your hand. Maybe you received less venom than the usual bite."

"That's good, right?" Maybe she could keep her arm.

"Will it kill ..." Hattie swallowed. "Will she lose her arm?"

"That depends." Dr. Robinson pursed his lips and met Kate's gaze. "Rattlesnake bites are serious. People often die, but not always. If they live, they often lose large sections of necrotic flesh. We could amputate at your elbow. It will improve your chance of surviving."

"No." She shivered, and her voice trembled. "If I didn't get a full bite, maybe my arm will recover."

"It is very swollen. You also have the symptoms of a serious bite—fever, sweating, difficulty breathing. Have you experienced nausea?"

She nodded.

"This bite threatens your life." His brown eyes held her gaze.

"Please. I need my arm. Please don't amputate."

He drew a deep breath and released it. "I make no promises. My job requires I save your life. If you did receive a smaller amount of venom, it may not kill you, but infection could. If it spreads, I may have no choice."

"Can we at least try—see if I heal without amputating now?"

"I will try it your way." He untied the knot in the cloth strips around her elbow and removed it.

Kate's heart raced, and she clenched her chattering teeth. Without the binding, would her upper arm and shoulder swell? Had she made the right choice? Instead of amputating her forearm, would the poison kill her entire arm?

G.W. cleared his throat. "Will she be able to stay here?"

"Of course. She needs care," Sara said.

Dr. Robinson nodded. "It will give her the best chance of survival. I can provide prompt treatment for any infection." He started to bandage the wound with a fresh dressing.

Hattie stepped forward and knelt beside her, grabbing Kate's good hand. "I'll pray for you. We'll leave your trunks here."

"What? Are you leaving me?" She clutched Hattie's fingers.

"Yes. You won't be well enough to travel for a few days. Right, Doctor?"

He nodded. "At least."

"We can't ask Allen and William to wait that long." Hattie's eyes glistened with moisture. "We all need to get to the Big Blue River to stake our claims."

Tears flooded Kate's eyes. "I understand." She had known Hattie for less than a month but had enjoyed their time together. Losing her friend now ... Stupid. Her stupid carelessness had left her alone.

Hattie squeezed her hand and released it. "When you finally arrive at Topeka, send us a letter or message. We'll come and see you."

"I will." But would she even live long enough to travel to Topeka?

Hattie rose and walked beside G.W. to the door. She glanced back and waved before stepping into the sunshine.

Dr. Robinson finished wrapping her hand and laid it beside her. He packed the items on the chair into a black leather bag. "I will check on you later. I have another patient to see. It's a good thing your friends brought you here before I left." He smiled and strode to the door.

Sara bent and tucked the blanket tighter. Kate touched her arm. "Will you write my parents if I die?"

"Of course, I will, but you shouldn't dwell on that thought." Sara placed a wet cloth on Kate's brow. "I was surprised to hear you planned to come to the territory. After our discussion last year, I thought you wanted to stay in Boston to attend college and support abolition."

That had been her dream. Once. "My circumstances and plans changed."

"I'm glad they did. Do you like our new home?" She gestured at the unfinished walls. A buffalo robe hung across the doorway to another room.

Kate managed a weak smile. "It's quite large by the standards of other houses I've seen in the territory—or will be when finished."

"Yes. It has taken longer than expected to complete. I stayed at the Baptist mission on this side of Kansas City for several days as Charles wanted to finish it before I arrived. But the sawmill here is cantankerous and suffers from regular mechanical problems. Even worse, a pro-slavery man, Dr. Wood, led a group of men and chopped off the studs. The workmen had to start over. They should arrive later today. I hope they won't disturb you too much."

"I'm sure they won't." They could pound and saw as needed. The noise would remind her she still lived.

Sara retrieved a broom and began to sweep the floor. "You said you came to Kansas because your plans changed. Would you like to share what changed?"

Would Sara understand or question her reasons? "My employers heard about my desire to teach and provided the needed funds to emigrate." Though not the entire story, that much was true.

"How generous of them." Sara finished sweeping and lifted a bucket. "I'm going to fetch more water from the well. I'll check on you after I return."

Kate *had* dreamed of attending college, but Arthur had changed her plans. She should have objected when Amelia invited him to call on her. Why hadn't she found an excuse to dissuade him sooner? Kate closed her eyes, and darkness rushed through her mind.

5

A pounding rhythm. Muffled voices. More bangs and thumps. Dust fell onto Kate's face. She turned her head and opened her eyes. A hairy brown hide emerged through her blurry vision—the buffalo robe hanging in a doorway, the Robinson's doorway. Light and air streamed through an open window.

How long had she slept? She struggled to sit up, but dark spots danced in her vision. Her head throbbed. She groaned and slumped back onto the pillow.

"You're awake." Sara walked from the kitchen, a mug in her hand. "Would you like a drink?"

She nodded.

Sara knelt and helped raise Kate's head and shoulders. The sip of water cooled her dry mouth. She swallowed a large gulp, but her stomach twitched from the drink. She pushed the cup away.

"You need to drink more. You've run a high fever."

"Not now." She settled back onto the sheets.

"Are you hungry?"

"No. I doubt I could hold anything down. What time is it?"

"About two in the afternoon." The sound of voices drifted through the floor above. A series of raps followed. "I hope the workmen are not disturbing your rest."

She must have slept through some of the work. "No. You need to finish the house."

"Can you stand another drink of water?"

She grunted. With Sara's assistance, she sipped at the mug until it was empty. Her stomach fluttered but did nothing more. She sank back onto the pallet.

Darkness surrounded Kate. She groaned and thrashed. Hot, wet cloth encased her. She struggled against a weight and sat up. Blankets slid from her neck and piled onto her lap. Sweat drenched her face and body. Where was she?

She lifted her right arm toward her face but stopped. The limb felt like a log, numb and stiff. Oh, yes, the snakebite. She was at the Robinson's in Lawrence. A lighted lamp appeared as Sara ducked around the buffalo robe and approached.

A cold draft crossed Kate's shoulders. Her wet chemise clung to her skin. "Where's my dress?"

Sara knelt beside her. "I removed it and your corset. I thought you would rest better without them, and I wanted to soak the blood stains."

"I don't remember." How could she fail to remember someone undressing her?

"Your fever has been very high. I'm glad it has broken. You were mumbling in your delirium."

"I was?"

"Yes. I think you believed Charles was your grandfather. You called him Grandpa when he examined you this evening."

"What did I say?"

Sara smiled. "Nothing important. Let me get you some water." She rose and retrieved a mug from the kitchen table.

A dull pain filled Kate's head. "What's the time?" she asked when Sara returned. Kate grasped the mug with her good hand and lifted it to her lips.

"Early morning. You slept all afternoon and evening, though I did get you to drink more water."

Kate lifted and drained the mug.

"Do you want more?"

The water sat easily on her stomach and had cooled her throat. She nodded. Sara refilled the mug, and Kate slowly drank from it. What had she talked about during her fever? She must have thought Charles was Grandpa Williams since he was her favorite. She finished the water and handed the cup to Sara. "Thank you."

"If you need anything more, just call me."

Kate nodded and lay her head on the pillow. Sara pulled up the blankets so they rested over Kate's legs. Sara lifted the lamp, smiled, and crept back around the buffalo robe.

What had she said about Grandpa Williams? It didn't matter. She sank into dreams.

Kate fingered the gold watch chain draped from the button to the pocket in Grandpa's dark vest. Her head rested against his chest. The acrid smell of tobacco smoke seeped from his clothes. But it wasn't Kate sitting on his lap, or rather, it was her—as an eight-year-old child.

"Grandpa, why is my lip like this?" She touched the birthmark.

A smile appeared in his thick white beard, and the lines at the corners of his light gray eyes deepened. "Why do *you* think your lip is like that?" He lifted a fingertip and touched her cheek.

"Bobby says Momma craved strawberries before I was born, but she didn't eat them, so my skin got marked."

He chuckled. "Did you ask your mother about it?"

"Yes."

"What did she say?"

"She didn't want any strawberries. She said God just made me this way."

"Do you like that answer?"

She didn't, but would Grandpa be disappointed if she said so? He talked a lot about God and his goodness. She shrugged.

"You don't like your birthmark, do you?"

"No."

"You must not blame your mother. It isn't her fault." He lifted his bushy white eyebrows and patted her back. "Not your fault either."

She tugged Grandpa's watch out of the pocket and studied the timepiece. The knob clicked when she twisted it. She poked the pocket watch back through the slit in his vest. "Am I ugly?"

"Of course not." He hugged her. "Why do you ask such a thing?"

"Bobby says I'm ugly."

"Who is Bobby? Is he a boy at your new school?"

"Uh-huh. He points at me and calls me ugly."

"Your birthmark does not make you ugly. Ugly is as ugly does. Remember that." He grasped the point of her chin and wiggled it.

She ran a finger along the watch chain. "He always laughs and points. He says I'm ugly as sin. He calls me Purple Lip Katie."

"My child, Bobby is the ugly one because he calls you names. Do you understand?" His eyes peered into hers.

"How can he be ugly? He doesn't have a birthmark."

"Katie, you can't change the way you look. You can only change the way you act. Do good. Help people. Make this world a better place and you will never be ugly."

"This world?" She cocked her head. "What do you mean?"

A laugh rose from Grandpa's belly and jiggled the leg where she perched. "You will understand someday. You will never be ugly if you help people. Promise me you will always work hard to help others."

She stretched her arms across his chest and pressed her marked cheek against his vest. "I promise." The thud of his heart soothed her ear.

Shivers racked Kate's body as she opened her eyes sometime later. Sunlight lit the room, and the blankets were folded away from her right side. Dr. Robinson and Sara knelt beside her. Again. How many times had he examined her wound? How long had she been here?

The doctor removed the bandages from her hand and scowled at the wound. "I don't like the look of it." Dark skin lined the edge of each swollen cut, and pus filled their centers. He bent and sniffed the wound. "Or the smell."

Sara studied him with a grim face. "Infection, isn't it?"

"Yes."

Kate trembled. "I'm cold."

"I know." Sara smiled, though it didn't reach her eyes. "I will pull up the blankets when Charles is finished."

The doctor scrubbed a soapy cloth across her hand. She closed her eyes, and images floated through her mind.

"Purple Lip Katie," Bobby whispered, a sneer curling his lips.

A blonde, curly-haired girl of thirteen whispered to two other girls while watching Kate from the corner of her eye. They smirked at her and laughed.

"Kate."

She danced with a tall young man in a dark coat and light pants. He stared over her shoulder, enduring his obligation. Good manners required him to dance with her since her parents had hosted the event. The music ended, and he excused himself, gazing at the floor as he strode away.

"Kate."

Bobby laughed at her tears. "Purple Lip Katie." He repeated the name in a sing-song voice again and again.

"Kate." Someone shook her shoulder.

Her eyes opened.

"I need you to wake up for a moment." Dr. Robinson knelt beside her.

She licked her lips with a dry tongue. "How long have I been asleep?"

"A few days have passed since you arrived."

"What?" How could it be so long?

"I have bad news. Infection has started in the snake bite. I need to remove the dead tissue to prevent it from spreading."

Sara stood bent over the kitchen table, scrubbing with a rag. Shivers traveled up Kate's body, and her eyes closed.

"Kate, I need you to wake up." The doctor's face peered down at her, and his hand brushed her forehead.

"Yes?"

"We're going to move you to the table so I can remove the infected tissue."

A putrid odor hung in her nose. "Ampu ... amputate?"

"Yes. As much as needed."

She grimaced and rubbed her aching head with her left hand. Sara stripped off the covers, and Sara and the doctor wrapped arms around her and raised her to her feet.

"Can you walk to the table?" His face hovered in front of her.

The room spun, and she slumped. She shook her head, but her thinking remained slow and heavy as she felt herself floating.

A hard, flat surface pressed against her hips and back, and a breeze flowed across her body. Her legs shook. She squinted at her wounded hand against the brightness. She tried to wiggle her fingers but felt no pain, no sensation. Nothing moved on her fat, red hand, edged with black flesh. Her hand was dead already. He wanted to cut it off.

A sweet smell drove away her thoughts as a cloth touched her nose and mouth. The sweet odor filled her, and blackness rushed into her mind.

6

Kate clutched Sara's hand and leaned against her, legs quivering like blades of grass in a breeze. Together, they shuffled through the doorway and onto the porch. The morning sun hung above the horizon and warmed her face.

"The sky promises a beautiful day." Sara eased her in front of a ladderback wooden chair.

Kate gingerly lowered herself onto the hard seat. "Thank you."

"The breeze is cool this morning. Let me fetch a shawl." Sara disappeared into the house.

At least Kate still had her arm, which hung in a makeshift sling of blue calico. The bandaged remains of her hand lay against her heart. Two fingers. She had lost two fingers—her ring and little finger. The doctor had also removed some tissue from her forearm. Ugly scars would climb her limb once the stitches healed.

Earlier, Dr. Robinson had remarked she should thank God he had caught the infection early. He was right, of course, but the new handicap disfigured her and provided another thing people would pity about her. She would thank the doctor for his care but could not bring herself to thank God.

Footsteps rapped across the porch until Sara draped a brown, knitted shawl around Kate's shoulders. "That should keep the morning air at bay. I also repaired this for you." She laid Kate's bonnet in her lap, the ties reattached with matching thread.

"Thank you, Sara. You've been so kind to me." How could she ever repay her friend? For more than a week, Sara had nursed her, scrubbed her soiled clothes and sheets, and spooned soup into her mouth.

"Think nothing of it. After I clear the dishes, I'll sit with you for a few minutes." She smiled and bustled through the door.

Kate drew a lungful of air. A chestnut horse, saddled and tied to the porch's far corner post, snorted and tossed his head. Beyond him, the land dropped away from the house into a wide, shallow valley. In the distance to her left, the valley met the river next to a sawmill puffing smoke. The faint whine of the mill mingled with the whisper of the breeze through the grass. A delightful view. Did Topeka also nestle in a treeless valley surrounded by the rolling prairie?

A cluster of buildings south of the mill and river marked the town of Lawrence. A few of the structures stood finished, but many were skeletons of lumber. Tents and shacks filled other lots. Columns of smoke rose from campfires and leaned to the north. Was Topeka as unfinished as Lawrence? She would have arrived by now if she had avoided the rattlesnake. Hattie and G.W. must have reached the Big Blue River. Had they found a good tract of land to claim?

Below her, a line of five wagons headed south out of the new town, just as she had a little more than a week ago. It seemed much longer. Were any of the wagons headed to Topeka? Could any provide room to carry her and her trunks? Perhaps she could catch a ride on another day. People were always moving west.

Dr. Robinson clomped onto the porch, followed by Sara. He pushed his hat onto his head and carried a black leather bag. "What a beautiful morning," he said.

Kate nodded. "Yes. I noticed the wagons leaving town."

"More free-state settlers headed west." The doctor lifted his head and grinned.

"I want to go with them." She spoke with as much firmness as she could muster.

He peered at her. "I'm sure you do."

She offered him her most gracious smile. "Would you please contact someone at the company guest house and ask them to look for travelers headed west on the trail who could transport my things?"

Sara frowned. "Kate, you're still too weak to walk so far."

"Sara is right." The doctor nodded. "You need to recover before continuing your journey."

"I'm well enough if they carry my trunks *and* me. I wouldn't need to walk much."

"Hmm." He stroked his beard-covered chin. "That would work if they had the room, but you risk another problem."

"Oh?" She had already faced enough problems. She needed to find a way to Topeka. What made him reluctant to help her in this way?

"You have not defeated the infection yet. Rather than amputate your hand or forearm, which would have been more prudent, I cut away as little tissue as possible, as you desired."

"I thank you for your attention to my wishes." She had lost quite enough of her hand. "But the wound looks much better."

Dr. Robinson and Sara stepped to her side, and Kate tensed. He rested his hand on her shoulder. "It does, but not good enough. I don't know if Topeka has a doctor. If the infection spreads again, I may need to amputate more. You must remain in Lawrence until all the incisions and stitches heal."

Her stomach tightened. Amputate more? Her pulse throbbed against the bandage. She swallowed, her throat dry.

Sara bent and rubbed her hand across Kate's shoulders. "Don't look so anxious. You are recovering very well. You will regain your strength before long, but you must be careful and allow your body to heal."

"I understand." Would she ever reach Topeka? Unless she taught school, she would receive no income. Her purse was light enough as it was. How long would her recovery delay her? She needed to unpack, organize lessons, enroll students—

"Please excuse me. I have a patient to see." The doctor faced Sara. "It may be dark when I return."

He stepped off the porch and strode to his horse. The gelding stamped a hoof and swished its tail. Dr. Robinson swung a leg over the saddle, settled the bag, and nudged the horse into a walk. Sara watched him with arms crossed. She sighed, and her shoulders dropped.

"You must not like him traveling so far," Kate said. "Is he often required to return after dark?"

"Sometimes, but it can't be helped." Sara sat in the chair beside her. "People are scattered throughout the territory. Once I finish establishing the house, I plan to accompany him unless we entertain guests." Her eyes watched her husband ride south.

Kate leaned close. "Do you call all that you've done for me *entertaining*?"

Sara chuckled. "No, our guests usually do not fight for their lives. Charles and I always show hospitality to an occasional patient or traveler needing a place to stay. As it happens, some of our friends will arrive today or tomorrow."

"Oh, how nice." Had her illness intruded on the Robinson's plans? Another reason to find a way west. She had not yet discussed payment with the doctor either. Would the cost of his care increase the longer she stayed? She cleared her throat. "When your friends arrive, I will be in the way."

"No need to worry about my guests. I'm sure they will arrive late in the day." Sara patted her arm. "But I wanted to discuss the possibility of you staying with a couple here in town to finish your convalescence. I've invited them to come this morning to meet you."

"Of course. You need to make room for your guests."

"Thank you for understanding." A buckboard rolled around the house, drawn by two black horses. "Oh, look, here they come now."

The team labored against a load of lumber. The wagon jangled and creaked to a stop with a man in a light shirt and dark pants and a woman in a dark green dress and white bonnet sitting on the seat. The square-jawed man with a sparse brown beard swung the woman to the ground and began to unload the lumber. The woman stepped onto the porch, a smile lighting her face. Brunette hair peeked from her bonnet and framed her large brown eyes.

"Elizabeth." Sara rose to greet her. "I would like you to meet Miss Kate Collins. Kate, Mrs. Elizabeth Kimball. She traveled with Charles and me from Boston in the first group of emigrants this year. Her husband Samuel arrived last fall."

She pulled another chair forward to face Kate and returned to her seat. Elizabeth thanked Sara and perched on the edge of her chair.

"A pleasure to meet you." Kate smiled.

"I hope you feel better." Elizabeth leaned forward. "May I call you Kate? Sara told me about your situation. How horrible! A rattlesnake bite. I'm deathly afraid of them myself. Samuel killed one at our place last fall. Isn't this a beautiful spring morning?" Words streamed from Elizabeth like water flowing over rocks in a babbling brook. Her head tipped and nodded like a songbird perched on a branch.

Sara touched Kate's knee. "I trust Elizabeth and Samuel. With our friends visiting and other plans Charles made ... well, I hoped to discuss this with you before they arrived. I asked if Elizabeth and Samuel would care for you until you regain your strength."

"What a splendid idea, don't you think?" Elizabeth clasped her hands together. "Of course, our home is not nearly as fine as Sara's, but I would love to have you. It is quite lonely here. More men live in town than women, though more women are moving to join their husbands like I did, and we always have things to do. I'm sure you would be wonderful company. I hope you accept our offer. You will, won't you?"

How could Kate refuse? The invitation did not solve her lack of transportation west, but the arrangement freed Sara of her care. "You are most kind. I would be very grateful to stay with you."

"Wonderful! We'll leave as soon as Samuel finishes unloading the wagon." Elizabeth beamed like Kate had done her a favor.

The women chatted as the two carpenters building the Robinson's house arrived on horseback and helped Samuel unload the lumber. Then, one of them helped Samuel load Kate's trunks. Elizabeth climbed aboard with Samuel's help as Kate shuffled to the wagon wheel. She clasped Samuel's offered hand, lifted her foot to the wheel hub, and tried to climb aboard, but she swayed and nearly fell.

"I'm weaker than I thought."

"May I lift you aboard?" Samuel asked.

Elizabeth peered down, her face lined with concern. "It might be better."

Kate nodded, and he scooped her into his arms and lifted her. She clambered over the side and collapsed into the seat beside Elizabeth. "Thank you, Samuel. You have the pleasant scent of sawdust."

He grinned, and Elizabeth giggled. "He always smells that way. He and his brother run the sawmill." The wagon rocked as Samuel climbed into the seat on the other side.

They rolled down the arm of the hill that pointed toward the sawmill. Kate clutched the cast-iron seat arm with her good hand and pressed her wounded arm against her chest. Even though Samuel held the horse to a walk, the gentle sway of the wagon lightened her head and stomach. Elizabeth pointed out different construction sites, buildings, and camps in the valley and delivered a running commentary on the town as they traveled.

A stream descended on their left, holding a small trickle of water. They turned away from it to the east.

"Plots have been drawn for all of this land." Elizabeth waved her arm. "Some of the lots have sold. Imagine how different the town will look this fall. It's so exciting."

"Yes, it is." Despite her queasiness, Kate marveled at the thought of houses springing up where grass stood. "All of these people arriving to vote for a free state."

Elizabeth rolled her eyes. "Not all. We have some pro-slavery people even in Lawrence, but give us time. I've heard several groups will come from Boston this year."

They turned north and followed wagon ruts. Ahead, smoke rose, and the mill's sound alternated between a high-pitched whine and the engine's chug. On the right, they passed unfinished buildings, tents, and wagons. "We're on Kentucky Street."

Elizabeth beamed like a mother proud of her children. She nodded at a wagon pulled into a lot where two wide paths met. "Samuel's brother lives on the corner. That's his wagon. He's been sleeping there since I arrived."

"Tell me, why are so many houses unfinished?" Kate asked.

"The sawmill keeps breaking down." She pursed her lips and shook her head. "The mill also prioritizes the aid company's lumber. I suppose that's only right since they own it. Ah, here's our place."

Samuel pulled the reins, and they stopped beside a pile of lumber stacked next to wooden boards set across a stone foundation, without any walls, rafters, or roof.

Kate's stomach soured. "You *live* here?"

Elizabeth giggled. "Oh, we don't sleep here, not yet anyway. Our order for lumber will be completed once Dr. Robinson's home is finished. We'll be able to finish ours then, even though the company has other projects."

Kate squinted. Elizabeth had said Samuel's brother slept in his wagon. Would she also need to sleep in a wagon? "Where do you live now?"

Elizabeth smiled and pointed to a small structure in the back corner of the lot. Slabs of stacked sod formed walls four feet high on the long sides. A thatched roof rose above it, pitched steep like a tent. A stove pipe rose from the far end, and a door stood in the near end.

"Can you believe it? Samuel lived here all winter. It's cozy, but we have room for you." Elizabeth wrapped an arm across Kate's shoulder and hugged her. "We'll have great fun."

"Samuel killed a snake here. Where was it?"

"Oh, that." A deep chuckle rose from Samuel. "The rattlesnake curled up inside near the stove. The warmth last fall must have drawn it in. I think it crawled under the door."

Kate's jaw trembled. A rattlesnake. Where she had agreed to sleep.

"Oh, don't be afraid." Elizabeth patted her leg. "Samuel sets his tool-box across the door every night to stop them crawling under."

Kate's stomach quivered. A toolbox might block the door, but what about the sod walls? Snakes lived inside holes in the ground. Could they dig through a sod wall? The whine of the mill chewing a log rose to a shriek. Kate stifled the urge to scream along with it.

7

January 22, Boston

The evening was still young, but darkness covered the streets, the only light shining from windows or the carriage lanterns. The cold air bit Kate's cheeks, and she slipped her gloved hands under the heavy lap robe.

"Are you warm enough?" Arthur sat beside her, the carriage's canvas top raised to shelter them, though the cold rain had stopped earlier in the afternoon and spared the driver who sat in the open.

"Yes, thank you." His arm and shoulder rested against her. She knew heat couldn't pass through their coat sleeves on such a cold night, but the shoulder nestled against Arther felt cozier than the other. She cleared her throat. "Why did you leave the sleigh bells attached to the harness? We are well past Christmas."

His smile reflected the faint light. "They make a rather happy jingle. Just the way I feel when you accompany me."

A flush of warmth spread through Kate. Hopefully, the shadows hid her blush. She shouldn't enjoy his attention as much as she did. A smile formed on her lips despite her efforts to stop it. "You flatter me, Mr. Eliot."

"Please, use my given name." He pouted with an exaggerated frown. "This is the fourth time I have called on you."

It was customary for courting couples to use a more familiar manner of speech, but should she? "You flatter me ... Arthur." A tingle crossed her shoulders.

His smile stretched into a grin. "May I address you as Kate?"

"Well ... I suppose so." She swallowed and avoided his eyes.

Outside his window, a large stone building appeared to crawl by. A wide walk led up steps to a set of arches supporting the columns of a portico. A domed roof perched atop the wide building, its outline dim against the night sky.

He turned and followed her gaze. "The Massachusetts State House. We draw near our destination."

"Thank you for choosing to escort me to the abolition meeting. You know my keen interest in the subject."

"It's my pleasure. Abolition is a cause worthy of support." He cocked his head. "Have you ever visited the Belknap Street Church before?"

"No, I have not. Didn't William Lloyd Garrison found the New England Anti-Slavery Society there?" They turned onto a narrow street and joined a line of plodding carriages.

Arthur nodded. "Yes, you are correct. Many meetings are held there. Everyone refers to it as the Black Faneuil Hall."

Several people hurried along the narrow sidewalks next to tall, brick buildings walling the street. Arthur spoke to his driver, and they stopped. He tossed the lap robe off his legs and stepped to the ground. She laid the robe on the seat, slid to the side of the carriage, and grasped his lifted hand. He smiled as she stepped onto the cobblestones.

He offered his arm, and she rested her hand in the crook of his elbow. A bride took the arm of her new husband in the same way. She startled. Why did she think that?

"Is something wrong?"

"What? Oh ... no, it's nothing." Nothing she wanted to share. Nothing she dared to hope.

They walked to a building nestled among others and entered a large hall. Arthur took her coat and woolen scarf and carried them to one of the coat racks standing along the wall. He hung them along with his coat and left his top hat on the shelf above.

She joined a line of people climbing the narrow stairs, Arthur behind her. She stepped off at the next floor and through a doorway into the back of an auditorium facing a pulpit elevated at the far end. Rows of curved pews covered the floor, filled with men and women of both negro and white complexion. More people sat in pews on the balconies that hung along each side.

"I think we can squeeze in there." Arthur led her to the center aisle, and they slid into the last row. "We arrived in time."

The room buzzed with conversation.

"Yes." Kate's stomach fluttered. What kind of message would she hear? Would the speaker rail in a deep voice like a preacher drumming on emotion, or would he present reasoned arguments to show the evil of slavery? Did anyone in this crowd support slavery? The colored men and women were well-dressed. Some must have been slaves, but their clothing gave no indication.

A man rose, climbed to the pulpit, and raised his arms. The murmuring quieted. He extended a welcome and noted distinguished guests, then introduced the speaker and concluded by saying, "I present to you, William Wells Brown, once a slave but now an esteemed author and an eloquent speaker for humanity."

Applause rippled through the room, and she joined in. Arthur glanced at her, no doubt checking to see whether she was enjoying the evening.

Mr. Brown mounted the stage and grasped the lapels of his dark suit. He began the story of his life—born in Kentucky, the son of a slave woman, fathered by her white owner. His voice rang off the yellow walls as he told of the master's move to Missouri and life on the plantation.

"A bell tolled each morning at four o'clock. Field slaves rose and ate. I was allowed to sleep longer since I was a house slave and still a young boy. The field hands had to arrive at the field by four-thirty or be whipped. Even though the fields were a distance away from the slave cabins, I could hear the crack of the whip and the cries of the slaves from my bed on many mornings."

How horrible! When Kate was a child, Mother entered her room and opened the curtains each morning while humming a hymn. What did Arthur experience each morning as a child?

"The negro-whip the overseer used was a cruel instrument," Mr. Brown said, "with a handle three feet long, the butt end weighted with lead. The lash consisted of braided rawhide six to seven feet long and tipped with wire. The overseer used the whip often and always carried it."

A whip tipped with wire? A lump formed in her throat. Had Mr. Brown ever felt the sting of such a cruel device?

"One morning, my mother arrived at the field ten minutes late. I lay in my bunk and heard the whip crack. My mother screamed."

A shudder shook Kate's shoulders, and her heart thudded in her chest. A wire-tipped whip would certainly deliver wicked cuts.

"I leaped from my bed and rushed to the door but dared go no farther. She groaned and cried for mercy with each crack of the whip. I stood at the door of the cabin and wept. After ten lashes, the sound of the whip ceased. The sun had not yet risen."

He was just a boy ... to hear his mother lashed with such a cruel whip. What if Mother had been whipped in the same way, her dress ripped and her flesh torn?

Mr. Brown continued telling of his life as a slave in Missouri and the abuse he experienced or witnessed. Once, he attempted to escape with his mother, but they were captured. The owner sold his mother, and Mr. Brown watched a boat carry her down the Mississippi.

Kate drew a deep breath of warm, stuffy air. Slavery caused so much suffering. This wasn't the type of evening most men calling on a woman would plan, but Arthur had chosen well. They agreed on the importance of abolition. She glanced at Arthur, his face grim and jaw a straight line. His brown hair hung over his ear, turning out at the end.

Mr. Brown's desire for freedom eventually drove him to escape and follow the Underground Railroad to Cleveland. There, he helped many escaped slaves find their way to Canada. But he claimed freedom was not enough. He implored the crowd to pursue personal elevation. True freedom required moral and mental improvement. He encouraged the colored people in the crowd to look to their religious relations and urged all to abolish slavery.

Vigorous applause rose when Mr. Brown finished. Arthur shouted his approval along with other men. Mr. Garrison climbed to the pulpit but only spoke a few words. The meeting adjourned, and they joined the flow of people shuffling to the steps and down to the lower floor. In the large room, many stood and talked as they waited in coats and hats.

Arthur found their things and handed Kate her coat. "Please stay here in the warmth. The line of carriages will be long. I'll come back when mine arrives."

He was such a courteous man. She draped the coat over her arm and stood near a wall.

A short, plump woman around Mother's age approached her. "May I ask, did Arthur Eliot escort you this evening?"

Kate's smile froze in place. "Yes, he did."

"I thought I recognized him. He comes from a respected family." Her gaze traveled to Kate's feet and back to her face. "Is he calling on you?"

The woman's abrupt question edged toward rudeness, and Kate's shoulders and arms tightened with tension. She fought the urge to touch her birthmark.

"Yes, he accepted an invitation to call on me."

"He is a remarkable young man. You should be thrilled to receive his attention."

"Yes, he is a fine man." Her mouth dried, and she swallowed. "And I am ... very pleased."

The woman lifted her chin and sniffed. "Yes." She glanced toward the door. "Ah, good. My carriage has arrived. Please excuse me." She walked to an older man near the door and received his help donning her coat.

Groups of people conversed in the room, and a few she recognized from meetings she had attended at the Forbes home, but not this woman. The matron hadn't introduced herself or even asked for a name, which was ill-mannered, to say the least. She had only inquired to confirm Arthur's identity.

Arthur, a handsome young man, had chosen to spend time with Kate. Of course, she enjoyed their conversations and was grateful for his attention. They shared a passion for literature. But he was not serious about marriage, at least to her. She knew this fact just as she knew the sun would rise in the morning. Something had happened to him, but she knew not what. Had he been rejected? Who in their right mind would reject him? She knew she was merely Arthur's safe choice for a social companion.

Abolition and other social reforms were her future, not marriage to Arthur. It would be wonderful to share that purpose with him as his wife, but how could she surrender her plans to the dictates of a husband, even if he was kind? Arthur didn't support suffrage.

She should devise a way to test his devotion. It was a common practice in courtship. A test would give him an excuse to stop calling on her. She would miss his attention and their discussion of books, but it would only be fair to him.

She should focus on tutoring Richard and Phoebe and continue volunteering to support abolition events. Mr. Brown's stories had stirred her heart. Could she do more? Would college provide opportunities to take action against slavery or just assignments and lectures?

Arthur stepped into the room. A sparkle of raindrops covered his top hat and coat, and as his gaze found hers, his face lit. She quickened her steps toward him and extended her coat.

"Would you please help me?"

He bent in a slight bow. "It would be my honor."

She slipped her arms into the coat. His knuckles brushed her shoulder, and a tingle rose on her neck. She would break the courtship if he didn't, but not tonight. What harm was there in enjoying his calls a few more weeks?

8

April 27, Lawrence

A murmur of voices stirred Kate awake. Above her, a light brown thatch lay across a grid of limbs, forming a peaked ceiling. She pushed a quilt off her chest and sat up.

The blanket Elizabeth had hung just past the head of Kate's bed the night before lay folded on a larger bed near the iron cookstove at the opposite end of the narrow room. At her feet, a wooden door stood in the whitewashed sod wall. Light streamed under it and around the curtains of a small window in the side wall. The toolbox Samuel had placed across the bottom of the door the night before was gone.

Snakes. Kate had worried about snakes while dressing for bed the night before, fully expecting a fearful and sleepless night, but exhaustion must have pulled her into a deep slumber. Nothing moved on the hooked rug covering the narrow aisle next to the bed. Trunks and crates lined the opposite wall. She swung her legs over the side and stood, careful of her wounded hand. A cool draft washed over her bare feet.

She reached for her dress and petticoats, wincing at the dull ache in her right hand. Sara had helped her the last few mornings as donning her clothing proved a struggle. Kate fumbled with a buttonhook to fasten her dress with one hand before slipping into her low-heeled boots and buttoning them. How would she ever manage laces and ties while her hand healed?

She slipped her arm into the sling and draped a heavy sweater around her shoulders as the mornings had been chilly. Kate swung the door open, and the scent of wood smoke wafted across her face. With her good hand, she steadied herself against the rough sod wall and eased around the shack.

Elizabeth stood beside a flickering fire between two rows of rocks, each the size of a loaf of bread. A blackened pot sat across one end of the rocks, steam rising from it. She brushed back a strand of dark hair that escaped the loose knot at the nape of her neck when she saw Kate approaching.

"Good morning. Did you sleep well?"

"Good morning," Kate stepped forward. "Yes, I slept so well I didn't hear you leave this morning."

"Help yourself to some water." Elizabeth gestured to a wooden bucket sitting on the ground next to a small table.

Kate dipped water from the bucket and filled a tall stoneware mug. The cool water soothed her dry mouth. She filled the mug again and gulped it down.

"I'm not surprised you slept this late." Elizabeth stepped closer and rested a hand on Kate's shoulder. "You looked exhausted last night. I was worried Samuel would wake you this morning, banging about with his toolbox. The man's just too big for our temporary home. When you slept through his commotion, I decided you needed to sleep as long as possible."

"I think I heard him talking earlier."

"Yes, his brother arrived for breakfast. They yakked about work and town gossip. They left not long ago for the mill." Elizabeth lifted a cast-iron skillet. "Are you hungry?"

Kate's stomach growled. A returning appetite must be a sign of her recovery. "Yes. I am."

"Let me make you a pancake. I made plenty of batter when I fed the men." Elizabeth placed the skillet across the rows of rocks holding the fire. "Eggs are hard to come by, but the store recently had some. Can you believe I had to pay fifteen cents a dozen? I need some chickens."

"That is expensive." Should she offer to help purchase food during her stay with the Kimballs?

Elizabeth poured thick batter into the skillet. "Sara said you came from Massachusetts."

"Yes. My parents live in Belchertown, but I lived with my aunt in Boston for several months before coming to Kansas."

"I'm not familiar with that town. We're from New Hampshire." She studied the skillet for a moment. "Samuel and I wed last fall shortly before he and his brother came to Kansas."

"Oh, that is ... it must have been difficult to see him leave so soon after your wedding."

Elizabeth sighed. "It was, but he wanted to come early to find a good place." She flipped the pancake with an easy motion. "Once the territory opened, all manner of people headed here. More people arrive every week or pass along the trail."

Kate nodded. She had been right to come to Kansas. She would help it become a free state.

Elizabeth retrieved a plate from the table near the shack wall, bent over the fire, and scooped up the pancake. She plopped the thick, brown cake onto the plate and handed it to Kate. Her mouth watered, and she inhaled the nutty scent as Elizabeth poured more batter into the sizzling skillet.

"Oh, Elizabeth, I don't need another. That one looks large enough."

She waved a hand. "Don't worry, I'm cooking another for me."

"Oh. Didn't you eat with your husband earlier?"

She smiled as warm as a summer sunrise. "I decided to wait until you rose so I could eat with you. We can get to know each other better."

A warmth expanded in Kate's chest. Elizabeth had already shown kindness by providing a place to stay, but she also sought a friend. "I would like that very much."

"Shall we eat here by the fire or inside the mansion?"

"Mansion?" Kate turned in a circle.

Behind the Kimball's shack, their neighbor's shed stood covered with odds and ends of wood. A stone foundation marked the location of a planned building. The Kimball's lot held a large foundation covered with floor joists but no walls or even studding. "I don't see a mansion. To what do you refer?"

Elizabeth giggled. "It's my name for our little hovel. I might as well pretend it's elegant, don't you think?"

Of course, Elizabeth would try to view the sod and thatch shed in a positive light. Did the woman ever complain or frown? "Let's eat here. It's much brighter than inside the ... mansion."

Elizabeth grinned. "I usually cook on the stove inside but stay out here when I can. It's so cramped in there."

A noisy sigh passed through Kate's nose. Her presence in the shack made it even more crowded. Her carelessness in retrieving her bonnet had crippled her, delayed her travel, and would incur expense—she still needed to ask Dr. Robinson the amount she owed—but her blunder also inconvenienced the Kimballs.

"The stove smokes until the fire takes off, and the flue draws well," Elizabeth said. "I enjoy the sunshine and fresh air, not smoky odors in my blankets. Samuel says the stove flu is safe, but ... well, there's less risk of a fire if I cook out here. A roof of sticks and grass—can you imagine how fast a fire would destroy it? What a mess it would cause."

Elizabeth lifted two cane-bottomed chairs and placed them closer to the fire. She bowed dramatically and gestured at the chair. "Would the lady like to sit?"

Kate chuckled and lowered herself as regally as possible. Elizabeth sat in the other chair with a loaded plate in her lap. She stared at the fire, and her smile melted into a sober expression. Was something troubling her?

Kate cleared her throat. "Would you allow me to offer the prayer?"

"Would you please?" Elizabeth's eyes glistened.

Kate thanked God for the food and the Kimball's hospitality. After she said "amen," she forked a bite of the pancake using her left hand and lifted it to her mouth. The taste of the pancake flooded her mouth—so good even without maple syrup. A chuffing sound rose from the sawmill about a hundred yards away.

Elizabeth gazed into the fire and pressed her hand to her chest. "My father always prayed at meals. I miss him and my family. Do you miss yours?"

"I didn't miss them during the travel, but when the snake bit me, I wanted my mother, which surprises me now. I thought I would have missed Aunt Amelia more."

"I would miss my mother if I faced a rattlesnake bite." Elizabeth forked a bite of pancake. "What about your brothers and sisters? Do you miss them?"

"I'm an only child."

Elizabeth's eyes rounded. "Really? I have three brothers and four sisters. I'm the oldest girl. I can't imagine being the only child. Were you lonely?"

"Sometimes. My friends lived nearby, so I had playmates and school-mates until we moved."

"That must have been hard."

"We left Boston and all my friends." Kate stared at the remains of her food. The memory still pained her.

"How old were you when you moved?"

"I was almost eight. I didn't like it, especially at first."

"Why not?" Elizabeth cocked her head and chewed like she pondered a mystery.

"Well, I was the new girl and ... you know." She pointed at her birth-mark. "The children teased me."

"How cruel." Elizabeth set her fork down and straightened. "I think your birthmark is lovely, especially when you smile. It looks like you've enjoyed too many fresh blackberries." She smiled.

Elizabeth could find something good to say about anything. "I've learned to accept my appearance. I know that true beauty is displayed by helping other people ... like you are helping me."

"Oh, thank you." Elizabeth beamed, and color flushed her cheeks.

"Now, tell me more about you and Samuel." That would be a safer topic than her birthmark.

"I've known Samuel for many years. He used to tug my braids at school, at least when I was younger. Do you have a husband waiting for you here in Kansas?"

Kate nearly dropped her fork. "What?"

"I came to Kansas to join my husband. Many men come before their wives. I thought you might have someone waiting here."

"No, certainly not. I came alone to teach school at Topeka. It's my way of supporting the free-state cause."

"Oh." Elizabeth's forehead creased. "I thought ... well, don't worry, you'll find one."

Kate sighed. "I'm not looking for a husband."

"Truly?" Elizabeth lifted her eyebrows and frowned. "What about Arthur?"

Kate gasped, and her stomach knotted. How did Elizabeth know about Arthur?

9

"I didn't mean to startle you." Elizabeth smiled. "I thought I heard you mumble that name in your sleep."

Kate lowered her fork to the empty plate in her lap. Did she always talk in her sleep? "I don't remember dreaming about Arthur."

"Who is he? A relative?"

The skin on Kate's neck tingled. What could she possibly have said? "Did I say much?"

Elizabeth's cheeks flushed. "It didn't sound like he was a relative." She shrugged. "But you mumbled, so I'm not sure."

A tightness grew in Kate's throat, and she swallowed. "No, he's not a relative. He's a young man studying medicine. My aunt Amelia introduced me to him."

"Introduced?" Elizabeth smiled like she had caught a small child in a fib and scooped up her last bite.

Kate's cheeks warmed. "My aunt invited him to call on me."

"Ooh." Elizabeth's eyes widened like she had heard a bit of juicy gossip. "Did he?"

"Call on me? Yes, for a few weeks."

"I'm so sorry." Elizabeth reached over and squeezed Kate's hand. "It must be an unpleasant memory. I shouldn't have pried into your affairs." She jumped to her feet. "Let me take your plate. I should clean up. I apologize for prying."

"No, you don't understand." Kate stood and followed Elizabeth to the table. "Arthur was a complete gentleman and comes from a well-respected family in Boston. He loved books much like I do, and he supported abolition. I enjoyed his company."

Elizabeth lifted the pot of hot water off the fire and poured some into a wash pan on the table. "But he lost interest and stopped calling on you."

"Quite the contrary. He was keen to continue seeing me. I think he would have ... may have proposed if we continued the courtship."

"You must have been thrilled. I was when Samuel offered to marry me." Elizabeth added soap flakes to the wash water and began scrubbing plates.

"I ... I was." Thrilled and worried. She shook her head, and her emotions swirled. "Arthur is a gentle and sweet man, but ..."

Elizabeth set the plate she had washed on the table and placed a hand on Kate's shoulder. "You don't need to tell me anything more." She bent and dipped another dish into the water.

"I knew he wasn't truly interested in me." How could he be? He could pick any woman in Boston's elite society. He must have received many invitations to court women.

"How did you know?" Elizabeth's words came soft enough that the buzz of the sawmill chewing a log almost covered them.

"I learned he had a lifelong friend, a young woman he admired, who had died of an illness. They were very close. I think I reminded him of her."

Elizabeth finished the last dish, frowned, and cocked her head to the side. She probably wanted to know more but was too polite to ask.

Kate brushed the table in small circles, the wood rough under her fingertips. "I know I didn't look like her. He described her with a different hair color. And, well ..." She lifted her finger to her lip. "A birthmark did not mar her beauty."

"Then how do you know you reminded him of her?" Elizabeth rested a hand on her hip. "Maybe he likes you."

"He talked about her passion for abolition. He complimented my devotion to the issue, saying I reminded him of her."

Elizabeth crossed her arms and hugged her elbows. "I don't understand. You had a caring man interested in you. Did you tell him to stop calling on you?"

"Yes." She straightened her shoulders.

"What did he say?"

Heat flushed Kate's neck and ears. Arthur hadn't deserved what she had done, but what else could she have done? "I ... he didn't ... I wrote him a letter."

"Did he reply?"

Kate's shoulders slumped. "I don't know. I left for Kansas the next day."

"Oh." Elizabeth stacked the plates, forks, and mixing bowl on the table. "Did Arthur know about your plans to come to Kansas?"

"I told him in the letter."

Elizabeth's head jerked back. "You planned to travel to Kansas to teach school without telling him?"

"You see, I ... I decided ..." Arthur was so kind. She couldn't let any feelings for him distract her. She had to nip them in the bud. Would Elizabeth understand? "I decided to come to Kansas a few days before our group left."

A gasp escaped through Elizabeth's open mouth. "We planned for months before we left."

"How could I risk marriage? A husband could move me anywhere."

"Like Kansas?" Elizabeth crossed her arms.

"You know what I mean. Wives are subject to their husbands. They don't own anything. A wife's property transfers to her husband when they marry. If a man decides to move the family, how can a wife change it? Even if Arthur allowed me to work for abolition in Boston, he doesn't support suffrage for women, which is also important.

"I just reminded him of his friend, Dahlia. I think he loved her, and they had an understanding about marriage. Now he mourns her loss. He told me her death prompted his study of medicine. Don't you see? He only called on me because I reminded him of her. He will find another woman. I know he will." Her eyes burned, and her throat ached.

"Oh, Kate."

"I know God wants me to help abolish slavery. So, I decided to come to Kansas and teach, to help establish free-state settlements. Everything was going well until that stupid snake bit me. Now I'm stuck here with a crippled hand." Tears wet her cheeks.

Elizabeth wrapped her in a hug. "I can see it was a difficult decision."

"Yes. He was so attentive. I will miss our talks about books." She gasped and stepped back. "Oh ... I'm sorry! I didn't mean to say I'm stuck with you. You and Samuel are so kind to help me. I ... I'm just stuck in Lawrence."

"So much has happened to you. I was wrong to pry. I didn't mean to stir painful memories."

Kate rummaged a handkerchief from her sweater and wiped her eyes and nose. She usually held her emotions in check. "I'm fine, truly."

"We should change your dressing today."

"Yes." She sniffed. "Would you wrap it differently so my thumb and fingers are free? I'd like to write some letters today. I assume Lawrence has a place to post mail."

"It does." Elizabeth smiled. "Let's step into the mansion where the bandages are."

Kate smiled, followed Elizabeth into the shack, and sat on the bed. Elizabeth propped the door open for light, gathered the needed supplies, and unwrapped Kate's hand. How strange to see only two fingers and her thumb. Pink tinged the muslin, and a spot of yellow stained it, though less than the day before. Dark thread stitched the outside of her hand and up her arm halfway to her elbow.

Kate dabbed her nose with the handkerchief. "I think it looks better."

"Does it hurt much?" Elizabeth studied the wound and winced.

"A constant ache. Sometimes it throbs. Holding it up with the sling helps."

Elizabeth laid a fresh muslin pad against the wound, lifted a rolled bandage, and wrapped Kate's hand and arm but left the fingers and thumb free. "There. I don't know about the wound, but you look stronger today than yesterday."

"I hope so."

"Would you like to use the table outside to write your letters?"

"No, I'll use the top of my trunk. The breeze might prove trouble-some." The shack would also give her privacy.

"I can take them to the aid company to post when you finish—unless you feel like a walk."

"Let me consider that." Fatigue already dragged at her. Could she walk any distance and have the strength to return?

Elizabeth gathered the old bandages and stepped out of the soddie, closing the door. Kate stood and stepped to her two stacked trunks, opening the one on top. Her writing supplies were tucked in the corner where she had packed them. She closed the trunk, sat on it, and placed the paper and ink bottle beside her. A lamp would make writing easier, but how could she manage the match and the lamp chimney with one hand? What if she knocked it over and caused a fire?

She set her jaw, fumbled the pen with her right hand, and lowered the pen toward the ink bottle. Her hand burned and throbbed. Writing in this position would not work. She knelt on the floor facing the stacked trunks and laid her right arm on the top of the trunk, rearranging the paper and ink. Dr. Robinson had said nothing about using her hand. Would this inflame the wound? She needed to risk it.

April 27

Dear Mother and Father,

I apologize for my crude penmanship. I have not arrived in Topeka yet. Several days ago, we traveled toward it, but a rattlesnake bit me on the hand. They took me to Lawrence to see a doctor. I have been very sick for over a week. The doctor amputated two fingers on my right hand to stop infection, hence my poor penmanship. I feel much better and hope to travel to Topeka soon.

I miss you. I treated you poorly by informing you of my plans by letter. Please write to me. I hope to continue my travel to Topeka soon. I will write more when my pain decreases.

Love,

Kate

A tear dropped onto the paper and smudged the last line, but the letter was still readable. Her hand throbbed, and a spot of blood had soaked through her bandage. She signed the letter, gritted her teeth, and wrote another to her aunt. After writing addresses on the back, she lit a candle, folded the corners down across the letters, and secured them with a daub of wax pressed with her seal. She returned the material to the trunk and stumbled out the door.

Elizabeth stood near the steaming pot on the fire. "Is everything well?"

"Yes, it was just a struggle to write." She handed the letters to her.

"Do you want to walk with me?"

"Would you post them, please? The morning has drained me."

Her friend glanced at the addresses. "No letter for Arthur?"

"No. The past is the past."

10

Kate picked up the lunch plates to carry to the table beside the shack. She had developed a routine with Elizabeth. After breakfast, she would walk around the growing town to the buzz of the sawmill and the pounding of carpenters. Permanent buildings rose next to tents and shacks that had survived the winter. Horse-drawn wagons jangled along the main street, some hauling lumber or limestone blocks, others carrying settlers arriving in Lawrence or departing for points west. Her walks grew longer each day as her strength returned.

After her stroll, she would help Elizabeth as much as her hand allowed, and they would talk like schoolgirls as they performed chores. Her wound still seeped blood into the bandage if she overused her hand, but the skin held by the stitches had changed to bright red.

She set the plates on the table as a horse whinnied and stopped at the edge of the lot. "Good morning," Dr. Robinson called from the saddle.

A lightness lifted Kate's chest. She must ask the doctor if she had recovered enough to travel again.

Dr. Robinson swung from the saddle and hitched his horse to a post at the corner of the house's foundation. "A pleasure to see you, Miss Collins and Mrs. Kimball. Such a fine day."

"It's good to see you." Elizabeth pulled her handkerchief out and dusted off a chair that sat by the fire. "Please sit."

He did so and removed his hat. "I'm here to see Miss Collins and check on her hand."

Kate smiled and took the chair next to him. "We were preparing to change the bandage."

"With the doctor here, you don't need me," Elizabeth said. "Please excuse me while I finish the dishes."

Dr. Robinson scooted his chair closer to Kate. "How do you feel?"

"Fine. I've taken a walk every morning and evening." She extended her arm, and he began to unravel the bandages.

"Very good. Do you feel you've gained strength?"

"Yes, I feel stronger each day." There was no reason she should avoid traveling to Topeka.

He unwrapped the last of the binding and eased the muslin pads from the wound. He frowned but nodded. "This looks much better." He placed a hand on her forehead. "No fever?"

"None whatsoever."

Elizabeth turned from the table toward them. "She's even helped me with chores the past two days."

He frowned again. "You haven't been washing dishes, have you?"

"No, but I have dried them. I also wrote two letters, though my penmanship was atrocious."

He smiled. "I'm sure people will understand. Please wiggle your fingers."

Kate tapped her thumb with each of her two fingers and managed not to wince at the pain. If only she had lost part of her other hand. Writing would be much easier, and the ugly scars would constantly remind her of her loss. Sleeves would cover the scars on her arm, but everyone would see the missing fingers and the knot of scar tissue on her hand.

"Can you curl them into a fist?"

She tried, but her fingers refused to bend more than halfway.

"Flex them daily and continue to curl them as tight as possible. They'll limber up soon." He rummaged in his bag. "I think we can remove the sutures."

Her heart skipped. "Does that mean I'm fit to travel?"

"How far have you walked?" He turned her arm so he could see the area better and used small scissors to snip each stitch and plucked them out with tweezers.

Each yank stung like a pinprick, and she fought to keep from jerking her arm away while she told him about her walks and highlighted how their length grew each day.

He looked at her briefly when she finished. "Yes, I believe it's safe for you to travel. Your wound still has a bit of drainage, but it'll soon close. Keep it clean and wrapped until it heals. You may want to cover it even longer to protect it, at least for a while." He wagged a finger and stared with a mock frown. "Don't use it too much until it heals fully."

She swallowed to stifle a giggle. "Dr. Robinson, can you ask at the guest house if anyone traveling west will carry my trunks to Topeka? I would pay a fee, of course, since I'm anxious to arrive and meet my students."

"Hmm." He set about wrapping Kate's hand in a fresh bandage. "I can ask if anyone will carry your things, but you may not want to go to Topeka."

Her stomach fluttered. The doctor's face was as serious as when he had talked about amputating her arm. "What's the problem? Has something happened to the town?"

"No, but they made other plans." He sighed. "A new settler arrived and opened a school."

She blinked back a wave of dizziness. "They ... they don't need me?"

"I'm afraid not."

Her mouth dried, and she licked her lips. "What about my position? The aid company agreed to pay me to teach school at Topeka."

Dr. Robinson stroked his beard. "They no longer need a teacher. If we find another settlement that needs a teacher, we will hire you if you're still interested."

"I am, of course ... but how can I earn my keep until then?" How could she fulfill her purpose? Where would she go? She must find a position somewhere. Her racing thoughts threatened to overcome her. She took a deep breath and asked, "Could I teach here in Lawrence? You need a teacher here, don't you? I've seen several children during my walks."

The doctor began putting supplies back into his bag. "We already have a teacher. Edward Fitch runs a school in the back room of my office."

Someone must need a teacher. The aid company had started several settlements, including the one where Hattie settled. "What about the settlement on the Big Blue River? I traveled with a couple headed there from Kansas City. You met them. They brought me to your house after the rattlesnake bit me. Do they need a teacher?"

"I don't know whether or not they do. Let me contact them and some other places. Come to the company office in a week."

She nodded. "I will. But I can't continue to depend on the hospitality of Elizabeth and her husband."

Elizabeth has stopped her chores to watch the conversation. She nodded, a slight smile on her lips, and resumed drying the plate.

"I understand." The doctor walked back to his mount. "Do you still want me to inquire about a wagon to haul your things to Topeka?"

"No, I'll wait. It may not be the right direction." She slipped her arm into the sling. "Now, what do I owe you for your care?"

"I usually charge two dollars a day. But I'll round it down for you to ten dollars."

She gulped. Eggs weren't the only expensive things in the territory. "Please wait here, and I will retrieve my purse."

She entered the shack, lifted the trunk lid, and pulled out her bag. She loosened the drawstring and gathered the needed amount. He had asked a steep price, but the doctor and Sara deserved every penny and more. The amount couldn't possibly cover the doctor's services, Sara's care, and her lodging. Kate counted the remaining coins—twelve dollars and thirteen cents.

She would need to offer a fare to whoever hauled her trunk. She should also give Elizabeth something. Lodging and supplies would need to be purchased when she traveled. It all meant she must find a teaching position soon. Kate closed the trunk, returned to Dr. Robinson, and handed him the coins.

"Thank you very much," he said. "I'll see you at the company office, hopefully with good news." He donned his hat, untied his horse, and swung into the saddle. "Mrs. Kimball, thank you for assisting Miss Collins."

"My pleasure." Elizabeth stepped to Kate's side as the doctor turned and rode away.

Kate turned to her friend. "Yes, you and Samuel have been a godsend, Elizabeth. I don't know what I would have done without you."

"You're welcome. It's our Christian duty, after all. I hope you find a teaching position soon." Elizabeth smiled, though it seemed to hold no joy.

Did something trouble her friend, or was she just sympathetic about the loss of the teaching job?

"With so many people coming to Kansas," Kate said, "one of the aid company settlements must need a teacher."

"And if none are available? What will you do?"

Kate frowned. "I haven't thought about it. I suppose one of the other settlements, one that the company didn't start, may need a teacher."

"Would you go to a town filled with slave owners or their sympathizers? I heard they've threatened and beat free-state men in other towns."

"Oh." She had forgotten people from Kentucky and Missouri were settling in Kansas, not just people from New England. The Missourians had threatened men when they stole the election in March, even had shot at one. "That would be a problem, wouldn't it?"

"Are there other jobs you could do?"

"Other jobs?" She had come to Kansas to teach and support free-state families. What else *could* she do?

Elizabeth chewed her lip, standing with her hands against her stomach.

"You're interested in my ... You seem ill at ease. Is something wrong?" Kate asked.

"No, I mean ... not really. It's just ..." Her cheeks flushed pink, and she wrung her hands. "The mansion is so small, and the sawmill hasn't completed our order. It may be weeks before our house is finished."

Kate touched Elizabeth's elbow. "What is it? Do you want me to leave?"

Her brow creased, and she tipped her head to the side. "It's not you. I enjoy talking to you. You've helped me as best you can while your hand heals. It's just ..."

"You're worried about the cost." Kate's shoulders relaxed. "I plan to give you some money. Would it help if I paid you now?"

Elizabeth wrapped her arms across her chest and hugged her elbows tight, her face twisting like she had eaten sour apples. "It's not that. It's just that ... I want to start our family."

"Oh." Warmth crept up Kate's neck. "I understand now."

A blanket divided the soddie's cramped quarters, which offered scant privacy. Of course, Elizabeth wanted to be alone in the shack with her husband. Kate would feel the same way.

"I don't know why the Lord hasn't blessed us with a baby yet, but ..." Elizabeth held up an open hand. "Please don't feel like I want to run you off, but I hope you find a teaching position soon ... or another job."

Kate took Elizabeth's hand. "I understand. I will find employment as soon as I can. Why, this is a fine afternoon to walk around town and inquire about a job."

Her friend's soft eyes filled with an inner glow as she squeezed Kate's hand. "Thank you."

Kate left Elizabeth and walked away from the lot toward the sound of the sawmill buzzing through another log. She turned down the dirt street separating the buildings from the river levee—Pinkney Street, they called it. She faced a dilemma. If she couldn't teach, what other jobs would earn her money *and* help defeat slavery?

She stopped, filled her lungs, and blew out a long, hard breath. Didn't God want her to teach school? If only she'd been more careful on the trail that day. The delay had destroyed her plan to teach in Topeka, but she couldn't blame the people there. They couldn't have known she would survive a rattlesnake bite.

The first days at the Robinson's were a foggy memory, but she realized she had almost died. Instead, God answered her prayers. She didn't have all her strength yet, though she could still work. But what could an educated woman do in a growing frontier town?

The men at the sawmill would not consider her, even if she had the strength. The aid company's guest house already had women to cook and clean. She didn't have enough money to purchase a lot and start a boardinghouse. Carpentry wasn't an option. She had neither the skill nor the strength.

A newspaper? Lawrence had a paper, *The Kansas Tribune*. Samuel had brought a copy of the paper home last night. She possessed the mental skills to write, and her hand could cope with the task even with two fingers and a thumb. Setting the type for the press couldn't be difficult. And the *Tribune* was dedicated to the free-state cause. The thought of working at the paper quickened her heartbeat. She squared her shoulders and marched toward the main part of town.

11

K ate stopped beside the building housing *The Kansas Tribune.*
Would the editor hire a woman, even one with a damaged hand?
She slipped her arm from the sling, lifted the cloth over her head, and
wrapped it loosely around her bandaged hand. The doorknob cooled
her fingertips as she twisted it before hiding her bandaged hand behind
her back.

She pushed the door open, and an earthy scent tinged with a sweet
fragrance greeted her. An iron press sporting a thick wheel stood in the
back of the room in front of bundles of paper. In the front corner, a
man sat at a rolltop desk. A mop of thick, brown hair hung to his collar.

He glanced up, his pen poised over a sheet of paper. "May I help
you?" His shaggy mustache hung past his mouth like the jowls of a
hound.

"Are you the editor?" Kate smiled widely despite the throbbing in
her hand.

He stood and approached. "I am. Do you wish to subscribe to the
paper?"

"No, I am looking for employment. Do you need any help with the
newspaper?"

He frowned. "No. I manage the paper quite well since it's a weekly.
When I publish daily, that might change, but that won't happen for a
few months—if subscriptions increase."

Breath eased through her lips. She shouldn't be disappointed since
this was the first place she had inquired.

He studied her. "What kind of position do you seek?"

"I came to Kansas to teach school, but a ... a delay necessitated other arrangements." She couldn't risk discussing her lame hand.

"Our paper carries ads for employment. Perhaps you'd like to subscribe. I'll include the last issue."

"Oh ... I left my purse back at my friend's. Did you have advertisements seeking workers?"

He shrugged. "It only had one this week, but it probably would not fit a woman. A stable near the hotel is looking for a hired hand. Have you tried other businesses?"

"Not yet. I thought my teaching skills could translate into writing for a paper."

"Well, I'm not the only paper editor in town. You might try the *Herald of Freedom* sponsored by the immigrant aid company. The *Kansas Free State* also publishes here in town." He frowned and tucked his chin. "You *are* a free-state sympathizer, are you not?"

She straightened her shoulders. "Yes, I am. Your position on slavery led me to believe your paper would be an ideal place to work. I came to Kansas as a teacher to support the free-state effort."

He nodded. "That's good, but I'm sorry I can't help you."

Kate turned toward the door and moved her hand to her stomach. "Thank you for your time."

"Wait." He pointed at her hand. "What happened?"

"A rattlesnake bit me."

Life sprang into his eyes as he turned to grab a pencil and paper from the desk. "You don't say! I would love to interview you and write your story for the paper. People enjoy stories about others facing dangerous animals."

How would people reading about her misfortune help her? Her story might engender sympathy, or it might draw attention to her lost fingers. Neither would benefit her search for a job. "No. I prefer not to relive the incident." She pulled the door open. "Thank you again. I'll check with the other newspapers."

Kate's footsteps clumped on the wooden porch in front of Liberty Hall. The building was used for meetings and housed the *Herald of Freedom* newspaper. Its editor had also informed her he did not need another worker. The editor of the *Kansas Free State* had said the same. She trudged south along a street wide enough that eight wagons could pass each other, though nowhere near that number rolled through the rutted dirt today.

Across the street, a man standing in a wagon handed large limestone blocks to another man on the ground, who placed them in front of a wide, knee-high wall. The building must be the aid company's hotel, the one she had heard about. It would become an impressive building.

Other buildings lined the street, some completed but several still under construction, their clapboard siding unpainted. The town must have undergone significant changes since its founding last fall. The coming summer and fall would bring further construction before it celebrated its first birthday.

Although Kate's morning and evening walks had strengthened her, the afternoon of standing and walking made her shoes feel as heavy as iron skillets. The air was pleasant, but the afternoon sun had warmed her enough that sweat dampened her skin.

Two wagons stood in the street, their teams flicking flies with swishing tails and stomping hooves. Three other horses, one black and the others brown, were hitched to the rail in front of a building with a sign declaring it a store. She hadn't considered a clerk position, but she needed to find something.

She pushed the door open and stepped onto a dirt floor. A line of barrels stood in the middle of the room, the one closest stenciled as nails. Shelves lined the walls, holding bolts of cloth, dishes, black pots, and various tools. A man with a handlebar mustache stood behind a counter stretched across the back wall.

"I'll be with you in a minute." He turned back to the couple facing him.

Four men stood in line behind them.

The sign on the wall behind the storekeeper advertised eggs for fifteen cents a dozen and cheese for twenty cents a pound. Butter was priced at thirty cents, but a scrawled note next to it read, "Out."

She scooted onto the edge of the nail barrel. Although not the most lady-like chair, the seat rested her aching legs and feet.

The storekeeper stacked items on the counter for the couple, tallied the total, and received payment. The other men purchased supplies, and, when they hauled them out the door, Kate rose and stepped to the counter.

The man smiled. "How may I help you?"

"I'm looking for employment." She tipped her head toward the door. "It appears you have many customers. Do you need a store clerk?"

He studied her, and his gaze rested on her sling. Kate swallowed. At least the cloth extended past her hand and hid her missing fingers. She should have placed both hands behind her back as she'd done before.

His eyes narrowed. "Have you ever clerked in a mercantile before?"

"No, but I'm proficient in arithmetic. I came to the territory to teach school, but the position has ... has already been filled. Would you like to test my ability?"

He sucked his lower lip and cocked his head to the side. "Clerking is more than doing figures. You have to help load and unload wagons. It's hard work." He lifted his chin.

"I can do the work. I'm not afraid to exert myself."

He sneered, and his mustache arched. "Think you could lift that barrel you was sitting on?"

Lift a barrel of nails by herself? She was strong for a woman, but not that strong. "Uh ... don't you roll those from place to place?"

He stared at her. "When we can, but we have to lift them at times."

How much did a barrel of nails weigh? If two men could lift one, she could help the storekeeper lift it.

She straightened her spine. "I could help someone else. Together we could lift it."

"I don't think so." His gaze dropped, and he pointed. "You look like you injured your arm."

Kate glanced down. "Not my arm. Just my hand, but it is healing. I will have my strength again soon. I can already use it to write."

The storekeeper crossed his arms. "I don't need you. Even a woman as tall as you don't have the strength to clerk my store—no woman does." He sniffed, and his nose wrinkled. "Are there any supplies you require today?"

Kate's jaw clenched, and she drew a deep breath. "No. Thank you for your time." She left the store with a firm pull of the door. It slapped the doorjamb and rattled as it banged into place. The storekeeper hadn't even given her a chance. Women clerked stores in Boston. In her hometown, the storeowner's wife clerked, often alone. It was obvious this storekeeper did not favor women. She huffed a breath. She wouldn't shop here.

Plodding horses pulled a wagon loaded with lumber past. She crossed the street and headed toward Elizabeth's. She had promised Elizabeth she would find a position, too confident that her search would only take an afternoon. Her shoulders slumped, and she rubbed the ache in the small of her back.

"Why is this so hard, God?" Her voice cracked, but no one was near enough to hear her.

She paused to watch men working on the various buildings and in the scattered campsites along the street. A growing town must have some kind of work a woman could do while she waited for a teaching position. But nothing else came to mind.

She wandered down another street and turned by a structure with a sign proclaiming it the New England Emigrant Aid Company Office. It was not a real building, just a sod-walled hall with a canvas roof, similar to the Kimball's soddie, only bigger. She would meet Dr. Robinson here in a few days.

She jumped aside as the door at the end of the building burst open and three boys dashed out. Four giggling girls strolled through the door next with books clutched to their chests. The town's school must meet here. Several more children of different sizes streamed through the door. The class must have been dismissed for the day.

A young man with black hair walked out and stopped when he noticed her. "Good afternoon." Red flushed his face above a white collar and dark tie. Sweat glistened on his forehead.

Kate nodded. "Are you the teacher?"

"Yes, I am Edward Fitch." His neatly trimmed beard edged his jawline, lending to his intelligent, handsome appearance.

Perhaps here was the opportunity she needed. "I see you have several students."

He smiled. "I do, twenty to be exact."

"Twenty? The town *is* growing. I came to Kansas to teach in Topeka but was delayed, and they hired another person. Could you give me a position in your school?"

A kind smile spread on his face. "No, I can handle a larger class. At any rate, the school term will end soon. If we have a massive group of settlers this summer, we may need another school in the fall. Only time will tell."

A weight bore down on her shoulders. Would she ever find employment, let alone a place to teach?

"I will keep that in mind. Good day." She stumbled past Mr. Fitch and wandered west toward the sawmill. Her eyes stung, and an ache gripped her throat.

Dr. Robinson said he would inquire about teachers needed in other towns. Should she wait for him to locate one or continue searching for a job? She had started her journey with just enough money to travel to Topeka and secure room and board for a couple of months, maybe three. Paying the doctor had reduced her purse. If she wanted to stay in Kansas, she needed to earn something.

If she left now, she might secure passage to St. Louis. She had that much. Would she find work there? St. Louis was a much larger city than

Lawrence or Kansas City. Perhaps she could earn enough to return to Massachusetts, maybe arrive sooner if she sent a message to Father. He could arrange to send money with someone or travel to St. Louis himself.

How easy life had been at Aunt Amelia's home. Boston had a public water system, a myriad of shops and vendors, and an endless supply of every luxury—even a public library. No one in Kansas had a wealth of books like it or like Arthur's personal library. What was he reading now?

She squinted against the sun, her steps dragging. She had come to the territory to strike a blow against slavery. In Boston, she had listened to a former slave tell of the abuse he experienced. She had also witnessed soldiers marching an escaped slave through Boston to return him to chains. The wickedness of slavery urged her to act. She had replaced her dream of a college degree with a desire to help Kansas become a free state. How could she abandon her mission after such a short time?

If she returned to Boston, what would she say to the Forbes? They had provided money for her to travel, believing Kansas should be free. Would they receive her again as the tutor of their children? What about Amelia? Her aunt had been livid to learn of Kate's plan. Would her aunt welcome her, or would she need to return to Mother and Father in Belchertown?

Tears spilled down her cheeks. A clear blue sky stretched overhead, but it might as well have been a Nor'easter. Everything had gone awry. Why had God allowed the stupid snake to bite her? She wasn't Eve, tempted by a serpent to eat the forbidden fruit. She'd just reached for her bonnet. Was that so wrong? Had she made a mistake coming to the territory? Was God punishing her?

She filled her lungs with a shuddering breath. Maybe God was testing her. Joseph faced a test when he was sold into slavery and later imprisoned. But God had elevated him to the second-in-command of Egypt.

She blew her nose and wiped tears from her cheeks. God *must be* testing her. She would stay in Kansas and wait for a teaching position, even though she would need to earn money in a different way for a short time. She would return to Elizabeth and pay for her board. It would reduce her coins enough that she couldn't return to Boston, but it would display her trust in God.

12

Kate shuffled into the Kimball's lot where Elizabeth knelt beside the fire with her head low, blowing on the coals. A small stream of smoke drifted toward the sawmill.

Elizabeth rose to her feet and shook out her skirt as Kate approached. "You've been gone a long time. I hope it went well."

"Yes, a long afternoon." She hoped the color had cleared from her tear-reddened eyes.

Elizabeth strode forward and wrapped an arm across Kate's shoulders. "You must be exhausted. Come and sit down. I'll get you some water."

"I will in a moment." She walked to the shack, entered, and took her purse from the trunk. Her stomach tightened as she counted out two dollars in coins. She needed to do this now. She slipped the purse back into the trunk and returned to the fire.

Elizabeth handed her a mug of water. "Now sit and drink this. You look like you walked all the way from Boston. Don't forget you're still recovering."

Kate thrust out her fist. "Please take this." She dropped the coins into Elizabeth's palm.

"What's this?" Elizabeth studied the coins, and her eyebrows drew together. "Why did you give me this?"

"You and Samuel have been so good to me." She squared her shoulders. "I insist that I pay for my bed and board."

Elizabeth shook her head and shoved her hand forward. "I won't hear of it, Kate. You're our guest, not our boarder. We don't need this money as much as you do."

"You *must* take it." She couldn't allow Elizabeth to dissuade her, not if she wanted to succeed in her mission. "So much has happened to me since I arrived in the territory. I couldn't understand why God allowed it. Now I realize my problems are a test. The coins express my appreciation to you, but they also demonstrate my commitment and faith."

"Giving me money demonstrates faith? I don't understand."

Kate drew a deep breath and licked her lips. "I miss home ... more than I thought I would. This afternoon, the thought of returning to Massachusetts tempted me." Elizabeth's eyebrows lifted at her words. "I don't have enough money to return, at least all the way, but what would that accomplish? Nothing good. I don't know how I would reestablish myself there. It's ... it's a long story, but I could—"

Elizabeth wrapped Kate in a hug. "You don't need to do this."

"Yes, I do. Please accept it," she said against her friend's shoulder.

Elizabeth held her at arm's length, her face clouded like a rain shower, before dropping her arms and slipping the coins into her apron pocket. "Did you find a job this afternoon?"

"No, but I will continue to look. I also need to find a room in one of the boardinghouses in town."

Elizabeth turned to place wood on the fire. "I walked past a new boarding establishment today that opened on the other side of town. I wouldn't call it a boardinghouse because they haven't built anything yet, but they have several tents. Mrs. Clarissa Hurd runs it. Her two sons, they're carpenters, will build the house. Since it's new, it may be cheaper than other places."

"Thank you, that's good to know." Kate lifted the mug and drained it.

Elizabeth had walked around town to investigate boardinghouses, something she didn't need to do. She was sweet and polite, but also eager to gain more privacy.

An establishment offering tents—canvas walls would not provide the same security as sod walls, but the canvas might shed the summer heat better than a roof of bundled grass.

"I will inquire if Mrs. Hurd has space for me this evening. How can I help you prepare our supper?"

Kate wound through the streets of the scattered camps and buildings. Elizabeth had given her directions to a part of town she had not yet visited, which lay on the east side beyond the main street and a few blocks south of the river.

Elizabeth's stew and biscuits had revived her energy. How could her friend bring perfection from a Dutch oven and a campfire? Kate strolled through the cool evening air stirred by a light breeze, such a pleasant evening even if she had to walk across town to find a new place to stay.

She approached a lot with neatly spaced tents and a crude sign in front reading, "Hurd & Hall Room & Board." On the front side of the lot, men sat on logs around a fire next to a white canvas tarp suspended by poles and ropes over a long table fashioned from rough boards. Two women dried dishes at the end of the table. The camp matched Elizabeth's description.

Kate stopped near the older woman. "Are you Mrs. Hurd?"

The stout woman with gray hair pulled into a bun at the back of her neck smiled and laid the dish towel on the table. "Yes, I'm Clarissa Hurd. You looking for a place to stay?" Her eyes held a shrewd, calculating cast.

"Yes, but I don't know how long I'll stay in town."

Mrs. Hurd eyed the sling. "Just you? No husband or children?"

Heat crept into Kate's cheeks. "Yes, just me. I came to the territory to teach school, but the position promised to me is no longer available. Do you provide room and board by the day, the week, or the month?"

Mrs. Hurd smiled. "I can do any of those. Would you like to see our accommodations?"

"Yes, please."

Mrs. Hurd gestured across the lot. "Let's start over there." She marched toward a pile of large limestone rocks, and Kate followed. The murmuring voices of the men seated around the fire stopped, and their eyes followed her. Were they wondering about her sling or her marked face?

"We just came to town." Mrs. Hurd stopped and turned. "My boys, George and Henry—they're carpenters—will start stacking the foundation tomorrow." She pointed at the center of the camp with both hands and drew a rectangle in the air. "Like so. It'll be two stories with rooms for eight boarders."

Would Kate even live in Lawrence long enough to see it completed? The breeze lifted a tent flap.

"I'm sure it will be nice, Mrs. Hurd."

"Call me Clarissa. I let the womenfolk do that, but not the men. I keep them respectful." She cocked her head and studied Kate. "Don't worry about the tents. My boys will have the house up in no time." She pointed at the three tents nearest them. "That's the men's side. Notice they have a separate privy."

She hadn't noticed the wooden privies with shake-shingle roofs, each standing in a back corner of the lot. "I'm impressed. How long since you arrived in Lawrence?"

Clarissa's eyes twinkled. "A couple of days. I told you my boys were quick." She touched Kate's arm. "Come on, you'll like the women's quarters." She marched through the open area toward the opposite corner. "No makeshift shacks for our privies." She jabbed a finger at Kate. "You won't find other boarding houses with separate ones for men and women either."

"You don't say."

They stopped before the middle tent of three. Clarissa pointed to the tent on the left. "That's full of my things and supplies. I'll thank you kindly not to enter it." She gestured to the tent on the right. "Lydia and I sleep there." She grasped the canvas flap of the tent before her and lifted it, revealing a work of art. "This is where you'll stay."

A brown trunk sat open in the back with an eight-legged metal cot extending out of it across the tent. A sheet wrapped the mattress, and blankets lay folded on top. Two darker trunks were stacked at the end of the bed, and two more brown ones sat on each side of the tent closer to the door.

"California beds with real mattresses!" Clarissa beamed. "They say George Washington slept on one much like this during the Revolution."

Kate stepped inside. "I'm surprised the tent has so much room."

"Oh, I should tell you, the bed in the back is already taken. The two trunks on each side hold more beds. Three women will share this tent, so it'll be tight quarters." Clarissa wore a bland smile.

Three women with their luggage would leave a narrow aisle. Tight quarters, indeed. Still, beds were better than sleeping on the ground where rain could run under the wall. The new canvas tent should shed water without leaking, but would it remain upright in a fierce wind? She wet her lips and stepped out of the tent.

Clarissa touched Kate's arm. "Remember, it's temporary. I'm sure the house will be ready in just a month or two."

She might not stay that long. In a few days, Dr. Robinson could report finding a teaching position elsewhere in Kansas. She turned to Clarissa. "Please tell me your rates."

"Lodging's fifteen cents and board's seventy-five cents a day. You can get both for a week at three dollars and fifty cents—in advance."

Kate crossed her arms, careful of her hand and sling. The weekly rate was almost half that of the daily rate for a week. The amount she had given Elizabeth was not as generous as she thought.

"I want to check the other boarding houses in town before I commit."

"You'll find the rates are the same, and you won't find a better place." Clarissa planted her hands on her hips. "I don't brook any male shenanigans in my home either. You can see this is a good place for a woman alone."

The look on Clarissa's face would give any man pause. Kate smiled. Maybe she could kill two birds with one stone.

"Clarissa, do you need any help cooking? I'm willing to assist you for a discount on your rate."

Clarissa shook her head. "Lydia provides all the help I need." She pursed her lips and squinted. "You realize people keep coming to town, don't you? I hear the aid company's got several more groups coming this summer. I can't hold a spot for you. You best take a place now."

"I do hope more people come." Kate smiled. "Still, I want to examine the other boarding houses tomorrow." Hopefully, she would also find a job.

"Suit yourself." Clarissa turned toward the table.

Kate strolled out of the camp and retraced her steps through town. She could afford to stay at Clarissa's for a week or two while waiting for word from Dr. Robinson, but it would be expensive. For that matter, she could remain at the Kimball's for a few more days, but she couldn't overstay their welcome. The snakebite had knocked her off course, and she needed to find her way again.

By the time Kate stepped up to the Kimball's fire, her legs were leaden weights. "Good evening." Even her voice sounded tired.

"Were you able to find the Hurds?" Elizabeth sat in a chair pulled close to Samuel's and facing the flickering fire. Samuel's black hat perched on the back of his head revealing his light brown hair.

"Yes, you gave excellent directions." She sat on the remaining chair. "I'll check the other boardinghouses tomorrow, but Mrs. Hurd impressed me." She sighed. "I'll also continue to look for work."

Samuel poked the fire with a stick. "I heard of a job you might try ... if it works for your hand."

"Oh, what is it?"

"There's a woman who washes clothes. She's got so much work, she's looking for help, so I've heard. I guess all these men in town need someone to clean the stench from their duds." A grin stretched his sparsely bearded cheeks as he gazed at Elizabeth. "Not everyone's as lucky as me to have a pretty wife to wash his clothes."

Elizabeth blushed, hands pressed to her heart. "Oh, Samuel."

Samuel was trying to be helpful, but wash clothes? Her hand had not yet healed. No, she would find something different than scrubbing laundry.

"Thank you. I'll check it out."

13

Kate shuffled away from a cluster of tents around a campfire—another boardinghouse with no room for her. The beginning of a large house stood nearby, rough studs reaching twenty feet into the air traced halfway around the structure. Four men worked to lift and brace additional pieces of lumber into place.

During the morning, she had visited five establishments—all she could find. Two had room for a woman lodger but charged the same rates as Clarissa Hurd's home and only had one privy. None of them would provide a discount for helping in the kitchen. She would return to Clarissa Hurd later today or tomorrow and secure a bed.

Her footsteps scraped the dried ruts in the road. The pinging of a blacksmith's hammer rang from under a canvas tarp suspended over an anvil. A shirtless man, a leather apron hung from his neck, swung a hammer against a metal rod glowing dull red. No need to inquire here. She had stopped at more than a dozen businesses—storekeepers, lawyers, even a shoemaker and a watchmaker. None expressed interest in hiring her. The town had plenty of work for carpenters, stonemasons, and other male trades, but little for women.

At the north edge of town, she stopped atop the levee. Stumps lined the riverbank. She would find no shade since men had already cut all the trees standing in Lawrence for lumber or firewood.

To her left, a team of brown mules dragged logs from the river toward the sawmill while men used poles to pull ashore more floating from upstream. Before her, the river rippled across a rocky ledge. In the distance to her right, a woman in a shirtwaist and dark skirt dipped buckets in the river. The woman who seemed to be her last hope of finding work.

Kate followed the top of the riverbank to a sign stuck in the ground, painted with one word: "laundry." Beside it, white shirts, dark trousers, and white underclothes waved in the breeze from a cord strung between two horizontal boards fastened to posts. Kate turned and descended the riverbank toward the woman climbing up with two water buckets suspended from a yoke across her shoulders. They met at a flat bench where a cauldron sat on smoking coals.

"Are you here to pick up laundry? I don't remember you." The young woman scrutinized her with sharp eyes. Wisps of hair the color of honey danced in the breeze beside her sweaty face. The woman was shorter than Kate but beautiful except for her frown.

Kate licked her lips. "No, I heard you may be looking for someone to help you with your business."

The woman squatted to rest the buckets on the ground and lifted the yoke off her shoulders. She eased herself straight, one hand on the small of her back. "Yes, I am." She eyed Kate's sling. "What's wrong with your arm?"

"A snake bit me, but it's almost healed."

She grunted. "You ever washed clothes before?"

"Yes, I helped my mother. My name is Kate Collins."

"Have you washed the clothes of people other than your own family?"

What difference did that make? Weren't dirty clothes the same everywhere? "No, I have not. May I inquire what your name is?"

"Martha Groot." She placed her hands on her hips. "What'd your father do for a living?"

Father's business was losing every penny of Mother's inheritance, but she couldn't say that. "He's an investor."

"Investor?" Martha shook her head and curled her lip. "Have you ever made soap?"

"No, my mother always purchased soap."

She sniffed and nodded. "So, you're well-to-do. You any good at mending?"

Kate bit her lip. She was an adequate seamstress, but holding a needle would be difficult until all the strength and flexibility in her fingers returned. "I can sew but ..." She shrugged. "I will be slow until my hand fully recovers."

"You talk like you went to school a lot."

"Yes. I attended school in Belchertown, Massachusetts. My mother also taught me the classics. I emigrated to Kansas to teach, but the snakebite delayed my travel, and the teaching position closed. I decided to stay in Lawrence and seek work." She stopped herself before explaining that she intended to take a teaching position when one became available.

"That must've been nice. Going to school every day. I didn't get to. I worked so my sisters could go." She pointed at Kate's sling. "Show me your hand, Missy."

Kate's lips and cheeks tightened. Martha had every right to determine if she could perform the work, but couldn't she remember her name? She demanded to see Kate's hand as if she were a child, even though they appeared to be the same age. Did Martha use rudeness to assert control?

Kate pulled the edge of the sling back to her wrist. The bandage covered her hand but did not hide the fact of two missing fingers. Her pulse throbbed in her hand as Martha bent forward, puckered her lips, and studied it.

"It looks painful. Are you sure you can wash clothes?"

"Yes, I can work." Kate lifted her head. She would make her own way in spite of her weak hand.

Martha straightened. "Can you build a fire?"

Did the woman think her an imbecile? "Of course, I can build a fire. Would you like one in a stove, a fireplace, or here on the ground?" She gestured at the coals under the caldron.

Martha studied the ground, her lips twisted. "I need help in the worst way. I got more work than I can handle, and no one else has asked all week." She stared into Kate's eyes. "I won't pay much since you only have one hand."

She needed to earn something. She couldn't use up all her money just in case she needed to travel some distance to the next teaching position. "What are you willing to pay?"

"I do laundry and a lot of patching rips and the knees of pants." Martha brushed a strand of hair back over her head. "You could focus on hauling water and firewood." She lifted her chin. "I'll pay you two bits a day."

Her offer was an insult. Men earned six bits a day as laborers. Twenty-five cents would only pay for one meal without any lodging.

"I can do the work, but your offer isn't enough. I'll haul the water, tend the fire, and wash clothes when my hand no longer needs to be bandaged ... for seventy-five cents a day."

Martha drew a deep breath and looked past Kate's shoulder at the top of the riverbank. "I'll give you four bits to start. When you can scrub as many clothes as I do each day, I'll pay sixty cents." She crossed her arms.

Kate glanced at the fire. How many clothes could Martha wash in a day? Two wash tubs sat beyond the fire, and clothes formed a mound on the ground next to one. How long would she need to labor in the sun bent over a washtub before a teaching position opened? Would this woman be a fair employer? Martha stared at her with a grim face. She would demand hard work just like she demanded to see her hand.

Kate should leave, but what choice did she have? She had tried everywhere in town. She swallowed. "I accept your terms. I can start tomorrow morning."

Martha nodded. "I start when the sawmill starts. Don't be late." She started to turn but stopped. "We may start when the sawmill does, but we keep working even if that finicky thing breaks down."

"I understand." Kate turned and climbed the bank.

After lunch with Elizabeth, she would walk to Clarissa's and pay for her first week. If she skipped lunch each day, her wages would only be five cents short of paying for her room and board. Of course, Sunday would require some of her savings since she wouldn't work that day. After Samuel returned with the wagon at the end of the day, she would eat supper with her friends before they hauled her trunks to her new lodging.

14

S amuel slapped the reins on the team's hindquarters, and the horses leaned into the harness. He steered the wagon around the corner, chains clinking with the soft thud of hooves on dirt.

"I think this is exciting." Elizabeth gushed like a schoolgirl from her place in the middle of the bench. "Are you happy to find a place to stay? I knew you would find a good place. I'm glad you're staying in town, at least for a while. I hope you find a teaching position close." She laid a hand on Kate's. "You've become a friend."

Kate managed a brief smile. "I don't know whether to be excited to stay at Hurd and Hall's or not. I would be much happier finding a teaching position." She squeezed Elizabeth's hand. "You became my friend as well. I enjoyed staying with you." Elizabeth's kindness and open heart made friendship easy.

"I can't believe it's already May." Elizabeth all but bounced on the seat. "How time flies. My momma's mayflowers should be blooming in Fitchburg. The daffodils are past, but tulips would still be in bloom. Don't you think Kansas is rather dull? Not much spring color."

"Yes, though I saw some small wildflowers on the prairie when we came from Kansas City." The town certainly could use some color other than black dirt and green grass. "I'm told the sunflowers bloom profusely during the summer."

"I want to plant flowers around our home." She turned to Samuel. "Can I do that now?"

He smiled. "Of course, but I can't promise they won't get trampled on as we build the house."

Elizabeth was as perky as a bird building a nest. And why wouldn't she be? She knew she had a home and could pursue her dreams of children and family. Kate had watched Elizabeth lift a white baby dress from her trunk to her face this morning. After smelling it, she held it to her heart before laying it back in the trunk. A sigh eased from Kate. When would she know the location of her home and be able to pursue her dream?

"I wish I had brought some bulbs with me. I have no idea where I'll get flowers here." Elizabeth shook her head.

"Flowers will be lovely. I look forward to seeing your home completed with bright blossoms in front of it." The idea of admiring blossoms made good conversation, but would Kate stay in town that long, or had Dr. Robinson already found a place for her to teach?

Kate squirmed and tugged the sling's fabric from her elbow, drawing her arm out. She lifted the sling off her neck and fumbled with the knot until she untied it. It was time to rid herself of such a visible sign of misfortune. The sooner she could use her hand to scrub clothes, the sooner she could earn more money. She folded the fabric into a neat square and clutched it in her left hand.

"You did that quite well," Elizabeth said. "Your hand has improved so much."

"Yes, it has. The sling has become such a bother. It won't be long before I can remove the bandage."

Kate listened to Elizabeth chatter like a songbird as they rode down the dirt streets until Samuel finally hauled back on the reins at Mrs. Hurd's encampment. Clarissa and another woman stacked clean dishes at the end of the table under the canvas fly, but Clarissa turned her head at their arrival and marched toward the wagon. Samuel swung Elizabeth to the ground and helped Kate step down.

"Welcome." Clarissa stopped with her hands on her hips.

"Mrs. Hurd, this is Samuel and Elizabeth Kimball," Kate said.

"Nice to meet you." Clarissa thrust out her hand, and Samuel shook it. She turned toward the fire and lifted her voice. "George. You and Henry come help with Miss Collins's things. Bring Robert to help you."

Samuel met the other men at the back of the wagon. Each took the end of a trunk and started for the women's tents. One of the men grinned through his auburn beard as he passed Kate. "Howdy. Nice to have another woman here." Clarissa swatted his arm and shook her head, a half-smile on her face.

Kate followed the men with Elizabeth and Clarissa beside her.

"I opened up the California bed on the right side just as you wanted," Clarissa said. "You'll be able to put your trunks just inside the door, though you'll need to stack 'em."

Kate nodded. "That shouldn't be a problem." Hopefully, she could meet the woman who shared the tent, and she would be as easygoing and friendly as Elizabeth.

Clarissa hurried forward and swept back the tent flap. The box holding the bed had been opened, and the cot unfolded. "Look at that mattress. Brand new. Never been slept on. You won't have to worry about any bed bugs. You'll be glad you chose to stay here."

Kate bent to peer into the tent. "Yes, it looks nice." Her tentmate's bed across the back looked the same as earlier, but the tent was otherwise empty.

"They go here, boys." Clarissa pointed to the end of the bed closest to the flap. "Miss Collins, which do you want on top?"

Kate pointed. "That one."

The men stacked the trunks, turned, and left. Kate opened the trunk and pulled out bedding and a small pillow.

"Let me help you with that." Elizabeth ducked into the tent, shook a sheet out over the cot, and tucked it under the thin mattress on one end while Kate did the other.

"I'll finish this later." Kate laid the bedding and pillow on the bed, reached inside her collar, and fished out a key hanging by a string around her neck.

"That for your trunk?" Clarissa said.

"Yes." Kate clicked the trunk's metal hasp in place and locked it before slipping the string around her neck and dropping the key inside her blouse. Locking the trunk seemed prudent since the canvas walls were her only protection, even if it might offend Clarissa.

Clarissa nodded. "I don't board riffraff, but you're smart to lock your luggage." She turned and strode toward the fire. "Alrighty, let's go meet everyone."

Elizabeth and Samuel followed, and Kate fell in step beside them. "I don't know how I can ever thank you for allowing me to stay with you while I recovered. You've been most kind."

Samuel smiled. "It's our pleasure. We all need to help each other in this new land."

"I hope you come back and see us." Elizabeth clasped Kate's hand. "We're just across town. Maybe I'll see you at church?"

"I'm sure we will see each other often. I won't be a stranger."

They reached the wagon, and Elizabeth wrapped Kate in a strong embrace. Samuel helped Elizabeth into the wagon and climbed up beside her. With a snap of the reins, the wagon turned into the wagon tracks marking the street.

Kate turned toward the campfire, where Clarissa introduced her to the woman she had seen earlier. Lydia Hall was as tall as Kate, with dark hair parted and pulled into a knot on the back of her head. Clarissa plopped down on a wooden keg facing the fire. The men around the fire stopped talking and gazed at her.

"I'm glad you've joined us," Lydia said. "Shall we sit?" She settled onto a wooden crate, and Kate perched on the edge of an uprooted stump placed near the fire.

"Listen up." Clarissa's voice carried like a sergeant barking orders. "This is our new boarder, Miss Kate Collins." She pointed at the man who had greeted her earlier. "My youngest, Henry." He grinned. Clarissa continued around the circle. "That's my oldest, George, and Robert Hubbard." Both had helped with the trunks. "And Tom Gordon." The man sitting on an upturned chunk of tree trunk had a weathered face and salt-and-pepper hair.

Everyone murmured greetings, and Kate politely replied. Henry, George, and Robert returned to their conversation, and she leaned close to Lydia. "Is Clarissa a widow?"

"Yes. She left two married daughters and three grandchildren back in Massachusetts." Lydia's long face and brown eyes held the tranquility of a summer evening.

"You stay in the tent with Clarissa, is that right?"

"We share it along with several trunks of household goods and kitchen supplies. I'm part owner of the boardinghouse."

Kate glanced around the fire. "The woman who shares a tent with me—is she here?"

"She often takes a walk in the evening. I'm sure she'll return soon."

"What happened to your hand?" George's loud voice came from where he sat on the log with his elbows on his knees.

The other voices fell silent, and everyone looked at her. The fire popped and crackled, reflecting in their eyes.

Kate tensed. If she refused to explain her injury, what would they think? She filled her lungs and told the story of coming to Kansas, the snakebite, and her surgery.

"I lost some parts too." George grinned through his ginger whiskers and held up a hand missing the ends of his middle and ring fingers. "Caught 'em in a belt at the shop."

"He worked in a cabinet shop in Lowell." Henry peered at her from under bushy red eyebrows. "He didn't mean you disrespect."

She nodded. "None taken."

"How long you been a teacher?" Robert's dirty-white hair hung long over his ears, and a scraggly beard covered his jaw.

She swallowed. Would they scoff if she told them she had tutored two children for less than a year? "A while."

"I sure hope you support a free state. We don't need any slavers here." Robert narrowed his eyes and leaned forward.

Her shoulders relaxed. "Rest assured. I support a free state. It is the primary reason I emigrated."

"Alright, that's enough." Clarissa scowled at Robert. "You don't have to question her like she's a spy."

Henry and Robert began grumbling about the Missouri men placed in the territorial legislature by the stolen election before she had arrived in the territory. George voiced his opinions, but Tom sat and listened, whittling a block of wood. As the dusk deepened, Clarissa added a chunk of wood to the fire.

"Good evening, gentlemen."

Martha Groot, the laundress, strolled up to the edge of the group, her appearance fresh compared to the sweat she wore at the river. Her hair was combed into a neat chignon. All the men except Tom grinned like they were eyeing their favorite pie. Tom just nodded. Martha sashayed past Henry, and her skirt swished across his knees. Such a blatant flirt! After the pretty young woman perched on the log, she gazed around the fire and stopped on Kate. "Oh. Have you joined us, Missy?"

The muscles in Kate's arms and back tightened. If the woman had forgotten her name, the polite approach would be to ask for it. But Martha knew her name. She intended the slight.

"Miss Collins is boarding here." Disapproval loaded Clarissa's voice. "You will share a tent with her."

Kate's stomach sank at the thought of Martha sleeping a couple of feet from her. Lydia glanced at Kate and lifted an eyebrow. Was that sympathy in her eyes?

Martha lifted her chin, turned, and graced Henry with a dazzling smile and words too soft for Kate to hear. Clarissa began talking to Lydia about plans for breakfast, but she glanced several times at Martha. Did she distrust the younger woman? Was Martha the reason Clarissa thought locked trunks a good idea?

Kate crossed her arms and leaned toward the fire. It was bad enough that Martha looked to be a demanding employer, but now she would share a tent with the pretty young woman, a woman who couldn't be trusted.

15

Kate marched toward the sod and canvas hall housing the aid company office. She couldn't swing her right hand in a normal stride, or it throbbed and swelled. She carried it pressed to her waist instead. The last few days of hauling water and firewood had left her with an aching back and sore shoulders, but her aches didn't slow her pace.

Dr. Robinson had set this day to meet and tell her about the settlements needing a teacher. She would march from his office to the riverbank and inform Martha of her new employment. Would Martha still dare to call her Missy then?

She reached the aid company door and stopped to brush the front of her dress. She had chosen her nicest, a light blue chintz printed with delicate, white branching leaves and flowers, more fitting for a teacher than her dark-colored work dress, which needed a good soak and scrub. She hadn't yet asked Martha about laundering her own dress since she would probably demand payment for the use of her tubs and soap. Kate pulled the bonnet from her head and brushed a strand of hair behind her ear. What had she been thinking when she chose not to pack at least one nice hat?

The door of rough boards swung open at her tug, and she stepped inside. Dr. Robinson sat at a desk on one side of the room, in front of a canvas curtain separating the back half of the structure.

He lifted his gaze from the papers on his desk. "Ah, Miss Collins." He set down his pen. "Right. I asked you to speak to me, didn't I?"

Her greeting died on her lips as he appeared to have forgotten about their meeting.

The doctor rose from his chair. "I'm glad you're here. It has already been a busy morning. Please sit." He motioned to three wooden chairs facing the desk.

"Good morning, Dr. Robinson." She settled into the first chair, her throat dry.

"How is your hand? May I examine it?"

"Yes ... of course." She lifted her hand to him. He had already removed the stitches. Why talk about her hand instead of teaching positions? She fought hard not to bounce her knee.

He turned her hand over and studied it from different angles, his eyebrows knit together. "The wound appears closed, but the skin is bright red and cracked."

"I'm working with Martha Groot, washing clothes. The soap irritates it."

"The woman with the sign on the riverbank?"

"Yes."

He nodded and released her hand. "You may want to rub some butter or lard on it at night to soften and restore the skin." He returned to his chair.

"Thank you for your advice." She couldn't afford butter, even if the store could find a supply.

"I must apologize for not expecting you. The sawmill broke again, and orders are backed up because of the huge demand. Even when the mill works, they often must wait for the Shawnee to deliver more logs. Men accosted me about the problem several times this morning."

She had noticed the absence of the mill's whine, but why did he choose to talk about the broken mill instead of a potential job for her?

The doctor spread his hands and shrugged. "The sawmill issues have distracted me from addressing the bogus legislature. I have been meeting with many of the free-state leaders to discuss a remedy to the fact slavery-loving men from Missouri will draft our laws."

"Dr. Robinson, have you—"

"The company has also arranged more groups to emigrate this year. I expect one to arrive in the next week or two."

She nodded and leaned forward. "Dr. Rob—"

"William Dutton leads it." He glanced at his papers and spoke in a lower voice. "I understand a smaller number joined than our earlier groups." He straightened and sniffed in a deep breath. "However, despite all this, I did inquire about teaching positions and have received news from our other settlements."

"Yes?" A flutter brushed her stomach. Had he found a teaching position for her? Would she need to travel far? Could it be near the Big Blue River where Hattie had settled?

He folded his hands and leaned his elbows on the desk. "Unfortunately, none of the other towns need a teacher at this time."

Her throat tightened. "Oh. I ... I see." The ache in her shoulders pressed on her, and she sank against the back of the chair. "Thank you." Must she continue to work for Martha, scrubbing clothes for a woman who demanded she work faster in the blazing sun? "Will you continue to look for me?"

A smile lit his eyes. "Yes, of course. The aid company still plans to provide teachers for the settlements we start, and others are also starting towns. More people come to Kansas every month. You remember how busy Kansas City was, don't you? I'm sure the need for teachers will grow."

More people came to the territory every month, but some would be teachers, just like those who had settled in Topeka. Had she missed her opportunity? Had she come to Kansas for nothing?

Dr. Robinson lifted his eyebrows. "Is there anything else I can do for you today?"

She clenched her jaw to stop it from trembling and rose to her feet. "No, but should you hear of a teaching position, please inform me."

"Of course I will." He picked up a stack of papers from the desk, already moving past their conversation.

Kate shuffled out the door, her eyes stinging, and stopped. The blue sky mocked her, and the breeze teased her hair. Her bonnet hung in her left hand. She lifted the cap, ready to throw it in the dirt and stomp on it, but gasped a shaky breath and dropped her arm. She stumbled toward the river. She would need to work for Martha today, after all.

But she couldn't. She halted and fingered the fabric of her beautiful skirt. Her work dress was still in the tent.

Tears filled her eyes, and she slipped the bonnet over her head and tied it. If she returned to the tent by way of the riverbank, Martha might see her. She clenched her jaw and turned back toward town. She would go another way. Martha must *not* see her like this.

She turned away from the river and shuffled down the street, wiping her eyes. Why did she face so many problems? She only wanted to do good, teach children, and help Kansas become a free state.

Why did God allow her problems to fester? Didn't he want her to make the world a better place? She had lost part of her hand. Lost a promised job as a teacher. Every day, she lost money paying for room and board while slaving for a hard young woman—one blessed with beauty unblemished by a birthmark.

A sob escaped her throat. Would her problems ever end? But it wasn't just her problems. Why had God allowed Missourians to steal the election? Didn't he care about the slaves? Why did he allow slavery to continue?

She stumbled over a wagon rut and stopped. The Hurd camp lay ahead. She lifted her handkerchief and blew her nose. All she could do was change her dress, haul water, and stoke the fire. She would plunge her hands, knuckles already roughened by the washboard, into tubs filled with water and lye soap. She tried to straighten her shoulders and walked toward the tents.

Lydia stood under the fly, kneading dough on a large, flat board. "How did it go? Has the doctor found a teaching position for you?"

Kate's throat burned and tightened. "No." She hurried to her tent, fell on her cot, and sobbed into her pillow.

16

The tent flap rustled, and Kate jerked, her muscles rigid. She couldn't face Martha now.

"May I come in?" Lydia asked.

Kate's shoulders relaxed. "Yes." She choked off a sob and sat up, hugging the pillow to her chest.

"May I sit?"

"Please do." She rummaged in her pocket for her handkerchief and wiped her eyes.

The cot creaked as Lydia lowered herself onto it. She waited in silence with her hands clasped on her lap. Kate blew her nose, took a deep breath, and let her hands drop on the pillow.

"I take it you received bad news." Lydia rested her hand on Kate's shoulder.

"Yes, no teaching positions are available at this time." She dragged the heel of a shoe across the matted grass.

"Will Dr. Robinson still consider you if another position opens?"

She drew a deep breath and released it. "He said he would." She was a fool to lose control of her emotions. The doctor had only looked for a week. What must Lydia think of her?

Lydia rubbed the back of Kate's shoulders. "This is just a temporary setback. I'm sure you will find a position soon. People continue to emigrate. New communities sprout all the time. I'm sure someone will need a teacher soon."

"You don't understand." She couldn't keep the waver from her voice.

Lydia clasped her hands and waited a moment. "Perhaps I ... Can you tell me what I need to know?"

"I came to Kansas to teach school. But every time I turn around, I face a new problem. Now I can't teach and must scrub clothes all day. Why won't God clear a path for me?"

"You think teaching school is God's will? Your mission?"

"Of course it is. Why wouldn't God support my efforts to do something good for others?" Fresh tears stung her eyes, and her throat burned.

"How do you know God wants you to teach? Maybe he has something else in mind?"

"But what could be more important? By teaching school for the aid company, I help attract free-state families to the territory. It is my way to fight slavery. Kansas must be free."

Kate laid the pillow on the bed. "What could be more important than abolition?"

"Abolition is important, but—"

"I can't vote. I can't run for office. I didn't want to simply attend teas and walk in protests. I came to Kansas to teach children about what's right and to help bring settlers to Kansas. Don't you think that's important?"

Lydia's mouth twitched, and she bit her lip. "Do you think God only wants you to do important things?"

"No. But we ... we should be kind to those in need ... like the Good Samaritan." Like Elizabeth had been to her. "God also wants us to confront evil, does he not? Don't you believe we should fight slavery?"

Lydia stared at the tent wall with pursed lips, then glanced at Kate and nodded. "Yes, I do."

"Then why do I face so many problems trying to teach? What have I done wrong? Why doesn't God help me?"

"Have you done something wrong?" Lydia gazed at her with soft eyes. "Do you think God is punishing you?"

"No, but it feels that way."

"I'm sure it does. Did you pray about coming to the territory?"

Of course, Lydia would ask that question since she read her Bible and prayed each day. "Yes, I've prayed many times while I tutored children in Boston and saved money to attend college. I've always dreamed of leading social reform, but I couldn't continue as a tutor." Words poured from her like water from a breached dam. "I needed to act, to help. The more I understood about the suffering of slaves, the more restless I became.

"I had heard Kansas needed free-state settlers, but I had no money to emigrate. How could I continue to tutor in Boston or allow Arthur to call on me when my help was needed elsewhere? So, I asked God to provide the money I needed to emigrate to Kansas. When I told Mrs. Forbes about my desire, she told her husband, and they gave me the rest of the funds I needed. God answered my prayer."

Lydia's brown eyes peered into Kate's. "Arthur? Who's Arthur?"

Her breath caught. Had she mentioned Arthur? Heat pressed down from the canvas roof, and she bolted to her feet. "I need some fresh air." She ducked through the tent flaps and rushed toward the front of the camp.

Her mind swirled. So much had happened in the last six weeks, but she didn't have time for dramatics. Martha would already dock her pay, but she couldn't go to work now, not in her good dress. She turned south onto the street, the direction away from the river.

Lydia caught up to her side, skirt rustling. "I apologize. I didn't mean to upset you by prying into your past."

Kate slowed her pace to a stroll. "No, you asked a question. I just ... I just needed some fresh air. Arthur is the man who courted me in Boston."

"I see."

"I told him I could not see him any longer."

Lydia nodded. "He was unsuitable to become your husband."

"No, he's a fine man."

Lydia tucked her chin and furrowed her brow. They passed a house where four men nailed siding to wall studs. The banging of their hammers held no rhythm.

Kate drew a slow breath and released it. "We enjoyed discussing literature together and agreed on most things. I have no complaints about the way he treated me. He will make an excellent husband for the right woman, just not me."

"Why do you say that?"

"Marriage is too restrictive. I want to remain a spinster like Lucy Stone. I want to abolish slavery and help women gain their rights. If I marry, my husband could decide to move us to a different city or spend all the money on foolish speculations." Her jaw tightened, and she crossed her arms.

"Have you seen that happen?"

Kate nodded. "My father. He means well, but my mother has suffered from his decisions." Mother wasn't the only one. Father had taken the inheritance intended for Kate's college and wasted it, but Lydia didn't need to know that.

"I've read about many of the women in the abolition and women's rights movements and know a few. Many are married," Lydia said.

"Lucy Stone isn't."

They walked in silence, passing other vacant lots until they reached the edge of town, and the grass stretched before them. They stood with the breeze in their faces, and Kate inhaled the faint smell of prairie grass. In the distance, a line of wagons headed toward them, their canvas covers swaying from the ruts on the road and the wind.

Lydia said, "Do you think Arthur wanted to marry you?"

"I fear he considered it. One day, we walked through the Commons. It was a beautiful afternoon with brisk air and blue skies, but sunshine warmed my back. Swollen buds cast a burgundy tint on the tree limbs, and yellow and blue hyacinths had started to ..." Arthur had looked so dignified in his black coat and top hat.

"It sounds beautiful."

"It was." Kate gestured at the landscape before them. "Not like this treeless prairie. He told me about Dahlia, a woman he loved and hoped to marry, but she had died of pneumonia a year before we met. He said my passion for politics and reform reminded him of her."

"He must have admired her greatly."

"He had gazed across the park as if looking out to sea. He never said it, but I know he loved Dahlia deeply." Kate dabbed a tear. "After telling me about her, we walked for several minutes. He turned to me and said he had become accustomed to me walking at his side and looked forward to many more days when we could walk hand in hand."

Lydia inhaled a quick breath. "Really? That sounds like a strong hint of his intentions."

"I thought so, but I didn't tell anyone about it. I thought he wanted to gauge my reaction to the idea of marriage. You think the same, yes?"

"I do." A small smile lifted the corner of her mouth. "What did you say to him?"

"I changed the subject. But I knew I needed to take action and remembered the aid company's efforts to help people emigrate. I visited their office to discover the costs and prayed God would provide a way."

"Did you discuss your hope to emigrate with Arthur? Did he agree or discourage you?" Lydia asked.

"No, we didn't discuss it." Perhaps she should have. She hadn't discussed it with Aunt Amelia or her parents either, so why involve him? "I mentioned my idea to the Forbes, the parents of my students, and they agreed to give me the rest of the money I needed to emigrate."

"What did Arthur say when you told him?"

Kate winced, hands dropping to her sides. "I didn't tell him in person. I wrote Arthur a letter the day before I left on the train." He deserved an explanation, and she provided one. She didn't have time to do more as she prepared to travel.

Lydia's eyebrows arched. "And you think breaking Arthur's courtship and coming to Kansas to teach was God's will?"

"It must be. The Forbes gave me the money, and everything worked out. I found a couple to travel with, and they carried my things from Kansas City. Everything came together so quickly that God must have answered my prayers ... until I reached Kansas, that is. Just one day from my destination, a rattlesnake bit me. I lost part of my hand and my job. Now I'm scrubbing clothes. This can't be the purpose of my life."

"Are you so sure?" Lydia folded her hands against her stomach. "Joseph was sold into slavery by his brothers, accused of mistreating Potiphar's wife, and thrown into prison. Do you think that was God's will?"

Kate scowled. "Well ... yes. God wanted him in Egypt to save his people during the famine." She shifted her weight. "But that was different. Joseph didn't understand why he went to Egypt until later. I know why I came to Kansas. I came to teach." She straightened her shoulders. "You may not understand what it's like to have such a strong sense of purpose."

Lydia laughed. "You may be surprised, but I decided to follow God's will, much like you. Ten years ago, my church in Lowell sent me and another woman west to teach the Choctaw at a mission school."

"Oh." Kate's stomach dropped. How presumptuous she had been. "I'm sorry, Lydia. I didn't mean to ... I guess you understand being sent to teach."

"I do. I taught for a few years and then realized I had to leave."

Kate frowned. "Why would you leave if you thought God sent you to teach the Choctaw?"

Lydia stared across the prairie, her face as tight as if chipped from granite. "The Choctaw owned slaves and would not heed any Christian teaching against it. Their refusal sickened me. How could I stay?"

Did the Indians own slaves? Kate's shoulders slumped. Had they learned this evil from Missourians or other Southerners? Lydia's attempts to teach them and their refusal to listen must have been discouraging.

"I returned to Massachusetts. I had worked in the Lowell mills before coming west. I didn't know what to do, at first."

Kate's mouth dropped open. Mill girls worked sixty to seventy hours each week, tending clattering machines. Most lived in dormitories. The conditions had been so bad that women had protested, seeking to limit the working hours the mills could demand.

Lydia shrugged. "When the Kansas-Nebraska Act passed, I decided to return to Kansas with Clarissa and open a boardinghouse with her. I have walked the path you are on, questioning God's will and providence. I questioned why he allowed the Choctaw to own slaves ... or any white person to own slaves, for that matter."

"What did you discover? Why does he allow such abhorrent behavior?"

"I discovered my need to trust God. He didn't owe me answers to my questions. I learned that when my circumstances changed, I needed to trust that he is wiser than I can imagine."

Kate's stomach soured. "But I haven't even taught school yet."

"Maybe you won't. You came to Kansas thinking you would teach and support the free-state effort, correct?"

"Yes, of course."

"Maybe God brought you to Kansas to prepare you for something else."

Anger rose in Kate's chest. She didn't need preparation. She needed his help to complete her mission. Instead, she had experienced problem after problem. "How can everything I've endured prepare me for anything?"

"Remember Joseph, Moses, and David? God prepared each of them through hardship. You must admit God might be using the problems to prepare you."

Kate squared her shoulders. Lydia had been kind to listen to her, but she was wrong. "Thank you, Lydia, for taking the time to talk to me, but I must change my dress and get to work."

"Let me know if you want to talk more." Lydia hugged her, and Kate's shoulders stiffened. Lydia turned and strode back toward the camp.

Kate plodded down the rutted street toward the boardinghouse. Joseph's experience was different from hers. If her life followed any biblical person, it had to be Job. The devil had wreaked havoc in the righteous man's life, causing tremendous suffering.

Was all she had endured a scheme by the evil one? After all, a snake had bitten her, and the Bible referred to Satan as a serpent. Still, if the devil had caused her pain, why had God allowed it? God had allowed Job's suffering, though the man never understood why.

She shook her head. Job also questioned God, but God never told him the reason he suffered. Is that what Lydia meant by saying God didn't owe her an answer?

17

A high-pitched trill rang in Kate's ears, and she squeezed her eyes tighter. The noise repeated, and she opened her eyes to the dim light of another early morning inside the rustling tent. A small frog sat on her pillow, inches from her nose. She jerked back and brushed it away.

She sat up, rubbing her eyes, and noticed Martha's empty cot. Kate slipped on her stockings, pantaloons, and petticoat, then tossed her work dress over her head and thrust her feet into her high-top shoes. She fumbled to fasten the buttons on her dress before grabbing the button hook to secure them and button up each shoe. Why did dresses and shoes have so many buttons?

She swiped her hand across her tangled hair. If she didn't manage it now, the work would turn the strands into a frizzled nest. She grabbed her brush and ran it through her hair, tucking her locks into a bun. Her shoulder muscles ached with the movement. When she had fastened the last bit into place, she grabbed her bonnet, tossed the tent flap aside, and shuffled toward the table.

The men sat hunched over plates. Lydia and Clarissa moved between the fire and the table, but Martha was nowhere to be seen. She was probably already at the river.

"Good morning," Lydia said. "Would you like a full breakfast?"

"Yes, please." Her stomach growled like a restless bear as she took a seat. Lydia set a plate before her, loaded with four crispy bacon strips atop a large, fluffy pancake slathered in butter and drizzled with honey. She placed a mug of steaming hot coffee beside it.

The men paused attacking their food long enough to greet her. The boardinghouse breakfast was quite different from the meals at home or Aunt Amelia's, which featured linen napkins and polite conversation.

"Kate, Martha left a message for you." Clarissa handed a plate to Lydia and pointed at a sheet-wrapped bundle. "She wants you to take those clothes to the river with you. A man dropped them off at first light."

"Thank you." Kate carved off another chunk of pancake. Martha could have taken the clothes herself.

"Anyone want another?" Clarissa held a plate stacked with four pancakes. Her sons waved, and she shoveled one onto each of their plates. "Kate?"

"No, thank you." She sighed. The bare conversation and the clatter of utensils on dishes were the same every morning. Only the food changed—sometimes pancakes, sometimes biscuits and gravy.

Kate finished, rose, and grabbed the bundle of clothes. She swung it to her shoulder and tramped toward the river. The wind at her back couldn't push the fetid smell of the clothes past her nose fast enough. Her strength had returned, though she still retired each night exhausted.

The scent of smoke stirred the air as people at other camps moved through the start of their day. Carpenters at two building sites stood gazing at their projects in gesture-filled conversation. The sawmill began its distant whine.

Kate reached the clothesline at the top of the riverbank. Today's wind would make using it a challenge. The carved wooden clothespins would need to be jammed on tight. At least the sun and wind would dry clothes quickly.

The river rippled slowly past below her. On the bank below, Martha rose from kindling a fire under the cauldron. She would have looked pert and pretty except for the set of her jaw. How could she rise so early, work so long, and still present herself fresh each night to flirt with the men around the fire?

Kate walked down the bank, and Martha pointed at the yoke with two buckets. "We need more water."

"I'll fetch it." Kate swung the bundle to the ground, hoisted the yoke across her shoulders, and trudged onto the sandbar. She scooped the buckets full, rose, and carried them back to the cauldron. The water splashed as she emptied the buckets into the black iron pot.

Martha stood with her hands on her hips and her head tipped to the side. "I wasn't sure you would last at this job, Missy, but it appears you've gotten used to hard work. I'm surprised someone as educated and cultured as you can keep up with me."

Kate straightened her shoulders. Martha had been testing her. "I'm determined to earn my wages."

"Yes, you are." Martha bent to the basket at her feet and pulled out a bar of lye soap and a knife. She shaved a few flakes of soap into the caldron. "The bucking will be ready soon. Let's get the rest set up."

Kate returned to the river for water, emptying the buckets into the wooden tubs near the fire. Martha had sorted the clothes Kate had carried and piled them near the tubs. She made another trip for water and set the yoke aside.

After tossing some clothes into the cauldron, Martha stirred them with a wooden paddle. Kate knew little about her, even after working with her for several weeks. She was less talkative than Elizabeth. However, the laundress seemed to be in a better mood this morning.

"Martha, why did you come to Kansas?"

Her employer huffed a breath. "It's a long story. Not very pleasant."

"We have all day." If Kate could develop a friendship with her, the long days would be more bearable.

"I just wanted some freedom."

"Freedom from what?" she asked.

"I have three younger sisters. Our mother died when the youngest was born. Then my pa got consumption."

"I'm sorry to hear that."

"I stayed home to care for Pa. That's when I started washing clothes. Since Pa couldn't work, it brought in some money."

"Where did you live?"

"We had a small farm several miles from Binghamton. That's in New York." Martha fished some of the wet clothes from the cauldron and plopped them into a tub.

Kate began scrubbing the clothes against a washboard. "You wanted to be free of your family?"

"No, I love my sisters." She clenched her jaw and stirred the caldron with a fierce thrust, splashing water that sizzled in the fire. "Pa died."

"Oh. My condolences," Kate said.

Martha grunted and stared into the pot.

"Why didn't you stay on the farm? You had a business. Did you have other family to help you?"

Martha's face turned as hard as flint. "No other family except a lecherous uncle, Pa's brother Zeb. He got the farm and wanted ..." She stabbed the paddle into the cauldron, pushing the laundry to the bottom. "Never mind what he wanted. He sold the farm. So Amanda, she's next oldest, and her husband agreed to raise our two younger sisters. I decided to get as far away as I could."

Kate lifted the pair of pants from the water and examined them for remaining dirt. "You wanted to get away from your sisters?"

"No, from Uncle Zeb." Martha scowled and shook her head.

"You came to Kansas because it was the farthest away."

"I didn't have money to get to California or Oregon. But Kansas is fine. There are opportunities here. Lawrence seemed like my best bet." Martha dipped clothes out of the caldron with the paddle and sloshed them into the second wash tub. She began scrubbing a shirt.

Kate bent again and rubbed the trousers against the washboard. "Why did you set up your business on this spot?"

"I couldn't afford to buy land. I approached Clarissa and Lydia about setting up my business at their place, but Clarissa wanted extra rent. Said if I made money on her land, she and Lydia should get a share. She wanted too much, so I set up here."

Kate shuffled the pants to work on the other knee. "You don't own the land where the clothesline sits?"

She grinned. "Nope. I chose to work here, and nobody has bothered me ... yet." She squared her shoulders and straightened. "I won't be here long. I plan to get a place of my own."

"Oh, I didn't realize the laundry business paid so well." Men only gave a few coins to Martha when they picked up their clothes. How could she afford to build her own house?

"I won't be buying any land." She smiled like a cat playing with a mouse. "There are other ways."

"What do you mean?"

Martha stirred the pot of clothes. "I'm going to marry a man with at least one lot and good prospects, more lots would be better. I can run my business a while after we wed if we need to let his business grow." She gazed at the horizon. "Might take a few years before I can stop scrubbing away other people's grime."

Kate sucked a quiet gasp. No wonder Martha flirted with the men at the camp. She had a plan to marry one.

"What's the matter? You think I want to wash clothes my entire life?" Martha planted her hands on her hips.

"No ... that's not it. I just—"

"Do you think the men around here are too good for me? They'd do better with someone like you?"

"Of course not." Martha appraised her like a trader studying a horse as she fumbled for an answer. "You're a beautiful and hard-working woman. I'm sure many men will consider you."

Martha's chest lifted and fell with a deep sigh. She licked her lips. "Yes, they will. I'll get my pick." She smiled. "But don't worry. There are far more men than single women in the territory. I'm sure you'll be able to find a husband, too."

"I'm not looking for a husband. I don't plan to marry."

Martha dropped the shirt into the water and stared at Kate, nodding slowly. "I see. You think no one will want you because of the ... um ..." She tapped her own lip.

"My birthmark?" Heat crept up Kate's neck. "That's not the reason. I'll have you know a fine young man courted me in Boston. He possessed a college degree and was studying medicine. He hailed from one of the most prominent families in Boston."

"Ah, he called on you and then ended the courtship."

"No." Why did everyone assume Arthur had ended their relationship? "I told him I no longer wanted to see him."

Martha stared with her mouth open and forehead wrinkled. "You did what? You told a wealthy man who wanted to court you to leave? What were you thinking?"

She had been thinking about her purpose, her dreams, but Martha wouldn't understand. "Marriage does not fit my plans." Kate tossed the wet pants into a basket and rose. She fished more clothes from the cauldron and slopped them into her wash tub.

"Why don't you want to marry?"

Would she need to have this conversation with every person in Kansas? She knelt again at her tub. "I don't want to give a man the power to determine where I live and to spend all the money."

Martha guffawed loud enough that the men at the sawmill upriver must have heard her. "You think that's how marriage works? It's not all about the legal things, you know." Martha smiled the same smile she beamed at the men around the campfire. "I don't worry about what men want to do because I can turn any man to *my* will. He will live where I want and buy what I want." She rose and stirred more clothes into the cauldron's water.

She pushed back a lock of her honey-colored hair. Even stirring a pot of laundry over a smoky fire did not lessen her beauty. But she believed her face and form were tools to get her way, to manipulate men.

Kate lifted a tattered shirt high to inspect it. If a man loved her enough to marry her, she would never manipulate him. Marriage should be a partnership of shared purpose where the husband and wife agree on their plans and decisions. She took a deep breath and plunged the shirt into the water again. She needed to stop thinking about marriage and find a teaching position.

18

May 7, Lawrence

John Whaley walked down a street of rutted sod in a new town sprouting with opportunity. Building sites lined the street—tents, shacks, horses, and wagons mixed with frame buildings in various stages of construction. The rap of hammers and the rasp of saws mingled with the voices of working men.

A treeless hill rose to the west. The breeze washed his face with the scent of grass from the shallow valley stretching south across the prairie. The woman at the aid company guest house said he would find a boardinghouse on this street. Several yards ahead, a stake held a hand-lettered board reading "Hurd & Hall Room & Board."

He wrapped a finger across his thick mustache and dragged it down his lip. It wouldn't do to have biscuit crumbs when making a first impression. He should have taken the time in Kansas City to find a laundress, but the town of Lawrence only lay two days travel farther, and the man hauling his things had been anxious to leave and find a claim.

He brushed his hands down his sleeves, dusted the thighs of his trousers, and approached the boardinghouse—if you could call it that. Two men wrestled lumber into place on a stone foundation that promised a large house. Tents lined each side of the lot with a campfire and table under a canvas fly between the foundation and the street.

Lawrence was John's fresh start, his new life. He had left his past behind. He hoped the boardinghouse would have friendly people and could become his new home until he established his own place.

Two women sat at the table. One read a book the size of a Bible. The other darned a pair of socks. John cleared his throat. "Hello. I'm looking for Mrs. Clarissa Hurd. Might one of you fine ladies be her?"

The older of the two—a squat, blocky woman with gray hair pulled into a knob on the back of her head—rose and walked a few steps to meet him, leveling a no-nonsense gaze at him. "I'm Mrs. Hurd. Who might you be?"

He grinned and swept off his wide-brimmed bowler and held it to his chest. "I'm John Whaley, fresh from the trail and looking for a place to stay."

"Are you looking to stay a night or two or something longer?"

"I'm looking for something longer."

Clarissa nodded. "Did you arrive this morning, or you been in town a while?"

He fought back a frown. What difference did that make? "I arrived yesterday as part of a group traveling from Boston with the emigrant aid company. They left on April twenty-four, but I joined them in Ohio. Most chose to look for a claim in a different part of the territory, but I came here."

"You stay at the aid company place last night?"

"Yes, I did." The woman was full of questions, not trust.

Clarissa squinted at him. "Did they kick you out? That why you're looking for another place?"

John chuckled. Clarissa was as stern as his old schoolmarm, but he'd find a way to make her smile. "No, I thought another establishment might be better." That should impress her more than his desire to find cheaper lodging. "I plan to settle here, and I'm looking for a permanent place that offers a good room and great food."

Clarissa set her hands on her hips. "As you can see, we don't have the house done yet, but it won't be long. When done, you'll have a room to yourself with a lock on the door. Until then, we have good tents and new California beds, but you'll have to share a tent."

He nodded and gestured with his hat. "I see you have things set up in an orderly way, Mrs. Hurd. You run a fine establishment."

"Yes, I do—for men of good moral character." She stared into his eyes as if challenging him to a fight.

"I assure you, ma'am, I'm an upstanding citizen and will give you no trouble." He had left his troubles behind in Ohio. He'd win her as a friend yet. He relaxed his stance and smiled as sweetly as two people chatting after church on a pleasant summer morning.

Clarissa turned toward the table. "This is my partner, Miss Lydia Hall." Lydia closed the book, stood, and stepped forward to greet him.

"Ma'am." He nodded at the tall woman with a thin face. She looked a mite older than he, about thirty years of age.

"We do the cooking," Clarissa said, "and it's some of the best you'll eat in Lawrence."

"I'm sure it's wonderful. You come highly recommended. I met Tom Gordon this morning and asked him if he was familiar with your place. I was delighted to hear he lives here and said your vittles are delicious."

A smile appeared on Clarissa's face like the sun peeking through rain clouds, and she placed a hand on her heart. "Tom said that?"

Warmth filled John's chest. He had broken through her tough exterior after all. "He did indeed."

"Tom doesn't say much," Lydia said, "but he always thanks us at mealtimes."

"Yes, and he enjoys eating. Let me show you our place." Clarissa waved a hand toward the men working on the house. "Those're my sons, George and Henry."

"Handsome men," John said. "I can see their resemblance to you from here."

The corners of Clarissa's mouth twitched. "Those tents are the men's." She pointed. "That side's for the women. We have two other women living here besides us."

"I hope they're as charming as you and Miss Hall."

Lydia suppressed a chuckle, but Clarissa cocked an eyebrow, her friendly nature quickly dissolving. "We have rules here, Mr. Whaley. Men will not go on the women's side or vice versa. Stay out of every tent but your own. Keep your things locked up. If you lose something or it gets stolen, Lydia and I will not pay for your loss." She poked her finger toward his chest. "Understood?"

"Of course. I understand." At least Clarissa had smiled for a moment. He'd work on plying her with his charms. "What are your rates?"

She told him the price of lodging and meals. He tried to dicker, just for the fun of it, but she didn't budge, as he expected.

He paid for his first week, then said, "I'll return this afternoon with my trunk. I'm going to explore the town today." Explore and look for a job.

Clarissa thanked him and turned toward the tents, likely to deposit the coins in her purse or strongbox.

"Miss Hall, one more thing, if I may?"

"Yes?" She smiled at him sweetly. At least she was the friendly sort.

"I need to find a laundress who can press a shirt and pair of trousers. Can you recommend someone?"

"Miss Groot, who lives here, does laundry." Lydia extended her arm and pointed north. "She does business at the end of the street. You'll see her sign on the top of the levee. I've heard good things about her service."

He dipped his head. "Thank you, ma'am. Good day." He turned up the street and settled his hat in place. Before finding the laundress, he'd need to find someone with a wagon to haul his trunk to Hurd and Hall's. A grin spread on his face. Another chance to make new friends.

The wagon rumbled to a stop before the Hurd camp, and John tipped his hat to the large, muscular man holding the reins. "Thank you, Mr.

Pierce. You sure I can't pay you something for hauling me and my trunk?"

"Call me Thomas." His face, trimmed with a neat brown beard, wore a smile. "Don't you worry about payment. It's my pleasure. Besides, it's only a bit out of my way. I've enjoyed my ride with you."

"I hope to see you again." John clasped Thomas's big, callused hand. "I'd like that."

John hopped off the wagon and hoisted his trunk from the back, a hand on each end. He lugged it toward the fire as the wagon creaked and jangled away.

Four men sat at the fire where Clarissa hoisted a Dutch oven with two hands. "One of you men want to help John?" She jerked her head toward him. "He's a new boarder. Robert, Tom, he'll share a tent with you two."

The older man who had recommended Clarissa's cooking hoisted himself off a log. "Hello again. Let me take an end. We're going to the middle tent."

"I took your advice, Tom. This looks like a good place."

"Yep. 'Tis."

The tent flaps were tied back from the door, and they plunked the trunk at the foot of a cot.

"Thank you very much. Where do you hail from, Tom?"

"I've been here and there. Came here after trying for gold in California." He turned back toward the fire.

"Supper's ready."

Clarissa's shout stirred the men at the fire to their feet. Tom quickened his pace, and John stretched his steps to follow. They slid into seats at the far end of the table.

Lydia and Clarissa set dishes of mashed potatoes, brown gravy, and red beans on the table. A whiff of the thick slices of sourdough bread made John's mouth water.

The flap of the middle tent on the women's side lifted, and a tall woman with brunette hair stepped out. A shorter woman with light brown hair followed. A radiant smile lit the shorter woman's face, and she carried her head high. John's breath caught. She was every bit as beautiful as Susanna. His stomach tightened at the memory.

"Gentlemen, I hope you had a good day." The shorter woman glanced at each man and turned her gaze to John. "I haven't had the pleasure of meeting you yet."

"Ladies, meet Mr. John Whaley." Clarissa set another dish of potatoes on the table and pointed at the shorter woman. "John, this is Miss Martha Groot"—she pointed at the taller woman—"and Miss Kate Collins." Clarissa tapped his shoulder. "We don't wear hats at the table."

Warmth spread across his face as he whipped off his bowler. "My apologies, ladies. Please forgive me. I've been traveling too long."

They smiled, murmured replies, and sat. One of Clarissa's sons, he wasn't sure which, blessed the meal, and everyone began passing dishes. Kate's large brown eyes appraised him, and a faint smile puckered a bluish blotch on one cheek, the only blemish on her fair skin. "Welcome to Lawrence, Mr. Whaley. I hope your journey was pleasant."

"Thank you. The steamboat had to creep up the Missouri because it was so low. I wanted to stay in Kansas City longer and find a laundress, but the man who agreed to carry my things wanted to press on."

"I can help you there, sir." Martha paused her buttering a slice of bread. "I run a laundry service. Missy here, I mean Miss Collins, is my employee." Kate pursed her lips, and her gaze fell to her plate. Had she clenched her jaw? Martha's slender eyebrows raised. "Do you have clothes you'd like washed?"

"Yes, but my immediate need is someone to iron a shirt, coat, and trousers. Do you provide that service?"

"Yes, just bring them to breakfast. I'll have them ironed for you by supper tomorrow."

"Miss Groot, would it be possible to do them first thing? I need them tomorrow."

"For you, Mr. Whaley, I will do them immediately after breakfast and have Kate deliver them back to the camp." Her soft eyes met his. "It will be my special favor to you."

Kate's face flushed as she scooped a bite of potatoes.

"Thank you. You are most kind." Susanna's behavior had bordered on flirtatious, much like Martha's. Was she just as deceptive? Martha turned to chat with one of the other men.

Kate said, "Mr. Whaley, where did you live before coming to the territory?"

"Ohio. I heard Kansas held great opportunities, so I joined a group emigrating from Boston."

"Since you came with an aid company group, I guess you support the free-state cause."

He shrugged. "I certainly don't support slavery. I just wanted a nice growing town where I can make a—"

"Mr. Whaley." Martha thrust a plate across the table toward him. "After your long journey, I'm sure you'd like another piece of this delicious bread."

Had she interrupted to silence Kate or gain his attention? He thanked her and accepted the plate. Martha snuck a peek at Kate from the corner of her eye and turned back to the other men. That woman drew the eyes of men like a flower drew bees, and she enjoyed it.

He passed the plate to Kate and frowned as she reached for it with a hand missing two fingers and edged with pink scars. "Excuse me, but I can't help but notice your hand. The scars look fresh. What happened?"

She told him about traveling to Kansas to teach, a rattlesnake bite, and the doctor's surgery. Martha glanced at them with a pinched expression twice but continued to chat loudly with the Hurd men.

Kate finished her story, and John leaned toward her. "Why didn't you return home after you learned the teaching job was no longer available?"

"I'm convinced God wants me here. I'm sure another teaching position will open somewhere in the territory."

John nodded, sat back, and sipped his coffee. Kate had grit. Nothing else could describe a single woman traveling from Boston and staying after all she had experienced. Her straightforward manner was another tell. He could trust her. But Martha? She reminded him too much of Susanna. He'd keep his guard up with the laundress.

19

Kate strode toward the camp with a freshly ironed brown suit coat and trousers draped over an arm with a white shirt carefully folded atop them. Martha had fussed at her to start work early and double-checked that she had pressed John's items well without scorch marks. She acted like Kate had never touched an iron and had never scrutinized work for other customers as much. Were John's handsome features the reason?

John rose from the table to meet her as she approached the camp. A fresh shave had removed the shadow from his jaw. "Thank you, Miss Collins." He held the shirt high and examined it. "Did you iron these?" His thick mustache matched his jet-black, straight hair.

"Yes, I did."

He grinned. "You did a wonderful job. These will serve nicely as I'm searching for a job today."

Warmth spread through her chest. "Thank you. I'm glad you're satisfied. May I ask your occupation, Mr. Whaley?"

"I clerked in a store back home. I hope to find the same type of job here." Sunlight lit the green in his eyes. "I noticed a few stores when I walked about town yesterday."

"I hope you have better luck than I did and find a position that matches your talents."

He cocked his head as if musing over an answer. She lifted her hand but stopped it short of her face. What must he think of her in her work dress?

"Miss Collins, you're most kind. I'm sure I will have a great day."

She excused herself and turned for the river. He might have a great day, but she wouldn't. Another week had passed without any word from Dr. Robinson about a teaching position. The papers she'd borrowed from Clarissa and Robert were filled with news of the bogus legislature, but not the news she sought, leaving her no option other than to work for Martha.

At least John had complimented her on her work. A pleasant man, he obviously enjoyed talking to others. Martha was a drudge to work with, but he seemed to care for those around him.

Kate walked toward the supper table and smoothed her fresh dress, which she had changed into after returning from work. John sat in the seat across from her usual place. A smile lit his face. "Miss Collins, I found a job as a clerk at the mercantile on Massachusetts Street. I owe my good fortune to you and your iron."

How nice to find the job he wanted so quickly. "Congratulations, but I don't see how I contributed to your success."

Martha brushed past her and sat in Kate's usual chair. "Mr. Whaley, did you find the pressing of your suit and shirt acceptable?"

Kate sucked a quick breath. Why had Martha taken her seat?

His forehead wrinkled. "Why yes, I did."

Martha gestured at Kate. "I checked over the work Missy did. I'm glad she managed to present your suit in acceptable condition."

Warmth flashed up Kate's neck at her employer's insistence on using a little girl's nickname.

"Missy? I thought Miss—"

"Oh, I'm sorry." Martha placed a hand at the base of her throat. "I meant to say Miss Collins. That's just a nickname. I meant no insult." She smiled up at Kate.

Kate's jaw clenched. Martha meant to insult her in John's presence. Kate lowered herself into the chair next to Martha. Clarissa offered a prayer, and everyone reached for the dishes of cornbread and beans.

Martha leaned toward John. "Did I hear you found a job as a store clerk? Where did you learn the trade?"

"My aunt and uncle helped raise me and taught me all about shop-keeping. They own a store back in Ohio."

"How wonderful."

Kate cringed at the syrupy tone of Martha's voice. Rather than converse with all the men from a place near the center of the table, it appeared Martha had decided to focus on John tonight.

"I'm sure you're a very attentive clerk," Martha batted her lashes as she dished beans onto her plate.

John's eyes narrowed. "Thank you, Miss Groot. That's how Uncle Levi taught me."

Kate accepted the dish from Martha and cleared her throat. "Your aunt and uncle must be proud of you."

"They are."

Martha shot a glance at Kate out of the corner of her eye. "John, tell me about your aunt and uncle. I'd love to hear the story. You have such a pleasant voice."

Kate's stomach soured.

"Aunt Ellen's like a mother to me." He glanced at Kate as he served himself a chunk of cornbread. "My mother died when I was a babe, and my father never married again. We lived a few miles away. I spent a lot of time at their store."

Martha leaned forward. "I am so sorry about your mother."

Was she sorry or just seeking his attention? Martha's airs around men differed so much from her attitude while working at the river.

John shrugged. "I really didn't know her. Aunt Ellen was always there for me."

"She must be a lovely woman." Kate spooned up a bite of beans.

"She is." He smiled at her.

"You said they had a store? What was it like?" Martha asked.

Kate chewed slowly. Martha's interest in the store was puzzling. She likely faked the interest as an excuse to converse with John.

"It's the biggest store in Franklin Township. They do a brisk trade since the train to Cleveland runs close by." His eyes softened as he peered into memory.

Martha carefully buttered a piece of cornbread. "Did something happen to them or their store? Is that why you came to Kansas?"

What an impertinent question. "You don't need to tell us," Kate interrupted. "We don't mean to pry." At least *she* didn't intend to pry. She wasn't as nosy as Martha.

"No, it's fine." John faced Martha with a straight face. "They're healthy and still run the store, though they're getting older. They want me to take over the business in a few years."

"So, you came to Kansas because you didn't want to keep store." Martha tilted her chin down and frowned.

"No, I enjoy it. I hope to own a store someday. I ... I just needed a change." He stared away from the table with tight lips and a lined brow.

Something pained him, but at least Martha didn't intrude further.

Kate cleared her throat. "I understand. I also needed a change once."

He glanced at her, and a half-smile twitched his mustache and warmed her heart.

Martha licked her lips. "John, do your aunt and uncle have children?"

Kate frowned at the question. Martha was digging for something.

John swallowed a bite of food. "No, they never had any children. I guess that's why I'm so special to them."

"I'm sorry to hear that." Martha bit into her cornbread, and the corner of her mouth lifted as she chewed.

John picked up his fork and began to eat again. Martha tried to engage him in conversation, but the more she wheedled and smiled, the shorter his answers became. Perhaps a memory had depressed him, or he might not trust Martha. Maybe he was wiser than Kate had thought.

She sipped her water. John supported the free-state cause. Did he also support women's rights and suffrage? Was he the type of man who would work for reform or ignore society's problems?

He was more outgoing than Arthur, even more attractive. No wonder Martha was drawn to him. What woman wouldn't be? He had such an easygoing manner. How would it feel to be wed to—

A cough raked her throat, and she sputtered and hacked.

"Are you alright?" John leaned toward her with dark eyebrows gathered.

She cleared her throat and wiped her mouth with her napkin. "Yes, some water went down wrong. I'm fine."

She shook her head. Why would she entertain any speculation about marriage to John? Daydreams didn't change a blemished face or mutilated hand, and besides, she needed to focus. She came to Kansas to teach, not marry.

20

Snorts and snuffles woke Kate, and she rolled to face the middle of the tent. She jerked away from the nose of a cow stretched through the tent door. After flipping back the blanket, she rose to her feet as the cow's eyes and ears slid through the slit between the tied flaps. "Whoa! Get out of here." She slapped the wet nose.

The beast snorted and jerked back, knocking the tent pole loose. Kate grabbed it before the canvas collapsed and dragged it back into place.

"What's going on?" Martha sat on the edge of her bed, rubbing her eyes.

"A cow tried to enter our tent." Kate pressed her face between the flaps into the dawn light. The cow ambled past the studs rising above the building site toward the back of the lot, nose to the ground. "It's just grazing, though it won't find much grass here."

The cow had awakened her earlier than normal, but she might as well dress. Maybe Lydia could use some help with breakfast.

Martha stretched. "This open range is a menace. That cow almost knocked over our tent, and it probably left a cow pie or two. When will they build fences like they do back home?" She stood and fluffed her pillow with two vigorous punches.

"What was it like where you lived before coming to Kansas?" Kate asked, reaching for her clothing.

"It's just a little place in upstate New York you've never heard of. Not much to tell about."

"Can't you tell me a little about it?"

Martha rummaged for a dress in her trunk. "No. We've got a lot of work waiting today, some of it's right filthy. I swear, how can some men live so long with their stench?"

Kate folded her nightgown and placed it under her pillow. Martha had never been talkative first thing in the morning, but this morning she seemed especially terse.

Kate winced as her hairbrush met a snarl. Another week had passed without news of any teaching positions. She had borrowed copies of different newspapers from Clarice and Mr. Hubbard, but neither contained the information she wanted. It didn't seem fair that John Whaley could find the job he sought in one day, his second day in town, and she had to break her back scrubbing clothes. Didn't God answer prayer?

A cow had invaded her tent, toads chirped on her pillow, and she didn't want to think about snakes that could crawl under the canvas walls. How long before Clarissa's sons finished the house and she could sleep in her own room rather than in a flapping tent with a bossy woman? At least Clarissa hadn't rented the last spot in the tent to another woman. How could John share a tent with two other men?

Martha squinted into a small mirror perched against her pillow and brushed her hair. She arranged it perfectly while practicing her charming smile. Martha shared the tent, but it seemed plaster walls separated them.

Kate ducked through the tent flaps and walked to the table under the canvas tarp. "Good morning, Lydia."

"Good morning, Kate. You're up early."

"A cow decided to investigate our tent. I knew I couldn't get any more sleep."

"Ah, that's the commotion I heard." Lydia cracked eggs into a bowl.

"Yes, perhaps I'll eat that cow someday, but this morning, I'll just relish the thought."

Lydia chuckled. "Beef sounds good. I think we plan to serve some on Sunday. Can you believe it's already the middle of May?"

"Time seems to drag for me."

"How so?"

Kate crossed her arms and stepped closer to Lydia. "I'm stuck performing menial work while I wait for a teaching position. I still don't know why God hasn't answered my prayers."

"It's difficult, isn't it? We often fail to understand God's timing. I sometimes wish he would just speak to me aloud or write a letter. Don't you?"

She nodded. "I find it hard to trust him when I don't understand things."

Lydia nudged her with an elbow. "That's what faith is—trusting God even though we don't understand everything."

Kate dropped her arms and drew a deep breath. "Enough about me. How can I help you this morning?"

"Do you want to set out the plates?"

"I would be happy to." Kate lifted the plates from the chest near the end of the table then circled the table, laying a plate at each place.

Clarissa approached from where she'd been crouched tending the fire. "Morning, Kate." Kate returned the greeting as Clarissa picked up a frying pan and turned back to the fire.

Lydia beat the eggs with rapid strokes. "Will you attend church with me tomorrow?"

She should go. Last Sunday, she had slept late and skipped church because she was so exhausted, and her back ached. Was missing church so wrong?

She cleared her throat. "I don't know. I may need to see how tired I feel tomorrow morning. It is a day of rest, after all."

Lydia's mouth quirked. "You do work very hard. I hope you have a good day and a restful night. I missed you last week."

"Thank you, I missed the service too." But had she?

"Elizabeth asked about you. I explained you slept late."

A heaviness settled on Kate's stiff shoulders. "I missed her as well." Seeing Elizabeth was one benefit of attending church. Her friend cared about her even if it felt like God didn't.

She filled her fists with forks and wandered around the table, placing them beside the plates. God could arrange her life in the same way she placed forks on the table, setting a teaching position before her. He was God Almighty, wasn't he? It would be simple for him. But no, rather than fulfill her purpose, she faced another day of toiling for Martha. How could she celebrate that by attending church?

Kate shuffled toward the fire with a chair from the table where Lydia and Clarissa washed the supper dishes. Tonight, the chair would give her aching back more support than her usual fireside seat on the stump.

Robert, George, and Henry drifted to the log on the street side of the crackling flames, talking about the construction progress and the qualities of different types of wood. Tom sat in his usual spot with his back to the men's tents, cradling a cup of coffee and watching the flames. Kate plopped the chair down on the house side of the fire—between the log and stump—then eased herself onto the seat and leaned against the back. Freedom from cooking and cleaning was worth every cent she paid, especially after a long day bent over a washtub.

"Miss Collins, I didn't get to speak with you much during supper." John sat on the log next to her and brushed a strand of his dark hair off his forehead. "How was your day?"

At supper, Martha had sat across from him and chatted endlessly. She had lamented that men traveled to town on Saturdays to drop off their laundry in the morning and wanted it ready in the afternoon, sometimes only an hour or two later. Martha had also shared opinions, stories, and the gossip she had gleaned from customers.

Kate smiled. "My day was much like Miss Groot's."

John grinned. "You use far fewer words to describe it." He leaned closer and lifted the back of his hand to his mouth. "She can carry a conversation farther than most people."

Kate chuckled. "Tell me, Mr. Whaley—"

"Please, call me John."

His warm gaze warmed her stomach. Although using surnames to address other people was the proper and polite form of address, the practice was awkward with people she saw every day. If Clarissa called the men by their given names, she could as well.

"All ... all right, John. How was your day at the store?"

"Very enjoyable. I met a lot of people, and we filled many orders. The owner was quite happy."

"You like talking to people, don't you?"

He laughed, a warm, musical sound. "You know I do. So many interesting people and stories."

"I heard Martha tell you the news she gleaned today, but she didn't ask what you heard. Are people talking about the Missouri men who seek to make Kansas laws?"

"The bogus legislature?" The corner of his mustache lifted, and his nose wrinkled. "Yes, people are incensed about it, though some seemed tight-lipped when talk turned to petitioning the governor for a new election. Probably pro-slavery men from Franklin or Lecompton." He shrugged. "I don't get too excited about politics."

She frowned. He wasn't offended that Missouri men had stolen the spring election? Politicians may be untrustworthy, but the political process was a necessary avenue to reform society.

"You do support a free state, don't you?"

He held his hands out to the fire. "Of course. I think slavery is a sad thing, but I fear people's passion for the issue will destroy the Union. Men stop thinking when they get angry. They do stupid things."

She chuckled. "I certainly agree that anger often precedes poor choices." Though anger wasn't the only thing capable of choking a man's ability to reason.

John leaned forward, forearms on his knees. "A man told me one such story today. Last fall, a woman knocked down the tent of a free-state man. He started to pitch it again, and a crowd of ruffians gathered and threatened to beat him if he continued. Then a bunch of free-state men arrived and promised to shoot the pro-slavery men if they didn't leave." He shook his head.

"The slavery crowd was clearly wrong to threaten the man and attack his property."

His eyes opened wide. "Yes, but that's not my point. If people on both sides don't stop stoking their anger, a war will break out. Don't you agree?"

Kate's shoulders tensed. "I want to avoid a war, but we need to abolish slavery."

Lydia settled onto her wooden crate on the other side of Kate. John nodded to her. "Glad you joined us, Miss Hall. You made a delicious supper."

"Thank you. Did I hear you talking about our unfortunate governmental situation?"

"Yes, and how people get fighting mad over slavery." John shook his head. "If we're not careful, this country will be torn apart by war. We need to settle the issue for Kansas without bloodshed. No need to fight about it since there aren't that many slaves in Kansas."

Kate felt herself stiffen further. "We don't want *any*. We must do something about the Missouri men making our laws. They want to force slavery on our new state."

"But people arrive every week. We'll have enough that they can't steal the election for the state constitution."

Lydia crossed her arms. "I fear supporters of slavery are also traveling to Kansas."

John picked up a scrap of bark and pitched it with a high arc into the fire. "The census taken last winter counted more than three hundred men living in the voting district around Lawrence, but only seven slaves. More people have arrived since, but I haven't seen any slaves among them."

Kate frowned. "Lydia, don't many support slavery who do not own—"

"A wonderful evening." Martha sashayed between Kate's chair and the fire, bent over the log beside John, and brushed it with her fingertips. He drew his handkerchief and dusted the log. Martha carefully arranged her skirt and sat beside him, a radiant smile on her face. "Did I hear you talking about slaves?"

Kate's gut drew tighter than a fiddle string. How could Martha appear at supper each night as fresh as a debutant awaiting a ball after working all day?

John sighed. "A distasteful subject that we don't need to continue. People fight about it too much."

Had John changed the subject to please Martha, or because he found discussing slavery distasteful? He usually enjoyed polite conversation, and he'd brought up the census, but Martha's arrival had shifted his interest.

"I asked Miss Collins about her day." John glanced at her. "It sounds like it was filled with hard work, much like yours, Miss Groot."

A light laugh lifted from Martha. "Yes, I'm sure it's difficult for her, missing part of her hand, but she makes do."

Heat rose up Kate's neck. She didn't need Martha's false sympathy. "I have regained the strength in my hand, though it's sometimes awkward." Not to mention the tingles and needling pain where her fingers used to be, but Martha had no business knowing about that or speaking about her as if she wasn't sitting next to her.

"You have become accustomed to our hard work." Martha cocked her head and looked at John. "I'm sure she never worked so hard in Boston, and she *has* attracted a great deal of misfortune—a rattlesnake bite, loss of fingers, not to mention being born with an ugly, blue blotch on her face."

Kate's breath caught, and her throat burned as the fire snapped and popped. The voices of the others fell silent, and their faces turned her way. Kate blinked back the sting in her eyes.

John glanced at her with a soft expression and looked away. "I think Miss Collins' birthmark is no tragedy. It can't hide her smile or mar her beauty." He grinned like he'd won a horse race.

Martha's lips drooped into a frown.

"Thank you, John, you're most kind," Kate said.

"You *are* most kind, Mr. Whaley." Syrup filled Martha's voice, and she touched his arm. "Tell me, does anything mar my face?"

Kate choked down a gag, bolted to her feet, and faced Lydia. "I'm going for a walk."

She strode out of the circle of watching faces as Martha's laugh hung in the air behind her. Why did the woman need to be so cruel? Kate wasn't trying to win John's affection. Martha had no reason to be jealous or make snide attacks.

"Wait, I will accompany you."

Lydia walked to her side. They turned and strode down the street and away from the murmuring voices.

"Martha can be unkind." Lydia's tone held no judgment.

"Yes, she can." *Cruel* was a better word for Martha.

"Ladies!"

Kate halted and turned.

John trotted up to them. "Perhaps I should accompany you."

"Accompany us?" Kate scowled. John was welcome, but what happened to Martha?

He smiled and shrugged. "I heard some other stories today. A couple of ruffians have intimidated people in our streets."

"I've heard no such thing," Kate said.

The corner of Lydia's mouth twitched as she squeezed Kate's arm. "Mr. Whaley, you're most welcome to join us. We appreciate your thoughtfulness."

"Oh." Tingles swept across Kate's face. "Uh ... yes, thank you, John."

John smiled, his rugged face softened by the setting sun. "Miss Hall, it is my pleasure to accompany you and Miss Collins on this fine evening."

His use of her surname sounded stilted, and she remembered his suggestion that she use his first name. "Please call me Kate."

"And call me Lydia."

A grin stretched John's lips.

As they strolled down the street in silence, John seemed content to walk and gaze at the houses and camps lining the street. Kate considered returning to the conversation about the bogus legislature and slavery that Martha had interrupted, but John had shied away from it earlier. Best to let the matter rest.

Lydia glanced past her at their companion. "John, would you like to attend church tomorrow? The Congregationalists meet in a home. I plan to attend."

"I'm sure it would do my soul well." He squared his shoulders. "Kate, will you go as well?"

"It depends on how I feel tomorrow. I was too exhausted last week."

John watched her for a moment before replying. "I would be delighted to join you, Lydia, though I'm more a Baptist myself."

Lydia laughed. "We won't hold that against you. Kate, why don't you come with us?"

She really should go. The walk to the meeting with John would likely be filled with pleasant conversation, and she always enjoyed Lydia's company. But attending a church service attracted her as much as another hot day scrubbing clothes.

"Perhaps I will. I'll let you know in the morning."

"Lydia, someone told me you taught school for the Choctaw Indians. What was that like?" John asked.

Lydia told the story of her mission. John smiled and asked questions, but he often glanced at Kate. Although a few people passed them as they walked, no one yelled or threatened them about abolition. What was John's true reason for tagging along with them? He didn't need to worry about their safety. She had walked the streets of town alone many times.

Perhaps Martha had offended him with her hurtful comment about Kate's birthmark. *Good*. The comment had hurt more than expected, even though she'd heard far worse comments in her years. Kate rolled her shoulders. Fatigue left her vulnerable to Martha's snide games.

The breeze brushed her face, and she glanced at John when he chuckled at something. He had claimed her birthmark didn't hide her smile or mar her beauty. Did he truly think she was beautiful or just offering a polite retort? He had left Martha and chose to walk with them. Did that show an interest in Lydia? She was older than Martha and John, and he was a single man—was he acting as a friend?

Kate tucked a wisp of hair behind her ear. No one had ever called her beautiful except Grandpa. Father had insisted she was pretty but nothing more. Mother had called her hair beautiful, or her clothes, but her mother's eyes often held pain when examining her daughter's face.

Lydia's soft laugh brought Kate's attention back to the conversation.

"Was that when you decided to help open the boardinghouse?" John asked Lydia, but his gaze shifted to Kate.

He seemed to have no trouble watching her or initiating conversations. He didn't pursue conversations with Martha in the same way. Warmth flushed her cheeks. Maybe he found her attractive.

Had Arthur considered her pretty? He had spent weeks courting her, though he never complimented her hair or dress. They had shared long chats about literature and abolition, both in Amelia's parlor and on strolls. He was always polite. Arthur had walked with his head high when she took his elbow. The memories filled her chest with warmth. His studies would be progressing, and he likely had begun courting someone new by now. Did he miss her?

21

Boston

The carriage rolled to a stop, and the horses champed their bits. Arthur stepped from the carriage, straightened the lapels of his dark frock coat, and turned to his driver. "Wait here. I intend a short visit."

Arthur swung the wrought iron gate on its creaking hinges and walked to the black door set in the middle of the two-story, red-brick house. His stomach crawled like ants scurried within it. He straightened his shoulders, lifted the brass knocker, and rapped it three times. Would he receive a friendly reception?

The door opened, and a tall woman with brown hair stared at him with lifted brows. "Arthur."

He gulped. Amelia was a picture of strength and confidence. He had forgotten how much Kate favored her aunt. Amelia could have been Kate's mother or older sister.

He swept off his hat. "Miss Williams, may I speak with you for a few minutes?"

"Yes, of course." Her brow furrowed, and she stepped back. "Won't you come in?"

He stepped into the hall and glanced at the bookshelves in the room to his right, loaded with volumes. Kate had read so many of them. He had admired them with her and selected favorites to discuss.

"May I take your hat?"

"Oh ... thank you." He handed it to her.

Amelia extended her hand toward the parlor. "Please take a seat."

He crossed between the fireplace and the sofa to the chair he had used when Amelia invited him to call on Kate. In the following weeks, he had shared many warm conversations with Kate while sitting there.

He cleared his throat. "I apologize for arriving without inquiring first. Curiosity has plagued me."

"Curiosity about ...?" She blinked twice and bit her lip.

"Kate's letter stating she was leaving for the Kansas Territory shocked me. It has been two months and I ..."

Amelia nodded. "She surprised us all. I had no idea she planned to emigrate, nor did her parents."

So, Amelia hadn't known, and Kate had also surprised her parents?

"I ... I visited the aid company after receiving her letter and confirmed she left. I—"

"Arthur, I must apologize for the way my niece has treated you." Amelia pressed her hands together. "I had no idea she would do this when I invited you to call on her."

"Please, you are not to blame." He lifted a shoulder in a shrug. "I thoroughly enjoyed my time with Kate, and your invitation honored me. I'm just wondering if you have heard anything from her."

Amelia's cheeks reddened, and she frowned. "I received a letter from her a couple of days ago." She drew a slow, deep breath. "She had not reached Topeka yet."

"Has something happened? According to the aid company, travel is difficult, especially if river conditions slow the steamboats."

"Oh, no ... that's not—oh, Arthur, a rattlesnake bit her!" Amelia put her face in her hands.

A cold wave dropped through his body. A rattlesnake? His throat constricted. She must have survived since she'd written a letter, but Amelia's eyes shone with tears.

"How is ... what ... you have not told me everything, have you?"

Tears shone in her eyes, and she shook her head. "They amputated two fingers on her right hand."

He sucked in a breath. "I see." He ran his fingers along the bones of his other hand. A settler might have amputated if a doctor wasn't nearby on the wild prairie. The procedure was more delicate than cutting up a chicken for the frying pan. Did Kate still have use of her hand, or was she now unable to care for herself?

Amelia sniffled and wiped her tears. "She wrote the letter from Lawrence and said she hoped to travel to Topeka soon."

"You've heard nothing more?"

"No, that's all I know. I'm hoping to receive another letter soon, but the mail takes forever to arrive from Kansas. The aid company sends groups every week or two from Boston, so sending a letter is faster, though it still may take three weeks."

He rose to his feet. "Thank you, Miss Williams. I apologize again for bothering you."

"I wish I could tell you more." She stood. "She seemed to enjoy the time she spent with you. I hope her sudden decision did not offend you."

He sighed. Kate hadn't offended, just puzzled him. "I've taken too much of your time. Thank you again." He strode across the room and lifted his hat from the coat tree.

"Thank you for coming. It was a pleasure to see you again," She called out after him.

He walked to the carriage and stepped aboard. "Let's go home." The carriage lurched forward as he settled against the leather seat. Blooming pansies decorated the flower boxes in the windows lining the street with white, purple, and yellow. Was Kansas as beautiful?

From what he had learned, settlers in Kansas lived in sod houses and tents until they could build something more durable. How was Kate living in such basic conditions with only the use of one hand?

He reached into his inside coat pocket, pulled out her final letter to him, and began to read.

March 26
Dear Arthur,

I apologize for the sudden nature of this letter. I have received an opportunity to teach school in Kansas and will leave tomorrow with a party led by the New England Emigrant Aid Company.

I have enjoyed our many conversations and outings, but our courtship cannot continue. I believe God has provided me with a way to influence the course of abolition, at least in Kansas. You are a gentleman, and I know you will find another woman worthy of your attention in Boston.
Kate

He read the letter three times and then watched building after building pass the carriage window until they arrived back at the family mansion. He folded the letter and slipped it back into his coat pocket, then leaped from the carriage and hurried through the front door without greeting the butler. With long strides, he mounted the oak staircase and entered his study. He slid into the desk chair and grabbed a sheet of paper, positioning it on the leather desk pad. He dipped the pen into the inkwell.

May 15
Dear Kate,

I visited your aunt today, and the news of your misfortune with the serpent and the resulting surgery appalled me. How you have suffered far from friends and family! I hope you recovered well.

I miss you and our long talks about literature and the political needs of our country. I wish not for another woman worthy of my attention since I was honored by yours. Should you choose to return to Boston following *your injury, I would be delighted to call on you again and hear about your adventures in the Kansas Territory.*

You could also hear about my apprenticeship as a doctor and plans for the future. Please consider returning to Boston. I know your aunt also misses you.

Arthur

22

May 29, Lawrence

Kate draped the last pair of wet trousers over the clothesline and shoved two pins in place to hold it—another batch of laundry finished, but more waited to be scrubbed. She untied the cloth bag of clothespins from her waist and dropped it into the empty wicker basket. Another task on another empty day.

Martha set a basket of clean, folded clothes beside the empty one, pulled a man's watch from her skirt pocket, and consulted it. "I'm going for lunch." She turned and walked toward the camp, curt as usual.

Kate pulled off her bonnet, her hair limp with sweat, and wiped her forehead. She lifted a tin cup from a nail in the clothesline post and dipped it in the bucket on the ground. The water had warmed but still wet her parched lips. She filled another cup and lifted it to her mouth.

"Kate, I have the most wonderful news." Several yards up the levee, Elizabeth hurried toward her with hands lifting her skirt over her ankles. Why would she run on such a hot day?

Her friend stopped and rested her hands on her hips, a breathless smile and a sheen of sweat on her face. "I really must talk to you. Samuel heard the most wonderful thing. I knew you'd want to know." Her eyes narrowed as she scanned the riverbank. "I'm not interrupting, am I? I thought I saw Martha walking toward your place. Will you stop for lunch? If you're going back, I can tell you on the way."

"No. I don't eat lunch. What's happened?"

Elizabeth's mouth opened, and she stared as if she were looking at a two-headed horse. "You don't eat lunch?"

Kate shrugged her shoulders. "I skip it, except on Sunday. That saves me a little money."

"Every day? It's no wonder you haven't regained weight. You lost a lot during your illness. You'll never gain it back if you don't eat."

"I'll be fine. Let's find some shade." She started toward the closest building. "Now, what have you heard that's so important you ran to tell me?" Whatever the news, it couldn't be that important if her friend had promptly forgotten it to fuss about skipping lunch.

Elizabeth smiled as wide as the prairie itself. "The school here in Lawrence has closed."

"Of course it has. The term ended," Kate said, leaning a hand against the rough siding of the building.

"No, you don't understand. Mr. Fitch decided to close the school permanently. He won't hold another term."

Tingles crawled up Kate's neck to the top of her head. "Why? Has Mr. Fitch left town?"

"I hear he decided to go to California, but don't know if he's left yet."

California? If Mr. Fitch had left Lawrence, then ... no, it couldn't be true. "Who told you this?"

Elizabeth pressed her hands together as if in prayer. "Samuel heard the news from someone picking up lumber at the sawmill."

"But who was it? How would they know? Was it someone with children in the school?" Kate drew a quivering breath and crossed her arms. If what Elizabeth said were true—

"Samuel told me the man's name, but I forgot it. I was so excited. I knew what this would mean for you. I left as soon as I could."

If true, this news would change everything. Dr. Robinson had promised to search for a teaching position nearly a month ago. Was it possible he had known Mr. Fitch was considering a change? Would the doctor reach out to her as his replacement?

Kate's ribs tightened as if squeezed by a snugly laced corset. "Why would Mr. Fitch close his school and go to California? He has several students here."

"It probably has something to do with his partner, Charles Stearns, and their boardinghouse."

Kate's breath caught. "That's right. He and Mr. Stearns boarded more than a dozen people when I checked their place for a room."

Elizabeth's eyebrows arched as she leaned closer. "Charles Stearns has been very critical of the aid company. He even wrote a letter to the *Boston Weekly Journal* last spring to express his views."

"How does that lead to Mr. Fitch closing the school?"

"Mr. Fitch has been rising early and working late to do all the cooking at their establishment in addition to his teaching. Mr. Stearns does nothing but stir up opposition to the aid company, so I hear."

Kate frowned. "Stearns is a pro-slavery man?"

Elizabeth huffed a chuckle. "Hardly. He's a strong abolitionist."

"Are you sure Fitch has closed his school?"

"That's what I've heard. He's been thinking of going to California and told Dr. Robinson he will no longer use the aid company's building for his school."

Kate steepled her fingers and rested them against her lips. Dare she trust news which seemed little more than gossip? "You haven't confirmed this with Dr. Robinson or anyone else, have you?"

"It must be true since Samuel says it. Oh—I remember now—a man named Colburn told Samuel. His children attended the school."

Kate's heart pounded like the hooves of a running horse. She clenched her hands together, fighting the urge to squeal. A teaching position here in Lawrence! Perhaps God was listening after all. Maybe the snakebite and her delay had been his plan all along.

"What are you going to do?" Elizabeth touched her upper arm.

What should she do? She could wait until Dr. Robinson contacted her. He promised he would search for a teaching position. But no, she couldn't wait. She dusted the front of her skirt. "I'm going to Dr. Robinson's office this afternoon, but I can't meet him looking like this." She wrapped Elizabeth in a tight embrace. "Thank you for telling me."

Her friend held her at arm's length. "Isn't this exciting? You must tell me what you find out. Promise you'll stop at our place once you know."

"I will. I couldn't celebrate the good news without you."

Kate rushed toward the camp with bouncing steps. This must be the answer to her prayers. Perhaps Lydia had been right when she'd claimed hardships were part of God's plan. Had he prepared her to teach in Lawrence instead of Topeka? It made little difference. Only one course would reveal any answers. She would find Dr. Robinson after she washed her face and donned a clean dress.

She lengthened her stride until she reached the camp where men and woman sat at the table eating, Martha facing John with her gaze fixed on his face. Kate squared her shoulders and marched to Martha, sitting near the end of the table.

"I won't work this afternoon, at least for a while. I may return later."

Martha's face clouded. "What about the work we have waiting? Are you unwell?"

"No." She spun toward the tents. Martha didn't need an explanation, and she didn't have time to give her one.

Kate tossed her bonnet on the bed, lifted a pitcher from the top of her stacked trunks, and splashed water into the basin. The ties holding the tent flaps open resisted her fumbling fingers, but at last, she dropped the flaps and tied them closed.

She peeled off her sweaty dress as Elizabeth's news played in her mind. If she taught in Lawrence, she would still live in the tent, at least for a while, but she wouldn't have to slave in the sun. Kate dipped a cotton cloth into the basin and lifted it. Martha's laugh carried through the canvas, answered by John's deeper chuckle. Kate shook her head. The woman didn't need to pester John at every meal, even if she had set her cap for him.

Kate drew a deep breath. She shouldn't think about Martha and John now. She needed to find Dr. Robinson. The tepid water wet her face but didn't cool it amid the sweltering air. She scrubbed quickly, moved the items off the top of her trunk, and retrieved her carefully folded, light-blue dress.

After fastening the last button, she grabbed her brush and studied her hair in her hand mirror. Several stray wisps of damp hair hung near her ears, but unpinning the coil on the back of her head, brushing her hair, and fastening it again would take too long in the stifling tent.

She tossed the brush and mirror atop her work dress slung across the bed, slammed the trunk shut, and quickly replaced the pitcher and basin. The flap ties opened with her jerk, and she ducked out into the breeze. It cooled her face, and she stood and filled her lungs.

If Dr. Robinson had left his office, she would march all the way up the hill to his house if needed. She turned and strode toward the street.

As she passed the table, John smiled up at her and lifted two fingers as if touching a hat brim in salute. "Good afternoon, Kate. Nice dress."

A grin burst across her face at his comment, but Martha's smile froze. How would she react when told about her teaching job? Kate shook her head. Martha wasn't her problem anymore. She would be a teacher.

23

Kate approached the sod-walled, aid company office, grasped the door handle, and swung it wide.

"Hello, Dr. Robinson?"

No answer came from the empty room except the creak of the ridgepole holding the canvas roof against the wind. The doctor often traveled to other parts of the territory or to Kansas City. She breathed a prayer that he had not traveled today and turned toward the street.

On the far side, a man held the hoof of a horse hitched to a wagon between his knees, studying the bottom of it. She grabbed her skirt and dashed to him. "Excuse me. Have you seen Dr. Robinson?"

He straightened, and his weathered face peered at her from under a large tan hat with sweat stains circling the inside of the wide brim. A wad of tobacco filled his cheek.

"The doc came out of that building and mounted a brown horse. He turned the corner and rode off that way." He pointed south.

"Thank you." She blinked away the sting in her eyes. He probably rode home for lunch.

Kate ambled back toward the aid company office as a sharp pain burned in the pit of her stomach. Maybe he hadn't returned home for lunch. What if he'd ridden off planning to spend the rest of the day elsewhere? The bright sun forced her to squint, and she shielded her eyes, the sweat on her forehead wetting her hand. A man on horseback rode away from her three blocks south, but it wasn't the doctor.

She had to believe he'd left for lunch rather than fret. She should have waited for him to contact her. Her swallow scratched down her throat. Why hadn't she stopped for a drink of water after changing her dress?

She paced back and forth in front of the aid company office, hands on hips. How long would it take him to ride home, eat lunch, and return? An hour and a half? He might talk to his wife, or someone might meet him there, so it could take longer. What if he didn't return today? She could head to the Robinson's house, but that would require a hike up the long hill, and she had forgotten her bonnet.

The man across the street had climbed into the wagon seat and watched her, elbows on his knees. Would he drive her?

She walked to the front wheel of the wagon. "Sir, will you take me up Mt. Oread to Dr. Robinson's home? I need to speak to him on an urgent matter."

His eyes narrowed, and he spat a stream of dark spittle that fell close to her skirt hem. "No. I don't truck with that man." His gaze dropped to her feet and back to her face. "I won't help any of his friends, either."

A tingle like a winter wind touched the skin of her neck and cheeks. Why was the man so hostile? John said supporters of slavery lived in town, and others came in for supplies. Could this man be one? She cleared her throat. "Thank you."

He scowled, slapped the reins on the horses, and drove away.

She drew a deep breath. Two chairs sat against the front wall of the company building. She could return to camp, but she might as well wait a little longer. She sat in the oak chair, and it creaked. The building cast a narrow shadow over her head and shoulders, though her knees extended into the sun.

"Please, God," she whispered, "You know I want to teach. Can I know today if it will be here?"

In the distance, the sawmill chugged and whined. Hammers rapped and voices called. A horsefly buzzed around her face, and she waved it away. A couple rolled past in a wagon, a boy and girl riding with two boxes and a keg in the back. The boy appeared to be old enough for school.

Was her ordeal over? The journey west, almost dying from snakebite, the loss of her fingers, scrubbing clothes for Martha—had it all been part of God's plan?

Martha had likely returned to the riverbank and started soaking another tub of clothes. No, enough time had passed that she could have scrubbed, rinsed, and hung them to dry. Kate folded her hands, laid them in her lap, and tried to relax.

The shade from the building crept across her lap. As it reached her knees, Dr. Robinson rode around the corner on his chestnut horse.

She leaped to her feet. "Dr. Robinson, I wanted to see you."

He pulled the reins, shifted his weight, and the saddle squeaked. "Ah, Miss Collins." He lifted his hat. "I have some news you will enjoy."

"Yes?" She squeezed her hands together until her fingers ached.

"It seems we now need a teacher here in Lawrence. Would you like the position?"

Her heart drummed, and she fought the urge to jump like a child. A teacher at last. "Yes, of course! I would be honored to teach here."

"Excellent!" He swung down from the saddle and tied his horse to the rail.

"When can I start?"

He chuckled. "You are quite anxious to begin, aren't you?"

"It's why I came to Kansas. I want to hold a term this summer." The sooner she began teaching, the sooner she could quit working for Martha. She swallowed the lump in her throat.

"Hmm. A school term in summer is not normal." He sounded like he stated a fact, not an objection.

"I think parents will appreciate a summer school term, especially those from New England. You know about the impact of the common schools in Massachusetts and Rhode Island, correct?"

"Of course. Schools are vital for the public good. Education is key to overcoming poverty and crime in society."

"And slavery."

He tipped his head and nodded.

She licked her lips. "If education is so valuable, why should we avoid it during the summer?"

A shrug lifted his shoulders. "Parents need their children to help farm or work their trade."

"Some may still do that, but we could try something new. Mr. Fitch had approximately twenty students in his school, did he not?"

"Yes, he did."

"I've heard some parents were disappointed he closed the school. We could ask them whether they would support a summer term."

Dr. Robinson tapped his fingers against his bearded chin. "What about the heat? The hall is not exactly cool, even today. We have yet to reach the hottest part of the summer."

"We would dismiss in the early afternoon."

He puckered his lips and narrowed his eyes. "I am willing to try this if you can enroll a dozen children for the summer term. If you can't, you can start a term in the fall."

"I'll have a dozen students within a week." She clutched his hand. "Thank you, Dr. Robinson. The children will receive an excellent education. May I see the classroom?"

"Of course." He held the door open, and they entered the building's outer room—the company office. He pulled back the canvas wall opposite the door, and she stepped into the back room.

Heat pressed down from the tent-like roof, but a breeze flowed from between the two open windows in each of the sod side walls. Soft light from the roof and the windows lit tables and benches of unfinished wood.

Kate's heart raced. This was *her* classroom. She strolled up the center aisle and trailed her fingertips across a table, feeling rough grooves. Someone had carved the initials O.S. into the corner of the tabletop. She continued to the small blackboard hung on the sod wall.

"I'm afraid Mr. Fitch supplied the books," said Dr. Robinson as he fanned himself with a handkerchief. "He only had a few and decided to keep them."

She smiled at the doctor. "I have a trunk full of books—ten sets of McGuffey's readers, several copies of New England Primers, and some arithmetic books. It also holds a small library of works by Hawthorne, *Canterbury Tales*, Shakespeare's *Hamlet*, and more."

The doctor smiled. "Excellent."

A few pencils lined the tables, but no paper, not even on the table in front of the blackboard.

"Do you have the names of children and families from Mr. Fitch's school?"

He held his hat in both hands, a sheepish look on his face. "No. The school was Mr. Fitch's. He's still in town, so you may be able to get a list from him."

"I see." She shrugged. "I will visit every house, shack, and tent in town if needed. I'm sure there will be interest in a summer term." If there wasn't, she would create interest. "Um ... will you pay me what we agreed before?"

"This will not be a subscription school like Mr. Fitch ran, so you won't earn more for more pupils. The aid company will pay you seventeen dollars per month, but you must maintain a dozen students or more."

Kate lifted her head and thrust out her hand. "Dr. Robinson, you have yourself a teacher." He gripped her hand, and her heart swelled.

Her feet couldn't move fast enough as she left the building. She hurried to Elizabeth's home and skipped toward her friend, who bolted up from her chair by the fire, a pair of trousers in one hand and a needle in the other. "Did you get it?"

"Yes!"

Elizabeth squealed, tossed her mending aside, and clutched Kate in a hug. "I'm so excited for you."

"But that's not the best part." Kate pulled back to arm's length. "I can start this summer as soon as I enroll a dozen students or more."

"Thank God! I prayed you wouldn't move far away."

Kate pressed her hands together. "I need to ask a favor of you and Samuel."

"Yes, of course, anything. What can we do?"

"I have a trunk full of books that need to be moved to the schoolroom ... to *my* schoolroom."

Kate lost track of time chatting with Elizabeth and drinking three mugs of water. Her friend promised they would arrive in the evening to haul the trunk. It was mid-afternoon before she sauntered down the levee toward Martha's clothesline.

Martha glanced up from hanging clothes, her face beaded with sweat. Additional mounds of dirty laundry lay near the end. "Good, you're back. We've got plenty of work to do." She glanced at Kate's dress. "If you're going to change, you need to hurry."

"I can't work today. I have a new job, a teaching position opened in town. I need to begin enrolling students."

Martha lifted her bonnet off her head and wiped an arm across her face. "Hmm, I knew you would find a teaching job one day. I just wish it had been a little later." She squinted at Kate. "Are you going to work anymore after today, or are you finished?"

Could she afford to quit now? She had enough money to pay Clarissa for at least a couple more weeks, besides, the sooner she recruited students, the sooner the aid company would pay her.

"I will not work for you any longer."

"I will settle up with you tonight, then." Martha grabbed a wet skirt from her basket, slapped it over the line, and stabbed clothespins in place, ending their conversation.

Kate turned and strolled toward the camp. Two families lived on the street farther south. She would visit them later today. Perhaps they would enroll.

Her feet barely touched the ground as she sauntered up to Lydia and Clarissa at the table. "You'll never guess what happened. I have a teaching position here in Lawrence. Mr. Fitch closed his school, but the aid company will pay me to teach. I plan to start before the middle of June. Can you believe it?"

Clarissa slapped the tabletop. "Good for you! You didn't give up despite all your hardships. You've worked hard for this. I'm glad for you."

"I'm glad God answered your prayers." Lydia beamed a smile.

"Yes, he has."

"Will you attend church services with me this Sunday?" Lydia asked.

"I look forward to it, but please excuse me. I need to go find some students." Kate strode down the street and whispered, "Thank you, God, for hearing my prayers."

24

Kate followed Lydia up the path from the street to a new house where the church had arranged to meet. The house had glass windows on the first floor, raised to catch the breeze, but boards covered the window openings on the second floor. They stopped at the end of a short line of people waiting to enter.

John stopped beside Kate. "It appears we'll have more people here than last week."

"Yes, it will be crowded this morning." Kate clutched her folded fan—mahogany ribs covered in creamy silk that she'd dug out of her trunk. Thankfully, Lydia had asked whether she owned one. She had refrained from using it previously, saving it for a dance, but none had been held. She figured she might as well use it to hold back the Kansas heat in this crowded room.

John wore an easy smile, his dark hair matching his black silk tie. He greeted a man standing near, shaking his hand. Other men also nodded and smiled at him. Everyone seemed to know John and like him.

A man with muttonchop whiskers and wearing a dark suit worked his way out through the men at the door and stepped onto the porch. He surveyed the people standing in line and those walking toward the house. "Oh dear, we may not have enough chairs." He excused himself and reentered the building.

The jingle of wagon harnesses accompanied the thud of hooves as two additional wagons halted beside the four in the street. Samuel and Elizabeth sat in one.

Kate turned to Lydia. "Please excuse me. I see Elizabeth."

"I'll save you a seat." John's voice followed her as she hurried toward her friends.

Elizabeth's large brown eyes glowed beneath a white bonnet. A white collar and cuffs trimmed her blue gingham dress. "Good morning, Kate. Isn't it a beautiful day? I love bright and sunny mornings, especially if I can share them with friends."

The day seemed even brighter with Elizabeth near. Kate smiled. "Yes, but I fear it will become quite warm in a crowd of worshippers."

Samuel nodded. "'Tis good of the Franklins to allow us to meet in their home. We'll need to squeeze tight to get everyone inside."

"Excuse me." A voice rose from inside the house. "Excuse me." The man who had worried about the number of seats stepped back onto the porch. "We're going to meet outside today," he called to those gathered.

A half dozen men walked out of the home, each carrying a chair. Samuel stepped forward to help them.

"Have you had success recruiting students?" Elizabeth asked while they waited for the chairs to be set.

"It has gone slower than I expected." Kate drew a deep breath. "I anticipated I could find a dozen students in one day, but only three children are confirmed, although four others—from two different families—might attend. Their mother would not commit them at this time."

Elizabeth squeezed her arm. "Please don't worry. You'll find the students you need. I'm sure of it."

"I hope you're right." Her idea of a summer session might prove to be a bad one. The faces of some parents had turned into puzzled frowns when she mentioned the idea. "I'm anxious to start."

"It's only been a day or two! You have plenty of time."

Another wagon pulled to a stop, and two men jumped out. They unloaded four wooden benches and carried them to join the chairs facing the house. Others approached carrying chairs from a neighboring house.

John strode up, his dark eyes fixed on Kate. "I've saved a place for us." He gestured elegantly toward the aisle formed in the chairs and benches facing the porch.

Kate followed John and took a quick count. Over forty people stood, sat, or moved toward the seats. Some would need to stand or sit in the wagons. On the right edge of the crowd, a large, bald man stood with a woman and two children. The older child, a boy, had the gangly appearance of one outgrowing childhood. The girl with a head full of brown curls and wearing a white pinafore tugged at her mother's hand. Kate had not yet talked to these parents about school, but she'd do so after the service.

"Here we are." John waved toward a bench where Lydia sat talking to another woman.

"But there's only room for a couple more people. Where will Samuel and Elizabeth sit?"

"Oh." John's brow furrowed. "I didn't realize—"

"You sit here." Elizabeth touched her arm, her glance darting to John and back. "Samuel and I will sit over there."

"If you please." John smiled and bowed.

Elizabeth winked at her, and Kate rolled her eyes. Her friend had the wrong idea. John's dramatic air was nothing more than a bit of fun.

Kate sat beside Lydia, and John sat at the end of the bench, grinning like he had won a prize.

A tall man with a neatly trimmed beard stepped onto the porch and began the service by leading the hymn "Holy, Holy, Holy, Lord God Almighty." During "Amazing Grace," John smiled at her, his deep voice lifting above those of the other worshipers. Warmth flooded her cheeks, and she unfolded her fan and waved air against her face. Was it the heat or John's attention that caused her to flush so?

She bowed her head for a prayer that meandered from thanksgiving for a beautiful day to petitions to make Kansas a free state and concluded by seeking comfort for a family who had lost a child. The leader read from the Gospels and offered a final prayer.

The family Kate had noticed earlier mingled with others as she stepped into the aisle and met Elizabeth. "Kate, would you join Samuel and me for dinner today?"

"Thank you. I would—"

"What? Will you not grace our table at Hurd and Hall's?" John's eyes widened, and his brow arched to match his mocking tone. "I understand Lydia and Clarissa will serve a fine beef roast that has simmered all morning with potatoes. You must join us."

"Oh, John." Lydia playfully swatted his arm. "I'm sure she wants to be with her friends. Now I must get home and assist with the meal." She strolled toward the street and smiled at Kate as she passed.

"Will I escort one lady or two back to the house?" John donned his hat.

"I will go to Elizabeth and Samuel's home," Kate said.

He nodded as his smile faded. "Good day, ladies." He lengthened his steps to catch up with Lydia, and Elizabeth giggled.

The family with the two children had started walking in the opposite direction. "Elizabeth, can you wait a few minutes? I want to speak to those parents about school."

"Of course. Samuel's helping with the chairs and benches anyway."

Kate lifted her skirt and hurried after the family. "Please wait. I'd like to speak to you."

The family stopped and turned. Another couple, who appeared near Kate's age, stood with the family. "Thank you for stopping. I'm the new teacher, Miss Kate Collins."

"I'm Thomas Pierce." The tall, barrel-chested man lifted his hat. "This is my wife, Susan."

"I am Hiram Vogel." The man was of average height, had a brown beard, and spoke with an accent Kate couldn't place. "This is my wife, Rachel."

"A pleasure to meet you all. I am starting a summer session of school. It will meet in the same place where Mr. Fitch's school met. Did you know he closed his school?"

"I heard that." Thomas nodded and frowned. "A summer session?"

"Yes. I will start it once I have a dozen students enrolled."

Rachel glanced up at her husband. "I don't know."

Kate had to do something to convince them. She turned to the tall boy. "What's your name? Would you like to come to school? I have books I know you will enjoy reading."

"Jacob's my name." He grinned. "I can't go to school because I'm Hiram's apprentice. I'm going to be a carpenter." He squared his shoulders.

Kate clenched her stomach to prevent a sigh, placed her hands on her knees, and leaned toward the little girl. "And what is your name? Would you like to attend school?"

The girl leaned against her mother's skirt and studied Kate with big brown eyes.

Rachel placed a hand on the girl's shoulder. "This is Esther. I think she's still a little too young to go to school. Perhaps in the fall."

There must be some way to entice the children or their parents. Kate squatted in front of the child. "Wouldn't you like to read books? I have McGuffey's readers and other books I know you will enjoy. Some have pictures."

The child's gaze dropped from Kate's eyes to her cheek, then the girl hid her face in her mother's skirt. Kate's scalp prickled. The girl was frightened by her birthmark. She stood and faced the girl's mother.

"Well, thank you very much for your time. I look forward to seeing Esther in the fall, maybe Jacob too."

She turned and trudged toward the house where the church had met. Samuel stood at the wagon and helped Elizabeth aboard. He turned and offered his hand as Kate approached.

"Thank you." She climbed aboard and plopped onto the seat beside Elizabeth.

"I take it your conversation did not go well."

"No, but I have several more people to contact. Some live out of town. I will find a dozen students. It's just harder than I thought it would be."

Elizabeth patted Kate's leg. "I know you will."

Samuel climbed into his seat, snapped the reins, and the wagon creaked forward. Elizabeth hummed a jaunty tune for a few seconds before a giggle burst from her.

"What's so funny?" Kate asked.

"You have an admirer."

"What? Do you mean John? He's not an admirer. John loves to talk and joke. Everyone is his friend."

Samuel chuckled. "Didn't look that way to me. He was determined to sit beside you and looked quite peeved when we invited you to dinner."

Elizabeth grinned. "I think he likes you."

Kate watched the crowd disperse, but didn't spot any families she had not yet approached. "You both have it all wrong. You don't know him like I do."

John was a handsome man and pleasant company, but she didn't need any distractions. After everything she had endured for the chance to teach, she needed students, not a beau.

25

Kate strode through the warm morning air toward *her* schoolhouse. She couldn't help but think of the aid company building as her own space now. Although it housed Dr. Robinson's office and the town held larger meetings there, it was used most often as a schoolroom—*her* schoolroom. She had also learned the company had started a permanent building to replace the sod-walled tent. It would be ready in a week or two. Her feet barely touched the ground. Her first day as a teacher would be a brilliant success.

She had worked tirelessly for over a week to recruit students. Many parents promised to send their children in the fall but needed them at home in the summer. After talking to every family in town and within two miles of it, she had only found nine students. Tears had stung her eyes until she'd met a covered wagon with a large family walking beside it.

She'd forced a smile onto her face and approached them. The Dorn family agreed to send four of their six children to school, making the class enrollment thirteen. God had answered another prayer.

A squeal had burst forth from her when she'd told Lydia and Clarissa. Lydia had hugged her, but Clarissa had clucked her tongue. "Thirteen's an unlucky number. You'd better find another student or two."

The thought was nonsense, of course. An old superstition. She didn't believe in throwing salt over her shoulder or searching through clover patches. Thirteen students would serve well for her first class. Richard and Phoebe Forbes had enjoyed her tutoring in Boston. Thirteen children would love her teaching.

She stopped and lifted the watch pinned to her blouse, a tremble in her hand. She was half an hour early, just as she'd planned. She filled her lungs and turned the corner.

A tall, rangy boy stood near the door of the schoolhouse, hands in his trouser pockets. He glanced up at her approach. "Are you the teacher?" Unruly black hair covered his ears.

"Yes, I am Miss Collins. May I help you?"

"I was told I could go to school here." Fine whiskers shadowed his lip. "When does it start?"

Warmth filled her chest. Fourteen students. "In half an hour."

He nodded and glanced away.

"You seem a little old for school," she said.

A blush colored his face. "I thought so, but my father says my reading and numbers need work."

"I see. May I ask your name?"

"Tom Patrick."

"Come in, Tom. You can have a seat at the back." She led Tom past Dr. Robinson's desk and through the canvas flaps forming the wall. "Tom, would you open the windows on each side so we can enjoy the breeze?"

He turned to the windows, and she marched to her trunk of books in the right front corner of the schoolroom. She fished out her key, opened it, and set four readers, a sheet of paper, and a pencil on the table at the front of the room that served as her desk. Tom finished opening the windows and sat on the left end of the back row.

The chatter of young voices announced several children a few moments later. Nine children ducked through the flaps and took seats at the tables before her, talking to one another. She shook her head at the noise. Of all the things to forget, she had failed to pack a bell.

Eight o'clock. Where were the Dorn children? She dropped her watch and brushed a strand of hair back over her ear toward her braided knot. Two small girls sat in the first row on the left, one with dark hair braided into thin ropes hanging from each side of her head and the other with light brown collar-length hair. Both watched her with solemn eyes.

As Kate was about to begin, a tall, black-haired girl thrust the flap aside and shooed three other dark-headed children through. The voices stopped, and every eye turned to watch. Kate released her breath and smiled as Harriet Dorn and her siblings stood looking around the hot room.

"Welcome, children. Please find a seat."

Harriet directed her two brothers and sister to seats and studied Tom for a moment before turning and sitting on the opposite side of the room next to a round-faced girl with auburn hair about the same age. Amanda Mackenzie, if Kate remembered correctly.

"Good morning, class. I am Miss Collins, your teacher." The little blonde girl at the front raised her hand. "Yes? Your name is Patty, correct?"

The girl nodded and pointed at Kate. "You have something on your face."

Her stomach tightened, but she squared her shoulders and lifted a finger to the corner of her mouth. "Do you mean this?" The girl nodded. "This is a birthmark. I've had it my entire life. It's just a mark on my skin, much like a freckle, only bigger and a different color."

The girl's face wrinkled like she had heard a tall tale. The dark-haired girl beside her raised her hand.

Kate sighed. Little girls could ask impertinent things. She needed to start the lesson, not discuss her face. "What is your question?"

"Teacher, what happened to your hand?"

She should have expected these questions, but had been so intent on starting the school. "A rattlesnake bit me. I nearly died. The doctor had to remove my fingers." Hopefully, that short answer would satisfy the girl's curiosity. Kate lowered her hand, and every eye traced its path to her side. "Children, I would like everyone to come forward and write your name on this paper. We'll start with the older students in the back." The exercise would help gauge each student's writing ability as well as help stop further questions.

Tom rose from his seat in the back corner and ambled forward. He lifted the cedar pencil and scrawled his name. Amanda followed and wrote her name in neat cursive.

Harriet lifted the pencil next and stared at it with an eyebrow raised. "Do I have the choice of writing instrument? I am accustomed to writing with pen and ink."

What a haughty request! Still ... "Yes, I will allow it for this exercise, although you will use a pencil for most assignments. Let me get you a pen." Kate retrieved her pen, inkwell, and blotter from the trunk, closed the lid, and placed them on her desk.

Harriet wrote her name with graceful loops decorating the capital letters. She blotted it carefully and straightened to her full height. "I use Spencer's cursive, which I learned at my school in Boston. It's new and better than other methods."

The girl turned on her heel and walked down the aisle past two boys with heads huddled together. They jerked upright as she passed and stared ahead with straight faces. Too straight. What mischief were they up to? Kate inhaled sharply and walked toward them.

Owen Spencer sat on the aisle, staring straight ahead, a bland expression on his face and uncombed hair the color of old oak leaves sprouting from his scalp. Beside him, Joel William sat with his husky shoulders hunched. Wood shavings littered the dirt floor at their feet.

"Boys, please stand and show me your hands."

They stood and offered empty palms. She took a step closer as Owen scooped something off the bench and hid it behind his back.

Kate thrust out her hand. "Give me the knife, please."

Owen's nostrils flared. "No. My pa gave it to me. You can't have it."

Heat crept up Kate's neck. Owen couldn't continue to deface the property because Dr. Robinson would hold her responsible for any damage, but she risked creating a scene on the first day—the first few minutes—of class.

"You heard the teacher. Give her the knife." Alex Dorn glared at Owen from across the aisle.

"Shut up!" Owen lifted a lip like a snarling dog.

Kate grabbed his arm. "Give me the knife." She stared into his eyes, willing him to back down before she did.

"Fine." He slapped a folded pocketknife with a bone handle onto her open palm.

"We do not destroy the property in this room. This is not your desk to carve as you wish." She marched to the front and dropped the knife on her desk. "Now, Owen, come forward and write your name. You too, Joel."

The boys trudged forward and wrote their names. Owen's writing was surprisingly neat. He eyed his knife and frowned at her, but he returned to his seat. Alex Dorn followed with his brother. Owen glared at Alex every step of his trip to the front and back to his seat. She would need to keep an eye on him.

The rest of the children followed without incident. Finally, Kate called the four youngest girls forward and knelt beside them. Two could print letters and two could not.

"Watch it!"

A thump and grunt launched Kate to her feet.

"Git him, Owen!"

Owen sprawled on his back atop his desk. Alex stood in the aisle, fists balled. Owen rolled off, growled, and launched himself toward Alex. The two became a flurry of flying fists. Yells and shrieks filled the room.

A blow cracked the side of Alex's head, and he stumbled back, tumbling into Isabella Mackenzie.

Kate rushed toward the fight. "Stop it this instant!" She grabbed Owen by the collar and jerked him aside. She planted her other hand on Alex's chest.

Owen spat through a bloody lip. "Blockhead! I'm going to stomp you!"

"Just try, hayseed." A bump had already risen on Alex's cheekbone.

"Miss Collins, do you need assistance?" The harsh voice came from Dr. Robinson, standing just inside the tent flap.

26

A chill crossed Kate's shoulders. How long had he been standing there? "Uh ... no, Dr. Robinson. I believe I can handle this."

He met the eyes of each boy, his face grim. "I will assist if needed." He turned and disappeared through the tent flap.

Every face turned and watched her. She dropped her arms to her sides. "Who started it?"

"He did," both boys said.

She turned to Owen. "What did he do?"

"He kept staring at me. I don't take nothing from nobody."

She crossed her arms. "How would you notice if you weren't staring at him?"

Owen clenched his jaw and stared at the floor.

"Alex, what did Owen do to you?"

"He came over and punched me." Alex squared his shoulders. "I shoved him back, and he landed on the table."

Owen didn't deny the accusation, just glared at Alex.

"I will not tolerate fighting in my class. Owen, do you see that chair between the windows?" She pointed at the chair against the wall on his side of the room.

He glanced over his shoulder but didn't speak or nod.

"You will sit in that chair until I tell you to get up. Alex, return to your seat."

Owen slumped into the chair and crossed his arms. Kate drew a deep breath and walked slowly to the front of the room.

She spent the rest of the morning asking children to stand before the class and read passages from different readers to determine their abilities. She loaned at least one reader to each family and assigned the older children to read. She called the youngest children forward to practice the alphabet and pronounce letters.

The heat coming off the canvas roof settled around her head at about ten minutes past noon.

"Children, we will break for lunch. Please eat outside. I will call you back in half an hour."

Books slapped shut, and the children chattered and hurried from the room.

"Owen, you may go, and you can sit in your normal seat after lunch."

"Yes, Miss Collins. I learned my lesson." He grabbed his cloth lunch bag from his seat and ran through the canvas flaps.

Kate slumped against the edge of the table. Her shoulders ached, and fatigue dragged at her feet. How could she be this tired? She hadn't slaved over a washboard all morning, only taught a few children.

"You've had an interesting morning." Dr. Robinson stood at the back of the room, hands on his hips.

Tightness gripped her throat. He might think less of her because of the small altercation with the boys earlier.

"Yes. I never expected boys to fight on the first day of school."

He chuckled. "Boys will fight anytime they can. I hope you maintain better control this afternoon."

She cleared her throat. "Do you have meetings after lunch? Do I need to plan quiet activities for the children?"

"No, I will not be here. I thought if necessary—"

"I'll be fine. The children will behave, I know it. My troublemaker showed penitence after I sat him in the chair."

"Good." He nodded and stepped back, the canvas rippling with his passage.

The front door creaked and closed. She walked to the water bucket in the office and drank four dippers of water, then sat by a south window and listened to the voices of the children until time to call them inside.

When she walked out of the building, head high, she found Harriet sitting on a chair. Two of the younger boys stood in the street, taking turns throwing dirt clods at the wheel of an empty wagon. The rest of the class was missing.

How could she have forgotten to pack a handbell? It would make calling the children so much easier. If she ordered one, it would take weeks to arrive. Perhaps she could find a cowbell to use. She clapped her hands. "Children, lunch is over. Please return to class."

Owen and Joel ran around the corner, peering up at her with eager faces.

"Can we go in first?" Owen asked.

"Of course, boys." She smiled at her victory in the test of wills.

The two boys grinned at each other and dashed inside. Harriet rose from her seat, frowning at the boys as they scampered through the door, and shook her head.

The rest of the children appeared from the sides of the building, and Kate followed them into the schoolroom. The children sat whispering to each other but stopped as she strode up the aisle. A lightness filled her chest. The children were beginning to recognize her authority.

She faced the class. "This afternoon we will work on arithmetic."

Owen stretched his hand high and waved it.

"Yes, Owen?"

"Miss Collins, this book you gave me's very difficult, 'specially if Daniel's going to use it too. Can I get an easier one?" He held up the book.

Kate beamed at him. Owen's time of reflection in the chair had produced positive results. "Your concern for your brother makes me very happy, Owen. Will you also help him at home with his reading?"

"Oh, I will." He grinned.

"Let me get you one." She strode to the trunk, lifted the lid, and reached inside.

A gray snake lay across the books, inches from her hand. She screamed and leaped back, slamming the trunk. Her pulse pounded against her chest.

The children snickered, hands to their mouths, except for Harriet, who shook her head, and Alex Dorn, who stared at his desk.

Owen tried to hide his grin. "What's wrong, Teacher?"

Kate clutched her hands to her chest. "There's a snake in my trunk."

"Let me see." Owen marched forward before she could stop him and lifted the lid. "Yep. You got yourself a bull snake. They're not poisonous." He reached down, grasped the snake, spun, and thrust the vile creature at her. "See?"

"Ahh!" She flinched. The snake hung more than half as long as he was tall.

"It's dead, though. See here? A wagon wheel caught it." He pointed to a spot just below the head where dried blood clung to the gray scales.

Kate trembled, and heat flushed through her face. Owen had put the snake in the trunk to humiliate her. He'd made her a laughingstock in front of the whole class.

"Did you put that thing in my trunk?"

"Who me? Why would I do that?" His bland face watched her, but a spark of triumph showed in his eyes.

Giggles rose, but Kate didn't turn to see who laughed. She hugged herself, but couldn't stop trembling. The boy deserved a thrashing, but could she prove that he did it?

"Class." Her voice wavered. "Class, I think we've had enough for today. Everyone may go home."

The children gathered their things and began to leave.

"I'll take care of this for you." Owen waved the snake. "Can I have my knife now?"

He must have brought the snake in after lunch. That's why he'd been so anxious to go in first.

"Yes, take your knife, but don't bring it to class again."

He stepped forward, and she dodged away from the snake. He picked up the knife, pocketed it, and dragged the snake down the aisle, whistling a tune.

Harriet, the only person left in the room, marched forward, arms clutching her reader, and faced Kate. "You did *not* handle that well. I thought every teacher knew how to establish discipline. How long have you taught school?"

Warmth flushed Kate's cheeks. "Long enough." She cringed at the weakness in her voice.

"I don't think so." Harriet rolled her eyes, turned, and left.

Kate stared at the empty classroom, and tears flooded her eyes. Her first day of class had been a failure. She collapsed in the chair behind her desk and wept.

Mucus ran onto her lip, and she dug out her handkerchief. She must control her emotions. Tomorrow, she would face the class again. She gritted her teeth, blew her nose, and wiped her eyes. Maybe Owen wouldn't return. She rose, locked her trunk, and closed the windows.

As she wandered out the door and slogged toward home, her mind felt numb. Teaching a class of fourteen students differed so much from tutoring two.

How did Mr. Fitch manage to teach *twenty* students? Had Owen been just as troublesome for him as he was for her? She could stop by Mr. Fitch's home and ask him, but not with swollen red eyes and a drippy nose. Would he even help her? He had closed the school—had Owen been the reason?

Her breath caught. She couldn't afford his help anyway. He might tell Dr. Robinson she couldn't handle herself, and then they'd hire someone else.

Lydia was her answer. Lydia had taught in a Choctaw school. She would know what to do. Besides, it would be easier to tell her about the day's disaster than a man she'd met but once.

She plodded up to the dining table where Lydia and Clarissa sat, sorting dried beans.

Lydia frowned. "You're earlier than I expected. How did school go?"

"Terrible."

Clarissa shook her head. "I warned you. Thirteen's an unlucky number. You should've recruited another student."

"Another boy enrolled this morning. I had fourteen students." Kate sat and slumped against the table. "It wasn't bad luck. I simply failed." Her tears flowed again.

27

"See you tomorrow, Horace." John waved at the man behind the counter and pulled the store door shut. The sun still hung above the horizon even though supper time was near. Across the street, a man waved, and he returned the gesture.

He sauntered toward the boardinghouse and greeted other men along the way, having learned many names in the few weeks since he had arrived. Moving to Lawrence had been a good decision, but it didn't relieve the ache in his heart. Susanna had agreed to marry him in June. Would the memory always weigh on him?

He reached the boardinghouse and stopped in the street. Henry stood on a ladder leaning against the house frame, driving nails into a rafter. George stood on joists near the ridge board. Clarissa had put them to work every day after breakfast, and they didn't stop until she called them to eat. A few more weeks and they would complete the house—unless they ran out of lumber. But two new sawmills had opened, so that shouldn't happen.

Tom moseyed toward him and nodded. "John."

"How's my tentmate? Did you have a good day?"

"Yep. You?"

"Yes, I did." No need to burden Tom with his memories. The man probably had a few heavy ones of his own.

John and Tom walked to where Clarissa bent over two large frying pans on the fire, while Lydia bustled about the table, placing plates and cups about. Kate already sat at her place.

"What you suppose we got for supper?" Tom tipped his hat back on his head.

"I have no idea, but if I know Clarissa, it'll be good."

"Supper's ready!" Clarissa's voice carried like a red-faced revival preacher's.

"You don't have to call me twice." John made quick work at the wash basin and hurried to his place.

Kate sat with a slack face and stared at the plate of biscuits in front of her.

"Good evening, Kate. Did you have a good day?"

"What? Oh." She shrugged. "It was a day." A smile flickered on her face and disappeared.

"John, I hope you had a wonderful day." Martha slipped into her seat, as pretty as ever. "Did you see a lot of customers at the store?"

"We did." John nodded. The less he said, the better. Martha was a beehive—a promise of sweetness but more likely to sting you. He'd seen her kind before.

As usual, Martha chattered at him throughout the meal. Kate ate a bite or two but pushed the food around on her plate more than she ate. Something bad must have happened in her day to cause her to look so discouraged.

Martha finally stopped yacking to drink some water, and he tried to draw Kate into the conversation, but her reply was as bare as bleached bones on the prairie.

Supper ended, and he excused himself, heading toward the fire with the other men. He stopped outside the circle of logs, kegs, and stumps. Robert and Henry sat in their usual places exchanging gripes about the bogus legislature. Why must they ruin a good meal by discussing politics? On the far side of the log, Tom sipped his coffee. He would be a good listener, but wouldn't have much to say.

A hand touched his arm.

Martha batted her lashes twice. "John, are you going to sit and enjoy the evening?"

She could carry a conversation well, but she looked and acted too much like Susanna. He was not in the mood for reminders of their relationship.

"I'm sure I will enjoy the evening ... but ladies first." He bowed and gestured toward the fire.

"Thank you." She smiled and moved toward the log.

"I'll be there later." He turned away from the pout on her face toward the table where Clarissa washed dishes and Lydia dried. Kate still sat in her place, elbows on the table and chin cupped in her hands.

"You must have had a very bad day." He sat across from her.

"It ... it was ... not good." Her gaze dropped to the table.

Lydia dried a plate and added it to a stack on the table. "Kate, maybe you should go for a walk. The pleasant evening air might help."

"Maybe I should." Kate rose and wandered toward the road.

Lydia peered at him with raised eyebrows and jerked her head toward Kate. She whispered. "She needs cheering up. Why don't you walk with her?"

Maybe a walk would help him banish his troublesome memories as well. He rose and caught up with Kate. "Can I accompany you on your walk?"

"Yes." She spoke the word with a sigh.

"Let's go south. I find the breeze in my face helps clear away discouraging thoughts." They turned and walked a few paces in silence. "So, what happened to ruin your day?"

"I failed on my first day of school."

"Oh. Are you sure? Failed is a strong word."

"A fight broke out between two boys, and a twelve-year-old girl thinks I can't teach. Dr. Robinson had to step into the class and restore order. He must think I can't teach either."

John blew out a breath. "You did have an eventful day. Care to tell me the whole story?"

They strolled past houses and camps as Kate told the details of her day. When they came to the edge of town, she stopped and crossed her arms, staring across the countryside.

"And then Harriet asked how long I had taught and rolled her eyes at my answer."

"What was your answer?"

Color flushed her cheeks, and her frown deepened.

"You can tell me. I won't tell Harriet." He caught her eye and winked.

Her chest rose, and she held her breath for a moment before releasing it. "Before I came to Kansas, I tutored two students for several months. They were well-behaved, but now I teach fourteen students, and one of them is full of mischief and picked a fight."

"It's only your first day. Boys often fight, especially if one is new to the school. They're like chickens figuring out who rules the roost. I bet those boys will work it out away from school."

She frowned and stared at the ground, a wisp of her dark brown hair lay against her clenched jaw.

What could he say to encourage her? Nothing came to mind, so he cleared his throat. "What're you going to do?"

"I talked to Lydia." Her arms dropped to her sides. "Did you know she taught school among the Choctaw Indians? She gave me some tips to manage my classroom, and I know what I will do to start class tomorrow."

John clapped his hands together. "Excellent! You've taken action to solve the problem."

The corner of her mouth lifted, and warmth filled John's chest. He had lifted the burden of her day.

"Enough about me." Kate clasped her hands and squared her shoulders. "How was your day?"

John frowned. "Also discouraging."

"Oh? What happened?"

"Well, nothing ... it's what *didn't* happen." He should change the subject before he said too much. No one knew of his loss in Kansas, not even Tom.

"I understand that kind of discouragement."

"You do?"

She lifted a finger to her birthmark. "When I was sixteen, things I wanted to happen at my cotillion didn't."

"Ah, I see." She understood rejection, maybe better than he did. He drew a deep breath. Perhaps it would be good to share his own struggles. "This is the day I was supposed to marry."

"Oh." Her large brown eyes peered up at him. "I'm so sorry. Would you ... that must be very difficult."

The trickle of release from telling her grew stronger. "I was engaged to a beautiful woman, tall with blue eyes and blond hair, Susanna. She loved to talk, and we enjoyed long walks dreaming about our future together. We planned to work with my aunt and uncle in their store and eventually take over the business, but ..."

Kate gasped. "She died."

John kicked a rock with the toe of his shoe. "No. Worse. She left without saying anything to me. She simply wrote a letter and left it for me. I got it an hour later, sooner than she intended, I think. She said she was taking the train and leaving town. I rode my horse into a lather—nearly killed it—and caught the train at the next town. She was ..." John swallowed hard. "... was with another man, older than me and wearing expensive clothes. She told me she was going to Cleveland to marry him."

"That's terrible."

The memory of her lifted chin and flashing eyes taunted him, and his throat burned. How could she leave him like that?

"Is that why you came to Kansas?"

"Huh?" John turned to her.

"Did you come to Kansas to escape her memory?"

"Yes, I had courted her since last summer and proposed on Valentine's Day, but she left me the last day of February." Sweat pricked his forehead. "Please, don't tell anyone. I shouldn't of ... I mean ..."

"I won't." She lightly touched his arm. "John, she's a fool. You're kind and have a good heart—I see that in the way you treat others. Even in your pain, you encouraged me." She smiled up at him with warm eyes.

He drew in a lungful of air and turned his face to the sun sitting on the horizon like a giant orange ball. Talking to Kate had helped, but his heart still felt like a brick. "Thanks for listening. Shall we return?"

She nodded and turned. They strolled back the way they had come. How could he return her kindness? She had listened to his story without condemning Susanna or pouring too much sympathy on him.

He knew what it took to come to Kansas alone. The whole ordeal must have been harder for her as a single woman. What courage and dedication she possessed to raise the funds and travel so far to teach. She wanted to help others, so different from Susanna.

28

K ate stood before her desk and clasped her hands. "Class, you are dismissed." The children scrambled for their things and scurried toward the door as she leaned against her desk. She had successfully completed her second day as a teacher.

Alex and Owen had eyed each other like two circling tomcats all day, but neither had attacked the other. Lydia's suggestion to provide consequences for the smallest infraction had surprised Alex, but he sat in the chair without complaint. Owen had smirked at his nemesis, but he had studied Kate after she'd sent Alex to the chair for whispering to Isabella. Owen would test her again, she was sure, but she had prevented any problems today.

Lydia had also suggested she use Harriet to teach the younger children. The responsibility had pleased the girl and allowed Kate to focus more attention on the troublesome boys.

The door slammed, cutting off the last of the children's babble. Dr. Robinson pushed the curtain aside and walked toward her, ending her silent praise for a job well done.

"Miss Collins, I see your class behaved in better fashion today."

"Yes, they did." She squared her shoulders. Perhaps her reputation as a teacher had not been destroyed. "May I help you, Dr. Robinson?"

"A rider brought some mail today from Topeka. You received three letters." He extended the folded papers.

Topeka? They must be letters from Amelia or her parents. She had never written a second letter home. How could she tell them she scrubbed clothes on the riverbank? Her heartbeat surged.

"Thank you!"

She held the letters and ran her fingers across the off-white paper, still crisp after their journey. Amelia's elaborate strokes formed the address on the first letter and Mother's bold script on the second. The handwriting on the third seemed familiar, but she couldn't place it. Who could have written her?

"Enjoy your letters and the rest of your afternoon." The doctor nodded and returned to his office.

She scrambled to a bench, dragged it closer to an open window, and plopped onto it. The back of Amelia's letter held a rose-colored seal. Her fingers traced the initials pressed into the fingernail-sized drop of wax. She lifted the edge of the paper, breaking the seal, and unfolded the letter.

May 25
Dear Kate,

I cannot imagine what you have endured in the middle of our American wilderness. My heart aches knowing you lost part of your hand. How I want to embrace and encourage you! I'm so sorry for our bitter parting last spring. I hope you know you are always welcome in my home. I enjoyed our time together and hope to see you again in the future.

Someone else would enjoy visiting you again, at least I believe so. Arthur Eliot stopped not a day after I received your letter. Shock filled his face upon hearing of your misfortune. I think he misses you.

I hope you enjoy teaching in Topeka. Your determination fills me with pride. I miss you.
Love,
Amelia

Tightness gripped Kate's throat, and she blinked at the sting in her eyes. Amelia's letter implied she shared blame for the harsh words they'd shared when Kate left Boston. But the blame was all Kate's. She had always been too headstrong. Would Amelia still be proud if she had witnessed the first day of school?

She drew a deep breath. Arthur must have visited Amelia to retrieve the books he had loaned. Kate pursed her lips. She should have returned them before leaving, but she had scurried to make all the arrangements for the trip. Discussing books with him had been a delight—she missed it—but she had to pursue her purpose.

Kate dabbed her eyes with her handkerchief and lifted Mother's letter from her lap. Would it contain a scathing rebuke about informing them of her departure by letter? The dark paper wafer sealing the letter tore under her finger.

Belchertown, May 28
My dearest Kate,

Your father and I are horrified by your suffering. We know you want to teach, but is the education of a few people in the middle of the prairie worth so much pain? Please come home. Your father tells me how arduous the journey to Kansas must have been. I am astounded you made the journey in the first place, though I shouldn't be. You have a strong will much like my own. Your father will meet you in Kansas City to accompany you home and provide any fares or fees needed. Please respond immediately. At the first word from you, he will depart. As you know, the journey will take about two weeks. He will meet you at the aid company hotel. We eagerly await word from you and hope you have regained your strength.
With all our love,
Your mother and father

Kate stood and turned to the window, the air cooling her face. Clouds of cotton drifted in the blue sky. She held the paper to her lips and inhaled a metallic whiff of the ink. If she wanted, Father would come and accompany her home. How could he afford it? She had used her savings and the generous gift from the Forbes to travel. Had his fortunes changed?

Their offer would have tempted her had she received it during her recovery, but returning home was impossible now. They wanted the best for her—or what they thought was best—but she had finally begun to teach, her purpose in emigrating to Kansas. Women could do little to stop slavery since they were denied the right to vote, but she had found a way to limit the spread of such evil. She assisted the aid company in attracting free-state settlers by teaching school. God had arranged for her to teach in Lawrence. How could she return now?

The handwriting of the third letter still stirred her memory without yielding a name. She flipped the letter over. A red wax seal, like men often used, held the folded paper together. An A and E circled by a twined ring were pressed into the wax. Kate gasped. *Arthur Eliot.*

Why would he write? He'd heard of her misfortune. Did he write to express polite concern or something else? She couldn't bear any distractions now that she taught school. Nor could she afford to think over much about home. No, that wasn't it. She couldn't spend time thinking about *Boston*. Lawrence was her home now. She jammed the letters into her skirt pocket.

Kate plodded toward the Hurd and Hull fire ring. She had reread Amelia's and Mother's letters twice after returning from school, but not Arthur's. Why was she so hesitant? He likely wrote a wish for her recovery after hearing of the snakebite and surgery. It is what a gentleman would do for an acquaintance. Why else would he write to her after she had ended his courtship?

She pulled his letter from her pocket. The address consisted of strong strokes and large loops. The seal was the size of her thumbnail, though something had flattened the ridges and lines on one side of the wax. Did a hand squeeze it too hard during its trip?

Her mind drifted to their last walk on the Commons in the spring. Had she misread his words? She could have imagined his interest in her. Maybe he wrote to clarify her misunderstanding of his intentions. Did she want to know? He was in Boston studying to be a doctor. His path was set, and so was hers.

She stopped and stared at short pieces of wood, the thickness of her arm, crackling in a pile of ash. Maybe Arthur wrote to recommend a book. She chuckled. No, she just wanted to savor a memory of their long critiques of authors. The letter was just a polite wish for her good health. Good manners dictated that he write her since their courtship was recent.

"You're standing a might close to the fire on a warm evening."

Kate startled. "What?"

John grinned from his seat on the log. "You've been lost in thought all evening."

Everyone sat around the fire at their usual places except Clarissa and Lydia, who were clearing the dishes.

"Yes, I know."

Her hand trembled. She needed to decide whether to read Arthur's letter or not. It was probably nothing, but ... She bent and flipped the letter between two burning sticks. A yellow flame leaped up and consumed the paper, lifting scraps of black ash into the air.

29

"That looks rather final," John said while stroking his mustache.

"What?" She glanced at him

He thrust his jaw at the blazing wood. "Looks like you burned a letter without reading it."

"It was nothing." She bit her lip and crossed her arms as she stared down at the paper in the flames.

He really shouldn't pry, but her behavior was curious. She spun toward the stump next to his log, smoothed her skirt, and sat. Something bothered her.

"I love getting letters," he said. "I got one from my uncle last week. I've read it again three times."

She smiled. "I received three letters today. I've also reread the ones from my parents and my aunt." She shrugged. "I knew what was in that one, so I didn't need to keep it."

"Good evening, John." Martha swept past and perched on the log beside him. "Have you heard about the July Fourth celebration? I understand the town has big plans."

"I have. People have been talking about it at the store. I hear it'll be a big doings with a parade, speeches, and a picnic. The town's now got a militia, and they plan to march in uniform."

Martha clasped her hands under her chin. "It sounds wonderful. I hope someone asks to accompany me. I'd love to attend."

Her eyes searched his, communicating her desire to be asked to the celebration, but he turned from her gaze. "Kate, have you heard about the festivities?"

Martha sniffed.

Kate nodded. "I've heard a few things, but I'm so focused on starting school I haven't given it much attention."

He smiled. "If you'd like to go, I'd be more than happy to accompany you."

Martha sucked a breath.

Kate's eyes narrowed, and she glanced at the fire. "You're quite generous, but—"

"I would *love* to attend with you, John." Martha touched his forearm, her blue eyes shining.

He had to admit, Martha was a beauty. Most men would want to court her, but she looked too much, acted too much like Susanna. How could he trust her? Even though Martha was a hard worker, unlike Susanna, they acted too much alike. Martha had her cap set for him, and he must avoid encouraging her.

Lydia and Clarissa entered the fire ring and sat at their usual places.

The muscles in his shoulders eased as an idea came to him. "Lydia, would you like to attend the July Fourth celebration?"

"You can go with us." Martha's voice rang with triumph.

John stopped a sigh from escaping his lips. If he corrected Martha, she might act wounded but would likely find a way to horn in at the parade or picnic anyway. Lydia could help buffer Martha's attention.

"Come to think of it, Lydia, I'm willing to accompany you, as well as Kate and Martha. We could make a day of it."

Lydia's eyebrows lifted. "I'd be happy to join you."

"John, how sweet of you to ask our friends." Martha's voice held honey, but her eyes didn't.

He turned to Kate. "The entire town'll be there. Why don't you come with us?"

Kate drew a deep breath, sat straight, and smiled. "I would be delighted to accompany you."

A lightness lifted his chest. "Excellent!" He could spend more time with Kate at the town's party, even if Martha tagged along, and Lydia's presence would make it less awkward. He'd be polite to all of them, which would take some juggling, but this way he'd get to know Kate a little better.

July 4

"Oh, John, this is so exciting!" Martha slipped her hand inside his elbow and pulled herself close, her frilly, green skirt crushed against his leg. She hung on his arm heavier than the loaded picnic basket in his other hand. Her perfumed scent tingled his nose.

Wagons rolled up the street toward him with waving people, and the cadence of drums drifted around the corner where the militia units had turned. People crowded both sides of the street, many wearing their Sunday best. Folks had done themselves proud with the town's first parade.

"An impressive sight." Lydia stood on Martha's other side in a dark dress with a white collar and a simple white bonnet. Her gaze darted to Martha's grip on his arm, and a bemused smile crossed her face. Did she find his discomfort funny?

Kate stood on his left in a light blue dress and a white bonnet, the brim of it arched across the top of her head, and a silk ribbon tied under her chin held it in place.

"People must have traveled from miles around to attend the parade." Another wagon rolled past and she waved. "Look. It's Dr. Robinson. I hear he's going to speak today."

Martha gasped. "What beautiful roses! Where did they find so many?"

Someone had fastened flowers to the harnesses of the teams drawing the wagons. Either they bound them to the leather with string or wove them in—either way, the task would have taken hours and likely pricked their fingers.

John pointed down the street. "Ladies, you will like what's coming next."

Cattle strained against their yokes. One, two … eleven. He shook his head. Eleven yokes of oxen were hitched to three wagons decorated with red, white, and blue bunting and filled with people. A large sign read "In Union Is Our Strength." The crowd clapped and cheered. Kate and Lydia joined the applause, but Martha's grip never loosened.

The union of states was the country's strength. The sooner people understood that and stopped threatening it with the dispute over slavery, the better.

"Look at their bright skirts!" Martha pointed at a group of men and women following the three wagons.

The women wore skirts with patterned panels of black, white, red, and green. Beaded necklaces hung from their necks. The men wore trousers, shirts, and colored turbans adorned with feathers. Several wore silver medallions.

"They're Shawnee," John said. "I heard their leaders would walk in the parade. I think that's another tribe." He pointed to another group with a different style of clothing.

"I think their clothes are beautiful. I'm glad they came." Kate glanced up and smiled, her brown eyes warm.

Martha tugged his arm. "John, I'm glad you invited me. You know so much."

How would he ever talk to Kate with Martha stuck to his side like a cocklebur on a long-haired dog?

The Indians passed, and the crowd thinned as people stepped into the street to follow the parade. Kate pointed toward an approaching wagon. "There's Elizabeth and Samuel. I asked them to give us a ride to the park."

"I'd rather ride in a wagon than walk, wouldn't you?" John said.

"Oh, John, you're so thoughtful." Martha beamed at him.

Kate had been the thoughtful one, not him. She bounced on her toes, waving and calling until Elizabeth spotted her and waved in return.

Samuel halted the wagon. A narrow bench ran along each side of the wagon bed.

John set the basket down. "Martha, if you would."

She smiled, took his hand, and hiked her skirt, stepping on the wheel hub. She climbed into the back of the wagon and sat on the bench on the far side.

He turned. "Kate, would you like a hand?"

"Thank you, John." She climbed aboard and sat on the nearest bench and greeted Elizabeth.

"Would you also assist me?" Lydia smiled like she knew a secret.

"Of course." He handed her up, and she sat next to Martha, who frowned. He forced the smile off his face. Lydia was a wise woman.

John lifted the basket over the side, scrambled aboard, and plopped onto the bench next to Kate. The wagon lurched forward, and he leaned closer to Kate. "Isn't this fun?"

She grinned. "I loved the parade. I hope the speeches will be just as good."

"Look at the hotel." He pointed across the street. Martha frowned and turned to look behind her. "They've made a lot of progress."

Martha turned back, a smile pasted on her face. At least she wasn't clinging to him any longer.

"It will be a nice hotel, once complete," Kate said. "The limestone blocks make it so stately. So much has changed and the town isn't even a year old."

Many of the buildings nearest the river stood complete.

He nodded. "It is exciting, isn't it?"

The wagon turned along the levee and rolled west. People filled the streets on each side, all walking to the park for the picnic. They rolled past the large, two-story mill building and through the shallow creek.

Kate turned to him and smiled. "I think it's wonderful that they reserved space for parks when they laid out the city. Don't you?"

"Yes, of course. A few hundred people already live here, and they have planned for growth. It'll stretch farther south and west, a couple more streets east too. Many of the lots are already sold, and more people will arrive before winter."

She said nothing, but her eyes peered into his, catching the light. Her smile transformed her face. She usually appeared serious, but today she showed the delight of a girl. Maybe Elizabeth's enthusiasm had rubbed off on her.

The wagon stopped beside several others. People climbed down and joined groups of people carrying baskets onto a grassy area. John hopped down from the wagon. Martha smiled down at him and handed him the basket. She must have leaped up immediately after he did. He raised his hand toward her.

Her brow wrinkled. "I'm afraid I may fall. Would you lift me down from the back?"

She was flirting, but a gentleman would do it.

He drew a breath and smiled. "I'll be happy to lift you down."

He stepped to the back, dropped the tailgate, and reached up, resting his hands on her waist. She placed her hands on his shoulders, and he swung her to the ground. She almost landed on his boots. Her blue eyes gazed up at him, an impish smile on her lips. "That was fun, wasn't it?"

"Excuse me, Martha, I must help the other women." He lifted his hand toward Lydia. "Would you like to climb down over the wheel, or shall I swing you to the ground too?"

"This will do."

He swung her to the ground and turned to Kate. "And for you?"

"Uh ... yes, please."

He swung her to the ground. "My lady, I hope your trip was pleasant." He smiled, and a blush colored her cheeks. "Shall we find a picnic spot?" He offered his arm and she took it.

Martha's eyes widened, and her lips pouted. He scooped up the basket and strolled after Samuel and Elizabeth.

30

"This looks like a good spot." Samuel stopped in a space surrounded by other groups spreading picnics on the grass.

"Let me help you." John handed the basket to Kate and joined Samuel in spreading a canvas tarp on the ground.

He motioned to Kate, who sat on a corner, and he sat on her right. Lydia quickly sat next to him. Had Kate asked her to buffer Martha? He hadn't spoken to Lydia, but he welcomed her presence. Martha sat across from Kate with Samuel and Elizabeth completing the circle.

Kate opened the basket and passed around the fried chicken and biscuits Clarissa had packed. Elizabeth opened their basket, and Samuel said a blessing. All around them, people ate and discussed the parade's sights and sounds. Martha smiled at him whenever she could catch his eye, but he ate in silence since Elizabeth chatted with Kate. He couldn't get a word in edgewise if he'd wanted.

After passing out cookies, Kate and Elizabeth gathered the picnic napkins and chicken bones into the baskets.

Elizabeth leaned toward Samuel. "Do you see a privy anywhere near?"

"Good idea." He craned his neck. "Everyone I see close has half a dozen people standing in line. We might want to go back to the mill or our place."

"May I go with you?" Martha stood as well.

"Of course," Elizabeth said. They rose and strode away.

Lydia also stood. "I see Mrs. Tedford. She's been poorly, and I haven't seen her for a few weeks. I'll be back before the speeches start." She wove through the groups of people toward the stage.

If Kate hadn't talked to Lydia, then the woman had read his thoughts and left him alone with Kate. He cleared his throat. "You said Dr. Robinson will speak today. What do you suppose he'll say?"

"I'm sure his address will discuss making Kansas a free state. Isn't that why we're all here?"

Kate didn't shy away from politics, but why would she? Her desire to end slavery had led her to emigrate.

John wiped his mustache with his finger. "I think most people come to the territory for land and a new opportunity."

"You're right, but we all want a state without slavery."

"Don't be so sure about that."

Lines creased her forehead. "You don't want a free state?"

"Oh, I want a free state, but not everyone does." He plucked a stem of prairie grass and held it between his teeth.

She frowned. "I find it hard to believe people in Kansas would want otherwise. Missouri, on the other hand, has many slave owners."

"There are towns in this territory filled with people who favor slavery—both north and south of here. Leavenworth is one. I hear about it at the store. Slavery interests are quite strong in several places. I fear we face a fight unless people come to their senses."

She peered over the crowd. "It may take a fight."

"You want war? Over slavery?"

"No, I do not, but I don't want to stand by while people are enslaved and our government tolerates the evil. We have to do something. Don't you agree?"

"Yes. I will vote for a free state, but ..."

At the far edge of the crowd, Samuel, Elizabeth, and Martha walked toward them. Were they already returning?

"But what?" Kate's eyebrows lifted.

"Kate, there's something I'd like to ask you."

"What might that be?"

The others would arrive in a couple of minutes, but how should he begin? "Well ... you're here without your parents or any family."

Her smile melted. "Yes, they live in Massachusetts."

"I hope I'm not being too forward ... if your parents were here, I would speak to them. As it is ..."

She frowned. "John, what *are* you talking about?"

"I would like to accompany you to other events ... to call on you."

"Oh." Her eyes opened wide, her head drawing back.

"I'd like to get to know you better, to—"

"John, teaching school is my focus. I've just started the school session, and the children have finally settled into a routine. I don't want any distractions right now."

"Distraction?" His company was a distraction? She seemed to enjoy the times they were together. He certainly enjoyed talking with her.

"You're most kind, and I enjoy our conversations, but ... you ... you must understand, I do not plan to marry. I have a keen interest in reform efforts—"

"John!" Martha swept onto the tarp and sat so quickly she nearly toppled into him. "I'm looking forward to the speeches, aren't you? After this, you must take me for a long walk so we can discuss them in depth." Her face held a look of triumph.

Kate's nostrils flared. "Excuse me, Martha." She turned her wide smile to him. "John, thank you for your courteous request. I will be honored to ... enjoy your company at future events."

"Why did you leave me?" Kate crossed her arms as the late afternoon sun cast her shadow across Lydia.

"Leave you? At the picnic?" Lydia asked.

After returning from the festivities, Martha had whisked John off on a stroll, and she asked Lydia to walk with her—in the opposite direction. They had now reached the edge of town.

"Yes. You left me at the picnic." Kate had waited until they were beyond earshot of the camp to voice her complaint. "Elizabeth and the others left, and you went to talk to a friend. You left me alone with John."

Lydia frowned. "I thought you'd enjoy time with him without Martha's constant interruptions. I could see he wanted to talk to you."

"I enjoyed talking to him, but ..."

"Did something happen?" Her friend's lips held a faint smile.

"He asked if he could call on me."

Lydia's smile grew. "Did you agree?"

"I tried to tell him I don't need any distractions from school and plan to never marry, but Martha showed up as smug as you please and plopped down next to him. Before I could help myself, I told John I would enjoy his company, *but* I didn't mean to agree."

Lydia frowned. "You don't enjoy John's company?"

"I do, but I ..."

"Will it be so painful to spend time with him?"

"No, not at all. John is very polite and an excellent conversationalist—"

"And quite handsome." Lydia's eyebrows arched.

"Well ... yes, but I'm just ... I don't know, it seems ..."

Lydia placed her hands on her hips. "What are you afraid of?"

That John's attention would confuse her like Arthur's had. She couldn't afford to be distracted. Unrealistic hopes couldn't grow in her heart again.

"My mission is to teach school and help Kansas become a free state."

"Can't you do both—teach school and see John?"

Kate crossed her arms. "I don't know."

"A man finds you attractive—"

"Ha! I'm not beautiful."

Lydia tipped her head and gazed out from under her lowered brow like she scolded a child. "You're prettier than you know. To my knowledge, most men don't ask to call on ugly women."

That was true, as she well knew. Martha—who was obviously more beautiful—wanted him, but he only tolerated her attention. Kate touched her lip. Did John find her ... pretty?

Arthur's interest could have been a fluke since she'd reminded him of Dahlia—not her appearance but her interests and convictions. Was John just lonely because of the rejection he had experienced, or was there something more?

A chuckle escaped Lydia, and she shook her head. "A man finds you attractive and asks to see you. You agree, but see a problem. Martha wouldn't."

Kate's mouth dried. "Yes, but Martha is searching for a man to marry. I'm not. He's probably just looking for someone to keep him away from Martha."

Lydia touched Kate's arm. "Maybe he's looking for a woman to marry and doesn't like the one thrusting herself at him." She turned and strolled back toward the boardinghouse.

A hot gust of wind swept Kate's face, but she shivered. Had John asked to see her because he was interested in marriage, or simply to keep Martha at bay? Lydia might be right. Should she tell John she had changed her mind, and that his attention was unwelcome?

The evening air remained hot and heavy and waved the grass, brown tinged green. She sighed. Boston would be beautiful now—green grass, flowers, and trees filling the Commons.

Arthur had delighted her with long conversations about politics and novels. What a delightful time they had enjoyed together. Of course, she cherished the memories, the way he made her feel. Would she enjoy spending time with John? She knew she would.

She'd broken Arthur's courtship because she'd decided to teach in Kansas. What harm could it do to enjoy John's attention now that she taught school? If his attention distracted her too much, she could end it.

31

"Sir, Mr. Coffin is here to see you."

Arthur turned from his study window overlooking the garden as Frederic stepped past the butler and strode across the study. "Greetings, my friend."

"Frederic, what are you doing here?"

"Well, chap, when I didn't see you at the Lowell's party on the fourth, and our paths didn't cross at the hospital, I decided to check on you."

"Here I am." Arthur extended his arms and shrugged. "Please take a seat." He plopped into the wooden swivel chair at his desk.

Frederic sank into the upholstered chair near the desk and gazed at the floor-to-ceiling bookcases lining the walls. "So many books. I simply must read one someday."

"Ha! You never read. You're always attending a party somewhere."

His friend grinned. "True, but I made you laugh—if you dare to call that snort a laugh."

Arthur shook his head. "Are you here to irritate me?"

"I never irritate you!" Frederic's face held mock horror.

"Not true."

Frederic smiled. "I simply amuse you." He drew a breath, and his smile disappeared. "But you haven't attended any social events since Miss Collins left you four months ago. Are you still pining for her?"

"My duties as an apprentice to Dr. Jackson consume my time."

"I don't believe it. Remember, I work at the hospital too. I'm concerned about you. It took you nearly a year to recover from Dahlia's death. Then you began calling on Kate and came to life. Remember?"

Arthur shuffled some papers on his desk. "Yes, I enjoyed my time calling on her. I miss her."

Frederic slapped his knee. "Miss her? You're melancholy and spend too much time sulking in this study."

"I do not sulk in this room. I ... I think and read here. Besides, I maintain my hours at the hospital and a few more."

Frederic sank back into the chair and steepled his fingers. "You know what I mean. You've withdrawn from all social activities."

What if he had? He couldn't pretend to be light-hearted and charming when he wasn't. "I am not a party maven like you."

Frederic's laugh filled the room. "An apt description! I maintain my duties *and* socialize. I'll have you know, it has paid off. I've received an invitation to call on Miss Alice Peabody." He smirked and puffed out his chest.

Arthur dipped his head. "Congratulations, I hope it goes better for you than for me."

Frederic's experience would be better because Miss Peabody wouldn't reject him before he became bored with her.

"How can I persuade you to attend a party with me next week?" His friend leaned forward.

"I ... I'm waiting for a letter."

Frederic fell back against the chair again. "From Kate? Didn't you write to her months ago?"

He made the time sound like an eon. "Yes, as soon as I heard of her misfortune."

"That's right, bitten by a snake and amputation of fingers." Frederic stroked his chin. "You still haven't received a reply from her?"

His throat felt dry. "No."

More than enough time had passed for the mail to arrive, so something must have happened to her or the letter.

Frederic thrust his hand out like a preacher. "There you have it! She rejected you, so let's attend the party."

"I'm not sure she received my letter."

Frederic's eyebrows drew together, and his shoulders sagged. "My friend, she has had ample time to send a letter. I know you don't want to admit it, but nothing prevents you from attending a party. Besides, Miss Peabody has a friend I'd like you to meet."

"It hasn't been that long. The territory contains miles of empty prairie with scattered settlements. It can take weeks for a letter to travel there, more to come back."

His friend leaned forward and shook his head. "Arthur, she's not interested in you. She prefers to run out to Indian country rather than see you. I know this hurts, but you need to face the truth."

The words did hurt, but Frederic had arrived at an unfair conclusion.

"You make it sound so ... so wanton. Kate set her mind to help the struggle against slavery. She decided to go to Kansas and teach. Have you any idea how difficult the journey must be, especially for an unmarried woman? Even after her misfortune, she remains committed to her task. I admire her."

Frederic held up his palms in mock surrender. "Whoa. I didn't intend to besmirch her. You're right. She's a brave woman."

"Yes, she is." His grumble didn't affect his friend's insistence.

"Arthur, I mentioned a friend of Alice Peabody. I understand no one courts her at this time. She's beautiful and loves to read. I know you prefer bookworms." He wore a disarming smile.

"Who is she?"

"Miss Louise Endicott."

"I've met her. She enjoys reading but ..." She was nothing like Kate.

"But what?"

"She's..." He shrugged. "I spoke with her once. She has a narrow view of life. She primarily reads *Godey's Ladies Book* and hasn't read many of the newer novels."

"You mean to say she can't hold a candle to Miss Collins." Frederic sighed deeply. "Arthur, why don't you just go to Kansas and speak to Kate? Maybe you'll listen when she rejects you to your face."

Kate wouldn't reject him ... would she? Did he care to know? "I can't go. You know that. I must complete my apprenticeship. You only say that to motivate me to join you at a party."

Frederic grinned. "Did it work?"

Arthur rose to his feet. "No. Now I really must prepare for my shift at the hospital."

"I'll keep trying to get you to a party." Frederic stood and extended his hand.

"Yes, you will." Arthur shook his hand, and Frederic excused himself.

Maybe his letter or Kate's reply had been lost. Kansas was half a world away. Had regular mail service been established? His shoulders fell. Even if deliveries were irregular, enough time had passed for the mail to complete the journey. Although the mail system might take a month or six weeks, the time had been twice that.

He sat at his desk and pulled a sheet of paper from a drawer. He couldn't travel to Kansas, but he could write another letter. He lifted the pen and stared at the paper.

32

July 23, Lawrence

Kate walked slowly through the class, her steps echoing on the new floor. The carpenters had completed the aid company's new meeting hall, and her school had moved in. The tall room allowed heat to rise, and the windows on each side provided a cooling current of air. There was still some unused space in the room, but her allotted space would allow twice as many students.

She turned in front of her desk and scanned the attentive faces of her class, sitting on benches at four rows of tables. The younger students had progressed rapidly thanks to Harriet's tutelage. Alex and Owen had formed a truce of sorts. A week ago, the boys had arrived covered in dirt, each sporting a swollen eye. Purple and hints of green still marked their cheeks, but they kept their conflict out of the classroom.

"Class, an important event occurred last week here in Lawrence called the Sand Bank Convention. Does anyone know what a convention is?"

Harriet and Tom raised their hands.

"Tom, can you tell us?"

He cleared his throat. "It's a group of people who come together for some type of business."

"Very good, Tom. People hold conventions to discuss different things, including how to end slavery, recognizing the rights of women, and banning alcoholic drinks. This convention discussed what to do about the government elected for Kansas by the Missourians."

Tom's hand rose again.

"Yes, Tom?"

"I was there last week, you know."

"Wonderful! Would you come to the front of the class and tell us what you saw?"

He grimaced but rose and tramped to the front. "A bunch of men gathered on the sandbar down on the river."

Kate's chest expanded. She had walked on that sandbar when she'd worked for Martha. "Is that all?"

His face wrinkled like his stomach ached. "Uh ... different men spoke. Some made lively speeches. They just talked about the bogus legislature more than anything." He shrugged.

"Didn't they decide to do something?" She nodded to encourage him.

"Oh, yeah. They called a convention at Big Springs later this year. They're going to get people from all over the territory to come."

Kate smiled. "Thank you, Tom. You may return to your seat."

He strode back to his seat, his cheeks red.

She faced the class. "The convention also decided to form a political party. It is important that the residents of Kansas rectify the stolen election that resulted in the bogus legislature because it will draft the constitution for our state. We want a free state, but they want to allow slavery. Thankfully, we have men like Dr. Robinson and others working to make Kansas free in a peaceful way. The Free State party is their first step."

Kate glanced at her watch. "Oh my. It's past time to dismiss. Thank you, children. I'll see you tomorrow."

The children grinned and came to life, gathering their things. She watched them a moment, feeling a surge of pride at how her class now hummed along. Once the children filed out, she straightened the desks, chairs, and other items around the room, lowered the windows, grabbed her things, and headed for the post office. Perhaps a letter had arrived from Mother or Amelia. Enough time had passed since she'd written them about her teaching position.

As she walked, she pondered how the town had changed so much. Most of the buildings in the part of town closest to the river were complete, most rising two stories. The constant sound of construction had moved south.

Even her home had changed. Clarissa's sons had finished framing the boardinghouse, installing doors and windows. They were still plastering the walls of the men's bedrooms, but they had completed her room. Clarissa and Lydia now had a kitchen with shelves and a cookstove.

"Kate!" Elizabeth hurried toward her, her face beaming.

"What brings you downtown?"

"The mail." Her friend blushed. "I'm so excited."

"A letter from home?"

Elizabeth leaned close and whispered. "I'm in a family way." She squealed, bouncing on her toes.

"Really? Congratulations!" Kate smiled.

"At least I think I am. I haven't told anyone, not even Samuel, but I couldn't keep it quiet any longer. Please don't tell anyone. I know it's early, and ... sometimes it doesn't last."

"I won't tell." Kate pulled her friend into a fierce embrace. "I'm so happy for you."

"Yes, I hope it's a boy. I know Samuel wants a son."

Kate peered at her friend's flushed face. "Elizabeth, should you walk so far in this heat? Why didn't you bring the wagon?"

Elizabeth waved her hand. "I'm fine. Don't worry so much. Samuel needs the wagon to make deliveries. I knew the mail would arrive today. When I saw you, I just had to stop and tell you."

They chatted a few moments longer, and Elizabeth resumed walking toward her home as Kate turned toward the post office. She approached a woman standing next to a wagon with an infant in her arms. Kate smiled as she realized Elizabeth would do the same in a few months.

"Mrs. Hopkins. How is your little one?"

"She's healthy and hungry most of the time." The baby's dark eyes rolled toward her mother's face, and a saliva bubble appeared in front of her fat cheeks. "Would you like to hold her?"

"Oh, may I? I don't get to hold babies often. Her name's Sadie, correct?"

"Yes, it is. I'm glad you came along. She gets heavy after a while."

Mrs. Hopkins held the baby out, and Kate nestled little Sadie against her chest. The baby squirmed and kicked until her gaze found Kate's face and peered into her eyes. Warmth spread through Kate's chest.

"Such a precious life. You're truly blessed to have her."

"I know."

Mr. Hopkins came out of the building a moment later, and Kate returned the child, said goodbye, and continued toward the post office. The pleasure of cuddling the baby surprised her. Sadie wasn't that heavy. She could have held her much longer. The thought of holding Elizabeth's newborn brought a smile. Wouldn't that be a treat?

She entered the post office and stopped at the end of a line of people behind a tall woman in a dark olive dress. She turned with a rustle of petticoats and nodded. "Good afternoon."

Judging by the woman's long, pleasant face bordered by short, dark spaniel curls hanging in front of her ears, she was several years older. Perhaps she had school-age children.

"Good afternoon. I haven't seen you before. Are you new to town? I'm Miss Kate Collins, the teacher."

"I'm Mrs. Clarina Nichols." The woman's voice was rich and full. "My sons and I arrived last fall, though I returned to Vermont for a few months. I don't make it to town for the mail very often."

Nichols? The name was familiar but not the woman's face. "Have I met you?" Kate asked. "I've heard your name before, but I don't remember where."

"Perhaps you've read some of my writing in the *Windham County Democrat,* or you may have read about one of my lectures or debates."

She stood beside a famous reformer! "Now I remember! You spoke at the women's rights convention in Worcester a few years ago. I read about it."

Mrs. Nichols smiled. "Yes, I have attended several women's conventions."

"What are you doing in Kansas?"

She laughed. "I live here. And I continue to work for a government of equality, liberty, and fraternity. I speak from time to time and lectured here in Lawrence last fall."

Such a prominent woman, one who had written, lectured, and debated for causes such as temperance and the rights of women for years.

"How wonderful! I must attend the next time ... but that's not what I meant. Why didn't you continue your efforts back in New England?"

"Shouldn't we help a new state form a constitution that recognizes the rights of women?"

Kate's heart quickened. "Of course, we should." How did she have the good fortune to meet Clarina Nichols in a post office on the Kansas prairie? "Uh ... you arrived with your sons. By chance, are they school-age?"

The reformer's eyes twinkled. "Not my sons who dwell here, but my youngest, George, is eleven."

"Would you like to enroll him in school?"

"I'm afraid we live too far south. It's not practical to send him here from Lane, but thank you for the offer."

Kate cleared her throat. "May I ask you another question?"

"Certainly."

"You've done such important things. How ... um ... I didn't think it possible to do such things while married and raising a family."

Mrs. Nichols touched Kate's arm. "It takes dedication and a husband who supports you. I'm blessed to enjoy my family while being able to right a few of the wrongs in our society."

"Next," the postmaster called.

Mrs. Nichols turned, spoke to the postmaster, and retrieved a bundle of mail. She turned back to Kate. "It was a pleasure to meet you, Miss Collins." She nodded and left.

Kate blinked and stepped to the counter, trying to calm her racing heart. "Do you have any mail for Miss Kate Collins?"

The postmaster grinned but shook his head. "Nothing came in today. Maybe later this week."

She turned, stepped out of the building, and strolled toward home, shaking her head. A married reformer here in Lawrence. Mrs. Nichols had worked for years leading social reform, even though she had a husband and family. Kate tapped her lips. Could she do the same? She already taught school—

"Agh!" A stocky man staggered around a house and rushed toward the street. He weaved and stumbled to a stop a half dozen paces away. Blood streamed down his face, covering one eye.

Kate gasped and froze.

"Get back here! We're not finished!" A large, balding man stomped around the same building toward the bleeding man.

"Hey! What's going on?" John's shout came from behind Kate. His hat fell from his head as he ran past.

"He hit me with a pry bar." The stocky man took his blood-covered hand from the side of his head and stared at it. Blood plastered his lank, black hair.

Kate's stomach churned. Who would attack another with a piece of iron?

Other men hollered and ran toward them as the balding man stooped and picked up a rock. "Get away from him. He's going to get what's coming to him for cheating me."

John held up his hands and stepped in front of the bleeding man. "Stop, Dr. Wood. You can't do this."

"Watch me!"

Dr. Wood lifted the stone, but other men rushed in front of him. Shouts filled the air.

"You have no right to attack him!"

"He cheated me!" Dr. Woods thrust a finger at the bleeding man.

"Get back to your house!" another man yelled.

Kate's legs shook, and she wrapped her arms tight across her chest as she watched men attempting to help the bleeding man while others tried to keep the doctor at bay. She sucked a breath and shivered.

"Throw that, and we'll beat the tar out of you!" A man in a wide-brimmed hat held out open hands like he was trying to stop a bolting cow.

Dr. Wood dropped the rock, but the argument continued with pointed fingers. John helped the bleeding man to the other side of the street and pressed a handkerchief to the man's scalp. More than half a dozen men now faced Dr. Wood, threatening him. He cursed them roundly, spun on his heel, and stalked past his house toward his backyard.

Kate swayed and clenched her jaw, stumbling a couple of steps and almost trampling John's hat. She picked up the hat and rushed to John and the bleeding man, her stomach crawling.

"John, are you hurt?"

Without looking at her, he said, "I'm fine. Robert's the one hurt."

Kate's head jerked back, and she blinked. Why had she asked that of John? He hadn't been the one attacked. "I'm sorry. Mr. ... will you be alright?"

The man winced and squinted at her. "Yeah. I'll have a headache for a while. It's Carr, Robert Carr."

"Mr. Carr, you may need to see the doctor about that gash. It's pretty deep and a wide one." Her words sounded lame, but she needed to say something.

Robert laughed a mirthless chuckle. "I just saw a doctor. He gave this to me." He lifted his hand to hold the handkerchief, now red, against his head. "Thanks, John."

How could a doctor beat another with a prybar? Kate fanned herself with her hand. "Why would he do such a thing?"

"He thinks I cheated him in a land deal. I didn't."

She shook her head. "But why would he hit you? Can't he take you to court to settle the dispute?"

"Oh, courts exist if you trust the judges." John looked at her with a wry smile. "There's been a lot of land disputes since the territory opened. Most get settled out of court, some with violence."

"Doc Wood's a troublemaker, always stirring up something." Robert spat to the side. "I heard he damaged Dr. Robinson's house while they were building it. That or he got others to do it. He's a slavery man."

"He owns slaves? Here in Lawrence?" She hadn't seen any evidence of that.

"No. No slaves, but he supports the ruffians who want to make this a slave state." John leveled stern eyes at her.

A man with a drooping mustache and long sideburns, wearing a dusty white shirt and brown trousers, strode up. "Robert, how are you?"

"I'll live."

The new man put his hand on Robert's shoulder and turned to John. "I'm his neighbor. I can get him home."

John nodded, and the other two men shuffled away.

"You look pale." John dipped his head and peered at her. "Why didn't you get away from the ruckus? You could've been hurt if things got out of hand."

"I ... uh ... don't know." She shook her head. How could her pleasant afternoon change so quickly?

John took his hat from her hand and pulled it onto his head. Then he tucked her hand into the crook of his elbow. "I'd better walk you on home."

They ambled down the street as Kate leaned against his strong arm. "Will the sheriff investigate this incident? Dr. Wood assaulted him."

John chuckled. "What sheriff?"

"I thought we had one."

"None close by. I wouldn't trust him if he were here."

Kate frowned, squinting up at him. "What do you mean?"

"The territory's sheriffs are appointed by the bogus legislature. Those slavery-loving clods only appoint men that support what they want."

"Oh." A shudder swept over Kate. She should have realized a sheriff would be antagonistic to free-state people. Judges too.

They walked in silence for a few moments until John patted her hand. "You looked so scared back there, but your color has returned."

"I did?"

"Yes."

"The incident frightened me. I thought you might be injured. I've seen ..." She flinched, fighting off the memory.

He placed his hand over hers in the crook of his elbow and gently squeezed. "You've seen a fight before?"

"Not a fair fight. Soldiers attacked a crowd." She hugged his arm. "They were hauling a runaway slave back to Virginia through the streets of Boston. They clubbed unarmed men with their guns and swords." A shiver crossed her shoulders. "It happened a few feet in front of me."

"I'm sorry you had to see that. I'm afraid we'll see more violence if people can't compromise on slavery."

Compromise? Was that even possible? Some wanted slavery, and others knew it was evil. How could a compromise be found, especially when pro-slavery men resorted to violence? "Thank you for walking me home, John. I needed it."

He doffed his hat. "Walking with you is always a pleasure. I saw you walk past the store a minute or two before I left work. I hoped to catch up with you, and ... well ... I'm glad I did."

She smiled at him. If she focused on good things, that might hold the memories of attacking soldiers at bay. John had reacted so quickly to help Robert, a courageous act. She had felt so ... exposed standing alone in the street, but with him beside her, she felt as safe as she did behind the door of her new room.

The memory of cuddling Sadie and the baby's smile drifted through her mind. Elizabeth's excitement. Mrs. Nichol's pride in her family and her career. A family was such a source of joy. She sighed. Would Amelia and Mother write soon?

33

Kate hurried down the street through air thick with the late July heat. Sweat beaded on her forehead, but she couldn't slow her pace. Why had she stayed so late working on lessons? The post office might close before she reached it.

Five days had passed since Dr. Wood's assault on Robert Carr, and people still talked about the altercation. Some also reported other pro-slavery men harassing people in the streets. The heat of summer seemed to shorten tempers.

She walked through the open door of the post office with a few minutes to spare. Thankfully, no one stood in line.

The postmaster glanced up and grinned. "Miss Collins, I wondered if you'd make it today. I've got something for you."

Her heart beat faster. Mother or Amelia had written, maybe both.

He flicked through several letters and handed her two. "I think this is what you've been waiting for."

"Thank you, Mr. Ladd." She scampered out and stopped in front of the building. Amelia's handwriting graced the first letter. Kate flipped it over and broke the seal.

Boston, July 5
Dear Kate,

Your recent letter brightened my day just before our July Fourth celebration! I am relieved that your hand has healed well. Congratulations on securing a teaching position in Lawrence. I'm sure you enjoy it more than washing clothes for Miss Groot.

I hope you also wrote to your mother and father. They visited me shortly after your first letter and attended an abolition meeting with me. They worry about your safety.

A recent issue of The Liberator reports that many believe Kansas will become a slave state because people from Missouri, Kentucky, Tennessee, and Virginia have flocked to the territory. It also said a pro-slavery mob burned the homes of two men in Douglas. I hope that is a long way from you.

The cause of Kansas has stirred many in New England to organize and pass resolutions condemning the travesty of the stolen election. I understand more people plan to emigrate.

You remain in my prayers. Keep safe and write again soon.
Love,
Amelia

Kate pressed the paper to her heart with both hands and let the breeze cool her brow. Amelia had written with a smaller script, but her letter was still too short. If only she could talk to her. Kate wandered down the street and reread the letter, savoring each sentence.

"Kate!" John crossed the street toward her. "I'm heading home. I didn't expect to see you here."

"I stayed late to plan lessons for Harriet to use. Then I stopped at the post office. I've received mail." She waved the papers.

"Congratulations. I know you've waited anxiously for word from home."

"Amelia congratulated me on my teaching position and ... well, I'll tell you more later. This one is ..." She lifted the other letter and froze. The script wasn't Mother's handwriting. The letter looked exactly like the one Arthur had sent before.

"From your parents?"

She turned the letter over, revealing Arthur's seal holding it closed. She crammed the letters into her pocket.

John chuckled. "I thought you were excited to receive those. Don't you want to read the other letter?"

"Um, I'll ... I'll read it later. I ... it would be rude to read it now instead of enjoying the walk home with you." She swallowed past the tightness in her throat.

He grinned. "I understand the wisdom of your choice and approve."

She forced a smile and nodded as John told her about a boy who'd leaned so far into a nearly empty apple barrel at the store that he'd fallen inside.

As they strolled home, John shared more stories and gossip from the store, but Kate couldn't concentrate on his words, thinking of the unopened letter in her pocket. When they stepped onto the front porch of the boardinghouse, Kate excused herself and climbed the stairs to her room.

She shut the door of the sparse room, feeling the warm breeze flowing through the open window across her face. She sat on the California bed and studied Arthur's seal. Surely, he'd know Amelia would write about any news of her family, so that couldn't be what his letter held. Maybe someone in his family had fallen ill.

On the other hand, if she opened his letter and read his words, would she miss him? A long conversation about a book with him would be so pleasant. No one here had a library like Amelia's, let alone Arthur's. Some people had brought a few books west, but they were heavy, and the space was limited, and everyone was often too busy building and working to sit and chat about literature.

She fingered the folded paper. What could possibly be so important that Arthur would write her now? She tapped the seal with her fingernail. Why did she hesitate? She already missed him, that's why, and reading his letter would make the feeling worse.

Kate bolted to her feet and jerked open the door. There was only one thing to do. She clomped down the steps and entered the kitchen, where Lydia stood at the stove tending a sizzling skillet.

"Lydia, would you excuse me a moment?"

Her forehead wrinkled. "Yes, what do you need?"

Kate grabbed a hand towel and used it to slide the skillet off the burner. She inserted the stove handle and lifted the round iron plate where flames flickered beneath. She thrust Arthur's letter into the fire and shoved the iron circle and skillet back into place.

Lydia cocked her head and stared. "Bad news?"

She gulped. "I ... um ... it's a letter I didn't want to keep." Lydia might understand why Kate had burned an unopened letter, but she didn't want to risk a long conversation. "I see we're having fried potatoes for supper. What else are you fixing?"

Lydia described the remainder of the meal, and Kate stilled her rapid breaths. After a few sentences of polite chitchat, she excused herself and walked to the front porch where John sat in one of the chairs facing the street.

"Would you care to sit with me until supper?" He gestured to an empty chair beside him.

"Thank you." She settled beside him, wishing she'd brought her fan from the room to quell the stifling heat.

"Did you enjoy your other letter?"

Should she tell John about it? Would he understand? She hadn't told Lydia, but he had asked politely. She shrugged.

He chuckled. "Your excitement has cooled. I wish this afternoon would cool as much."

At the July Fourth picnic, she had agreed to allow John to call on her. Social functions had been constant in Boston, but Lawrence had few unless it was a gathering to discuss politics and the bogus legislature, and most of those were filled by men more than couples. She and John had spent more time sitting on the porch or walking in the evenings than attending parties. What would it hurt if John knew about Arthur? He was in her past.

"About the other letter ... I didn't open it because it's from a man who called on me in Boston."

"Ooh." He sounded like an excited girl hearing juicy gossip. "Is it a love letter?"

Warmth flooded her cheeks, and she rolled her eyes. He was such a tease. "It most certainly was not."

"I'm not surprised."

Kate bristled. "Whatever do you mean?"

"I'm not surprised someone called on you." He shrugged. "Or wrote you a letter."

She slumped against the chair back. His face and tone were serious, matter-of-fact. She drew a breath and exhaled. "It surprised me when my aunt invited him to call on me and he accepted."

"It shouldn't have. You're an intelligent, kind, and dedicated woman. You're also pleasant on the eyes."

"Maybe, but not as pleasant as some." Like Martha or Elizabeth.

"So, what did his letter say? Is he begging you to return to Boston, or is he coming to join you in Kansas?" His eyes held a mischievous glint.

"He didn't say anything important. I stopped seeing him before I came to Kansas, so he will not emigrate."

"I see." John pulled a folded newspaper from under his arm and handed it to her. "I thought you'd enjoy the *Herald of Freedom* from last week." He pointed to a small article at the bottom of the page. "Didn't you witness the Anthony Burns hullabaloo in Boston? That's what you told me about, isn't it?"

"Yes." She took the paper and peered at the small print.

"It says he's free and traveling to Oberlin, Ohio."

"I'm so glad. Now we need to free the rest of the slaves."

"That may be the only good news in the paper." John gazed across the street. "Looks like President Pierce suspended our governor. I doubt the next one'll be any better. A pro-slavery mob destroyed the paper at

Parkville. There's also an article saying a war rages in western Missouri."
He turned toward her, his face serious. "I'm worried about you."

"About me?"

"I've heard four brothers are roaming in *our* town trying to pick fights.
They want to provoke a response so the ruffians from Missouri have an
excuse to attack us."

Her stomach churned. They would likely attack her school since it was
also the aid company's hall.

"Do you truly think more violence will come here?"

John blew out a long breath. "I hope not, but I fear it might. Nobody
wants to get along anymore. They made a mistake repealing the Missouri
Compromise."

"But that legislation never addressed the problem. We have to elimi-
nate slavery."

"Maybe, maybe not." His hazel eyes gazed into hers. "There's something I want you to do. I want you to stay at the school building until my
quitting time, then come to the store. I'll escort you home each day. The
Hopper brothers haven't shown up early in the day, and they haven't
pushed around any women ... yet. But they're insulting and dangerous.
They might threaten you to get a reaction from me or another man.
Who knows what they'll do if they're drunk? I don't want to take any
chances."

Her heartbeat quickened. John cared deeply about her safety. His
concern seemed more than the chivalry any man would show a woman.

"If you wish."

34

August 17

Kate strolled down the classroom aisle, glancing over the shoulders of the older students working on a set of arithmetic problems copied from the chalkboard. A steamship had reached Lawrence and delivered the seven-by-ten-inch slates the students used, as well as the larger chalkboard and special pencils made of white rubber. If only she could have used the new writing instruments on her slate when she attended school. The pencil-shaped pieces of rubber were much neater than a stick of chalk.

In the front of the room, Harriet sat with the younger children helping them write vocabulary words, which made Kate smile. Harriet would make a fine teacher someday.

The door hinges squeaked, and a woman in a gray dress and white bonnet stepped into the back of the room.

Kate walked to her. "Good afternoon, Mrs. Dorn. How may I help you?"

Sharp eyes peered from her tight face, and she made no effort to remove her bonnet. "I've come to take my children home."

"Oh, I see. We should finish for the day in about half an hour. Would you like to sit? Harriet is teaching the younger children writing."

Mrs. Dorn peered over Kate's shoulder at the children. "If it's all the same to you, I'd like to take them now."

"Is something wrong?"

She stepped close and lowered her voice. "There are ruffians in town. I planned to wait at the store, but knew they were trouble."

Tightness squeezed Kate's ribs. Ruffians would likely come to the main street where the school stood.

"Oh ... I see. Of course." Kate turned to the class. "Harriet, would you bring your sister? Alex and Michael, your mother would like you to leave early today."

The Dorn children gathered their things under the curious eyes of the other students.

Mrs. Dorn drew her children close and said, "Thank you, Miss Collins." Then she ushered them quickly out the door.

Kate lifted her hand and covered her mouth. Should she end the school day early since men prowled the town intent on causing trouble? Would they resort to violence? Other parents might come to walk their children home, but the children might be safer here unless the ruffians planned to search for the doctor. No, the children would be safer if she dismissed them early.

She spun and strode to the front of the class. "Children, I think we should all leave early today. Please be careful going home. I understand some pro-slavery men are in town hoping to cause an incident. You'd best avoid the main street and head straight home. I'll see you next Monday."

The younger children buzzed about gathering their things, no doubt happy to leave the stuffy schoolroom, but the older children exchanged tight glances.

Kate collected the slates and the book Owen had forgotten to take home, storing them in her trunk. It still wasn't time for John to quit work, but she wouldn't need to wait long if she went to the store now. She lowered the windows and stepped out to the street.

"Yeehaw!" Up the street, a wagon bolted away from the store at a dead run toward her. A squat man with a dark beard waved his hat.

The two horses careened past her, dragging the clattering, swaying wagon. A keg tumbled out the back and broke, scattering nails across the dust. A lanky man huffed past, trying to catch the runaway team.

The man who had spooked the horses stood in front of the store, roaring with laughter. "That'll teach you to oppose my right to own slaves!"

He must be one of the Hopper brothers.

Kate hurried toward the store, staying behind the hitching rails and close to the buildings. Across from the first man, another man wearing a dull red shirt stood with his hands on his hips, staring at three men in front of the building across from the store. John had said there were four Hopper brothers. Where were the others?

She reached the edge of the store building, and the squat Hopper tipped his hat to her.

"Why you must be the school teacher. I heard about you." He pointed. "Got the mark of Cain on your face. Why don't you come here, and I'll scrub that grape jam off your lip."

Kate skidded to a stop, her heart thudding against her chest. Was he full of bluster, or would he attack her?

The door of the store slammed open, and John hurried toward her. "Let's get you inside." He took her elbow.

She took a shaky breath. "I know I'm early. I thought I could wait here."

"Hey, store clerk!" Hopper swaggered to the hitching rail. "What ya' doing?"

John's jaw clenched as he turned and glared at the man. "You, sir, are a disgrace, stampeding that team. That wagon could've hurt someone or smashed something."

Hopper spat. "Why don't you come over here and school me so I don't do it again?" His voice never wavered, and he stared at John without blinking.

John dropped her elbow and clenched his fists.

She placed a hand on his arm. "John, don't—"

"You're not man enough." Hopper crossed his arms.

John pushed her through the door and followed her, shutting the door while Hopper howled with laughter. The man across the street with the red shirt grinned, walked over, and slapped Hopper on the back.

"I'm man enough, but not stupid enough." John's mouth worked in his red face like he chewed on something rancid as he stared through the window.

"Those idiots." Horace, the store owner, stood behind the counter, arms crossed. "One of these days, someone's going to clobber one of them. And then we'll be in a world of hurt."

Kate hugged herself to steady her trembling hands. "We must do something. Parents are worried about their children walking to school. Can we file a complaint with the sheriff?"

The action would be a long shot, but they needed to do something.

"Ha!" John snorted. "See the man in the red shirt? That's Sam Salters. The stupid legislature in Shawnee made him a deputy sheriff. They're looking for any excuse to arrest us or attack the town."

She should have known the law wouldn't help. Salters yelled and hollered in the street, challenging people along with Hopper. They ran off three saddle horses, but no one met their challenge. They carried their ruckus down the street, and people rushed from buildings to mount the horses that remained or drive wagons from the side streets in the opposite direction. Finally, the troublemakers swung up on their saddled horses, raced down the street, and shot their pistols in the air three times. Silence like an early morning hung over the street in their wake.

"Let's get home." John picked up his hat and clutched a rolled newspaper like a club. He led her out the door, and she took his arm. John was such a good man, concerned for her safety and wise enough to avoid a challenge that could unleash violence.

As they walked toward home, he searched the side streets and glanced behind them twice, his dark mustache and firm jaw lending his face an air of danger. How different from his normal jovial appearance.

Weeks had passed since she had agreed to his request to call on her. What would she have done today if he hadn't been there to help?

John glanced at her, his mouth tight. "I heard a free-state man in Leavenworth was beat, tarred, and feathered. The mob almost hung him before setting him adrift on a raft in the Missouri River. I don't want to see you hurt."

Kate's breath caught in her chest. "Would they dare attack a woman?"

"Maybe they would and maybe not, but you don't have to be the target of an attack to get hurt." John stopped next to a building, unrolled the paper, and stabbed it with his finger. "Read this right here."

She took the paper, found the spot, and read, "'Dr. Robinson is sole agent of the underground railroad leading out of Western Missouri, and for the transportation of fugitive "niggers." His office is in Lawrence, K.T. Give him a call.'"

She unfolded the paper fully. *Leavenworth Herald* emblazoned the top of the page. The sensation of a crawling spider climbed her neck. Violence had already escalated in the territory, and the writer urged people to attack the doctor.

John licked his lips, peering into her eyes. "I wish the school wasn't in the same building as Dr. Robinson's office. An attack on him might hurt you."

She gasped and gripped his arm. "You don't think anyone would harm the children, do you?"

John looked over her head at the street behind them. "Sane and decent men wouldn't, but drunk men? Slaveholders? I'm not so sure. More important is whether you want children to see a man shot or look at a bloody body."

Her arms trembled. It was just a matter of time before the worst kind of violence erupted in Lawrence. How could she protect the children?

"I must prepare a plan to get the children out if someone comes to attack the doctor."

"Or tries to burn the building while you're in it."

Her heart raced. She hadn't thought about that possibility. How did one plan to avoid a mob?

John grabbed her shoulders and held her at arm's length. "I don't want anything to happen to you."

"Nor I you ... or to the children."

35

Kate hurried down the street toward the school building. John had reviewed her plan to evacuate the children should an assault come and approved it. What else could she do?

A wagon rolled past her, driven by a man with a woman in the seat beside him. Half a block ahead, a man stepped into the street, and the wagon stopped. The hulking man swaggered around the team and stopped beside the front wheel.

He grabbed the brake lever. "You a Yankee?" Menace and a thick accent filled his bellow.

The woman cringed against her husband, and he put his arm around her. "What do you want?"

"I want to drive all Yankees out of the territory!" The man's shirtsleeves were rolled to his shoulders. His thick muscles flexed as he pulled the brake lever tight.

Kate eased to the side of the street away from the big man. He wasn't a Hopper—she'd learned to recognize each of the brothers. He must be the Hungarian who claimed to be a doctor. She'd heard he stalked the streets, harassing people and backing the Hoppers and Sam Salters, a thug like them.

"Sir, I got no quarrel with you." The wagon driver's voice was soft. "I got business in town."

The Hungarian drew a knife as long as Kate's forearm from a sheath and pointed it at the man. "If you cause any trouble for me or my friends, I'll cut your heart out and eat it!"

"N-no-no, sir. I j-just got some business to attend to, and I'll head back to my farm."

The Hungarian stepped back. "Head back to your farm and keep going 'til you reach New England." The man lashed the reins, and the horses jumped forward.

Kate angled for the horses on the far side of the street.

"Hey, woman. Where do you think you're going?"

She looked back. "I ... I'm going to the school. I'm the teacher."

He slid the knife into the sheath. "I've heard about your school. Filling children's heads with crazy ideas that slaves should be free." He pulled a revolver from his holster, aiming it at her. "It'd take too much work to come over there and skin you. I'll just shoot you."

Ice filled Kate's chest, and she stumbled back a step. John's store was in the next block, and she was on the wrong side of the street, too far for him to help her. She turned and ducked past the hitched horses.

A roar of laughter followed her. She hurried past men standing next to the building with crossed arms. Were they just going to watch? Couldn't they defend her, an innocent woman? The Hungarian accosted another person, and she scurried toward the school.

Lawrence had changed, and not for the better. Thugs roamed the streets threatening people. The sheriff and his deputy encouraged the action and even joined in. John had told her the town leaders were trying to ignore the bogus legislature, but how long could that continue? The legislature had just passed laws to punish people who opposed slavery. Helping a slave escape could bring a judgment of death. They had even outlawed speaking in public against slavery.

She crossed the street to the school building and opened the door. Dr. Robinson sat in his office writing. After warning him about the Hungarian, she opened the doors to the schoolroom with trembling hands and strode to the front, her footsteps echoing in the large room. She must remain calm. The children needed to find her with her emotions under control. Writing would be a good way to start the day. She slowed her steps and carefully positioned the slates and pencils on each desk, drawing slow, deep breaths.

When she'd finished, she smoothed the front of her dress. Should the class practice the evacuation plan again? No, doing so could increase the fear of the youngest children. Their eyes had filled with fear when she explained the reason for the plan the other day.

The door opened, and Tom clomped in and sat in his seat. "Hello, Miss Collins."

"Good morning." She kept her voice light. "How was your walk to school?"

He grinned. "A bit longer than usual."

"You avoided the Hungarian."

"Yes, ma'am. I circled and came down the street from the north."

"You were wise to do so." Kate glanced at her watch. The rest of the children should have arrived by now. "Tom, why don't you read while we wait for the others? There's a novel on my desk. I think you'll enjoy it."

She walked to the front door and stepped out. No children approached from any direction.

"Miss Collins." A man reined his horse to a stop before her and dismounted.

"Mr. Dorn, isn't it?" she asked, her gaze darting up and down the street.

His mouth quirked, and he nodded. "I've come to tell you Harriet and my other children will not be coming today. Not only that, they won't come to school as long as we have this problem." He jerked his head toward the Hungarian a block away, loudly confronting a man in the middle of the street.

Her stomach tightened. "I'm sorry to hear that, Mr. Dorn."

"I should also tell you that I spoke with the Colburns. They're not sending their kids either."

This couldn't be happening. The Dorn and Colburn children were half her class.

"If you're worried about the safety of the children, I've made plans to evacuate if trouble arises. The children have practiced—"

"I know. Alex told me. You may have plans for the school, but they have to walk through town too. Who knows where these ruffians will strike next? A spooked horse or wagon—they're dangerous, let alone men with guns and Bowie knives. My children will stay home until the town gets order in the streets."

She wrapped her arms across her chest. "I see."

Mr. Dorn thrust a boot into the stirrup and swung his leg over the saddle, gazing down at her. "Did any kids come today?"

Her cheeks warmed, and she cleared her throat. "One, Tom Patrick."

"Hmm. I think your school session is done for a while." He turned the horse and walked it around the corner into the side street.

Still, no children could be seen in any direction. What should she do? Attendance had been scattered over the last few days. The Colburn children had missed the past two days and the Mackenzie girls yesterday. Her watch showed it was well past time for class to begin.

She trudged through the doors, straightened her back, and stepped into the schoolroom. "Well, Tom, it looks like you will be the only student today. I can give you special attention with your arithmetic."

"Nobody else?" His face sagged. "Can I go home? My ma's concerned about the ruffians in town, besides Pa could sure use my help."

She sighed and nodded. "Yes, go home."

He rose and handed her the book. After warning him to be careful, she gathered the slates she had placed on the desks. How long would ruthless men disrupt her school?

"No students, I see." Dr. Robinson stood in the classroom door.

Kate nodded and stored the slates. "Their parents are afraid to send their children with the harassment in the streets. What can we do? Order must be restored."

He watched her, his face like granite. "I think we should close the school."

Her hands quivered, and she clenched her fists, standing tall. "Close the school? How will that solve the problem?"

"It won't, but it's safer."

If they closed the school, would she continue to receive her pay? Her wages covered her living expenses, unlike her work for Martha, but they didn't allow her to add to her meager savings. "If we close ... what ... what will happen to my wages?"

Dr. Robinson tipped his head to the side and raised his eyebrows. "I'm sorry, Miss Collins—"

"September is just two days away." Her words tumbled out. "When I recruited students in June, several families indicated they would send their children in the fall. I'm sure more students will attend soon. We shouldn't close the school." She should have already returned to those parents and confirmed enrollment. She would try to do so today.

The doctor shrugged. "I wonder whether they will now, what with all that's happening." He stared at the floor for a long moment, his mouth a tight line. "I think we should close the school, but I'll give you a week to confirm enrollment. If you have at least twelve students committed to attend, we'll keep the school open."

She released her breath. "Thank you, Doctor. I'll start meeting parents today."

He started to turn away but stopped. "Miss Collins, I've agreed to proceed as a trial. I may change my mind. Lawrence has become a target of the pro-slavery mobs. You may want to consider leaving the territory, at least for a while." He waited a beat before walking back into his office.

Leave? How could she leave? Teaching here was her mission, her act to end slavery. She wasn't allowed to vote. She couldn't serve as a conductor on the Underground Railroad. Teaching was all she could do.

36

September 4

Kate trudged past the skeletal houses marking the edge of town. Lawrence had spread south during the summer, completed houses lining the broad streets. But none of the new families had agreed to send children to school. She had hiked to the Dorn's place, so far it was a wonder Harriet and her siblings hadn't worn out their shoes from walking to school each day.

Mrs. Dorn believed firmly in education, but she and her husband stood by their decision to keep their children home during the increasing violence and tension. Rumors swirled that Missourians would attack Lawrence within the next two months.

Not a single family would risk sending their children to school. Many promised to consider it again in the spring, but the school would remain closed indefinitely. Kate could live off her savings for a time, but that couldn't last. Where would she find another job? Martha had not found another helper, but Kate cringed at returning to the hard labor on the riverbank with the terse woman.

She tramped the remaining blocks to the boardinghouse where the Hurd brothers had replaced the sod privies with frame structures. Her home was much more pleasant than a tent, but she couldn't afford to live there much longer without a job.

The midday heat and long walk had turned her dress into a sweltering tent. She crossed the porch, entered the house, and turned into the dining room. Most of her fellow residents sat at the table eating lunch with John in his usual place at the end of the table, talking to Martha who sat across from him. She still relished his attention, eyes shining. Henry Hurd filled Kate's usual place, vying for Martha's attention. Faces turned toward her as she entered.

"Kate, will you be joining us?" Lydia rose. "We're almost finished, but I can get you a plate. There's enough left."

Kate sighed. "Um ... no, not today. I'd just like water." She had skipped lunch as long as she'd lived here, except on Sundays. She needed to save money even more with the school closed. Lydia poured a glass of water and handed it to her.

Kate drained the glass and handed it back. "I'll just sit on the porch."

A sly smile spread on Martha's face as she leaned forward and spoke to John in a voice too low to hear. He chuckled at whatever she said.

Kate turned, stepped onto the porch, and plopped into a chair, praying she would not need to return to that woman's employ. She could look around town, though that hadn't yielded anything in the spring. A few more businesses had opened, but would they hire a woman, and one with a partial hand?

She could live on her savings while she waited for the school to open, but should she? If the ruffians attacked the town, she might need money to escape or replace anything destroyed. Her best choice was to work for Martha while quietly looking for another job. She knew Martha's work and had already proven herself capable.

The wind had cooled her face by the time Martha stepped through the door, giggling with John on her heels. "John, as always, you've been a delight. I'll see you tonight."

John grinned as Martha walked off the porch, then sat in the chair beside Kate.

"I take it from the look on your face that your efforts to recruit students didn't work out very well."

"No." Kate bolted to her feet. "Excuse me, but I must speak to Martha." She hurried off the porch. "Martha, may I have a word?"

Martha stopped in the middle of the street and appraised her. "If you're quick. I have a lot of work waiting."

"It appears the school will be closed for an indefinite time. Would you ... could I work for you again?"

Martha tipped her head, her gaze darting to John on the porch. "For the same pay as before?"

"Yes."

Martha frowned and inhaled. A caterpillar crawled through Kate's stomach as she waited for a reply. She ought to say something more to convince Martha.

"I know the job well. I'll be just as quick and thorough as before."

"Hmm." Martha glanced at her and back to John, sucking her lower lip. "I could use the help, but ..." Her eyes locked on Kate. "Even if your school remained closed, I think you'd abandon me the first chance you got. You're not right for the job, *and* I have another reason to refuse." She smiled without warmth, turned on her heel, and marched away.

Another reason? What other reason? Did it involve John and what he had promised? Kate retraced her steps to the porch and sat next to John, crossing her arms. "You seemed quite friendly with Martha."

He glanced at her out of the corner of his eye. "She talks a good piece. Always has news she's heard from customers."

More likely, she coveted his attention, but Kate couldn't say that. "So, you've warmed to her?"

He shrugged. "I want to be friends with everybody. At first, Martha was ... well, she reminded me of Susanna. But she's different in some ways."

Some, but not all. What did he see in her, other than her flawless face and waspish waist? Had Martha used lunch every day to entice John, while Kate had skipped lunch to scrimp and save?

He chuckled and touched her arm. "Don't worry. I'm still calling on you. You're far more interesting than Martha. I just want to be friends, that's all."

Interesting? Is that all he thought of her? She snorted before she could stop herself.

He rose to his feet. "I need to get back to the store. Would you like to walk with me? I'd like that."

She rose to her feet, and they strolled toward the main street, but John remained quiet. She shouldn't have worried. He had asked to call on her, not Martha. Besides, she had always known she might end their relationship before he did. Teaching was her priority, but she enjoyed his attention just as she had enjoyed Arthur's. She'd even dared to imagine teaching as a married woman.

She wasn't even a teacher now. After losing her students, how could she lose John too? He was such a good friend. Her eyes stung as she fought back the tears. Maybe she was just tired.

John cleared his throat. "I've heard rumors that the Missourians are looking for an excuse to attack us. Some think it will happen in the next couple of months. Shoot up the place and burn it before winter."

"I heard the same rumor today."

"The Hopper boys, Sam Salter, and that Hungarian doctor ... now we have a new sheriff, Sam Jones. I heard he led the rabble that stole the election in Bloomington last spring. Took five hundred Missourians to the polls and threatened to kill the election judges if they couldn't vote."

"It's not fair."

They turned onto the main street near the store where a large group of men clogged the street, blocking the way. John took her hand and edged around the group. Vile curses bellowed forth.

"The Hungarian." John's tone was grim. "Maybe you should have stayed home."

The crowd convulsed, and fists flew as men shoved and shouted. A man stumbled backward and crashed into Kate, sending her sprawling in the dirt.

37

John grabbed the man's arm and hoisted him off Kate. "Are you hurt?"

She lay sprawled in the street, her face twisted into a tight grimace. He reached down for her, but something crashed against his hips, and he stumbled. Kate scrabbled out of the way.

Another man, who must have knocked into him, charged back into the fight. The man who had fallen onto Kate stood rubbing his jaw. Kate moaned and sat in the street, leaning back against her hands.

John reached for her. "Let me help you."

Her large brown eyes latched onto his, and his heart thudded. He should sweep her into his arms and carry her to safety, but—

A violent curse lanced through the yells, cracks of fists, and noise of scrambling feet. The tang of dust filled his nose.

Kate lifted her hands, and he grabbed them, pulling her to her feet. "I need to get you out of here." He put a hand on the small of her back and guided her back to the side street, away from the fight.

She stumbled, but he caught her, and she leaned against him, her breath trembling gasps. He forced himself to walk slower until he stopped halfway down the block.

Kate turned toward the fight. The odor of horse manure wafted from a stain ground into the hip of her dress, and a smudge clung to her cheek. Dust powdered her tousled hair.

He licked his dusty lips. "Are you hurt?"

"I don't think so." She brushed the dirt off her hands.

"I fear our town's not safe anymore." He fished his handkerchief out and brushed the manure from her cheek. Her eyes widened, peering into his, and he tried to smile. "I'm sorry, but you have a little ... uh... horse apple on your cheek."

A blush colored her cheeks, and she wiped at the spot with shaking hands. "I'm sorry." Tears flooded her eyes. "John, what am I going to do?" A shaky breath cut off her wail.

"About the fight?"

"I don't have a job. I don't know how long before this ends and parents send their children to school again. Martha won't hire me again. Fights in the street. I—" She sobbed and buried her face in her hands.

He wrapped an arm around her shoulder, resting her head against his chest. "Don't worry. I'm here." Should he tell her what was on his heart? It hardly seemed the best time.

She drew a deep breath, held it a moment, then exhaled and straightened. "Thank you."

He withdrew his arms and offered his handkerchief. She took it and wiped her eyes. "Kate, you know I care about you, don't you?"

"Yes." A weak smile lifted her mouth, her watery eyes shining.

"When you fell, I wanted to ... well, I knew I needed to help you."

"I'm glad you did."

"You told me once you didn't plan to marry. In light of all of the difficulties, should you consider changing your plans?" It wasn't what he wanted to say.

She stared at him.

Had he said too much?

She looked down at his handkerchief and folded it into a neat square. "I ... I'm glad you were here today."

He took the handkerchief, his fingers touching the scar on the edge of her hand a moment before she turned toward the house.

The pit of his stomach fluttered. He had said too much. "Would you like me to walk you back?"

"No. I can get there myself." She walked a few steps before glancing back, a trembling smile lifting the corner of her mouth, but she resumed her steps.

John's stomach twisted, and he turned toward the main street. The brawl had ended, and most of the crowd had cleared. One man helped another out of the street. The Hungarian stood, shirt torn and nose bleeding, but no one challenged him. Two of the Hopper boys glowered at men walking away. "That'll teach you!" one yelled.

John shook his head. How could he feel so strongly about a woman so soon after Susanna's rejection? The pain remained, though not as intense. Kate wasn't as gorgeous as Susanna, but her warm eyes and smile lifted his heart, and she was kinder and more interested in helping others than Susanna. What a pleasure it'd be to watch her cook breakfast, to eat every meal across from her, to enjoy the sound of her laugh. He stroked his shirt where she had laid her head against his chest.

Had he shocked her with his comment about marriage? She hadn't answered his question about changing her plans or restated her position on marriage, but she had given him a quick smile. Had she changed her views?

Kate wandered down the street, stunned by John's question about changing her decision on marriage. What could she say? He hadn't proposed, but asking if she'd changed her mind about marriage seemed a much stronger hint of his intentions than Arthur had made. Should she have ended this courtship with John sooner? What would he have done if she had said her mind had changed?

Confidence and comfort—that's why she had allowed his courtship to continue so long. His friendly banter had helped pass many evenings, and seeing Martha's piqued face watching them offered amusement. Maybe Kate shouldn't have, but each time John chose to spend time with her rather than the honey-haired beauty felt like a victory.

He wasn't perfect—not as well read as Arthur, preferring newspapers over books. She missed the long discussions of literature with Arthur. Still, John kept abreast of the news, though he didn't have the same passion for abolition, and she'd never discussed women's rights with him. He was probably as cool to it as Arthur.

But John made her smile. He delighted in making others laugh and was such pleasant company. Who wouldn't enjoy time with him? She touched her cheek. His touch had been tender as he brushed the manure from her face, his eyes soft and warm.

Kate licked her parched lips. Should she consider marriage? Mrs. Nichols had lectured about women's rights for years before coming to Kansas while loving her husband and children. But would it solve all her problems? It would help with her income gap until the school could reopen, not that she would consider marriage simply for financial benefit.

What would sharing life with a good man, someone who would partner with her for reform, be like? Would a husband tell her she couldn't teach or attend lectures, maybe even forbid her speaking to support suffrage?

Kansas was so different than the streets of Boston. Even if the Missourians didn't bring militia across the border to attack, the Hoppers and the Hungarian still stalked the streets. The sheriff also favored them.

What would John do if she asked him to stop calling on her? Her breath caught in her throat, and she jerked to a stop. Could she tell John their courtship must end?

She placed her hands on her hips and drew a deep breath, wrinkling her nose. *Manure.* The green stain covered the side of her dress. The sooner she washed and changed her dress, the better. Maybe the fresh clothes would help her think more clearly. She strode toward the boardinghouse.

Arthur stood, hand on his top hat, studying the road stretched before
him, down a barren hill to rows of buildings lining the river. Did the
wind always gust so hard here? Red brick and buff limestone hotels rose
three and four stories. Wood frame warehouses crowded the river where
a steamboat sat, dark smoke arching from its stacks.

Across the street, more buildings rose along the street that ran straight
south, crossed at regular intervals with side streets. Kansas City was larger
than he had imagined, though not as established and fashionable as St.
Louis had been.

"Here ya' go, mister." An old man with a stooped back led a saddled,
brown and white horse from the stable. A toothless grin opened in his
grizzled beard. "That'll be eight dollars."

Arthur ran his hand over the well-worn saddle, the leather polished
smooth. "Why is the pommel so high?"

"Case ya' need to lasso a steer and wrap the rope around the horn."
He chuckled. "Course you best not try that wearing your fine suit and
all, but the horn'll be handy to hang your grip on."

Arthur shook his head. The cantle was also too tall, but he only needed
to ride the horse for a couple of days, not jump fences. And they said
fences were few in Kansas.

"You have nothing else?"

"Oh, I got fancier, but they be pricier. Just be happy I had an old Santa
Fe saddle for ya'."

"And you'll buy it back when I return?"

The man turned his head and spat. "Sure will, but the price might be
less." His eyes twinkled.

Arthur handed him the coins and looped the handles of his carpetbag
over the horn. "And the road to the Baptist Indian Mission?"

The man handed him the reins and waved a hand. "Just head that way,
straight down the street. You'll come to the edge of the city after a while.
You want to follow the California Trail. Just ask folks which one. Wagons
are leaving all the time. You should reach the mission by nightfall." He
turned and limped back into the stable.

Arthur stuck a shoe in the stirrup and mounted the horse, which looked back at the stable with ears pricked up. Arthur kicked the beast's flanks and reined its head around. The horse walked south with the saddle creaking with each step.

He'd endured two weeks of travel to reach the edge of the territory. The aid company said he could find lodging at the mission, and he could use a night's sleep in a bed. From there, he could reach Lawrence by tomorrow evening.

38

Arthur had left the mission in the early morning and rode into the afternoon. He had tried to make the horse canter, but the old mare only knew three gaits. He had forced it to gallop for two long stretches after paying to cross the bridge over the Wakarusa River. Sweat now darkened the hair of its neck. He should have been kinder to the animal, but the sight of Lawrence's buildings standing on the prairie at the bottom of a long hill drove him, and he drove the horse.

He slowed the mare to a walk at the edge of town, passing between tents, shacks, and skeletal houses. He crossed two streets where finished buildings lined both sides. Other streets ran parallel to the main street on both sides. Where had they gotten the lumber to build a town of this size? Which of the buildings was the boardinghouse where Kate lived?

Men and women watched him without a greeting or smile.

He met a wagon, and the driver eyed him as he passed. Maybe it was his clothes. He had traveled for two weeks with three sets of clothing crammed into his bag. Packing a trunk would have been more prudent, but would have complicated his travel, requiring a wagon. Besides, he didn't need it because he didn't intend to stay long.

He had managed to have his clothing cleaned on the riverboat, but the suits he had worn in Boston looked nothing like a settler's garb. At least he'd saved a clean suit for today.

"Whoa, girl." He dismounted and led the horse to a water trough, trying to ignore the ache in his hips. He had never spent so many hours in a saddle. The horse dipped its nose and sucked a long drink.

Across and up the street, men laid yellow limestone blocks on the second floor of a large building. Near it, a large structure of sod walls covered with a canvas roof stood. The description fit what he'd been told about the aid company hotel.

The horse finished, and he tied it to a hitching rail to rest. He strolled up the street looking for a friendly face. Someone must know where the school was or where Kate lived.

A large man stalked down the middle of the street, bellowing curses. Didn't the town have police to keep the drunks off the street? Other men hurried along next to the buildings on each side, watching the big man with tight faces. Arthur passed the drunk who had turned to accost someone on the opposite side.

A block ahead, a tall woman in a green dress strode toward him, a white bonnet perched on the back of her head. He sucked a breath. *Kate!* He rushed toward her with rapid strides until they met in front of a building advertising itself as a store.

"Hello, Kate. I'm glad I found you so soon."

"Arthur?" She blinked, and deep lines wrinkled her forehead. "What are you doing here?"

"I came to see you." The sun highlighted her brown hair, framing her face under the white bonnet.

"To see *me*? Whatever do you mean?"

He gulped, and the words he had rehearsed fled his mind. "I ... I heard about your snakebite and surgery."

She hid her hand behind her back, staring at him with round eyes. "Amelia told you?"

"Yes, she did. May I see?" Her eyes narrowed as he held out his hand. "I *am* studying to be a doctor." Though he had abandoned his apprenticeship to see her.

"Uh...yes, of course." She slowly extended her arm from behind her back.

He held her hand and turned it palm up. He traced the scars along the edge with his finger, and her hand trembled. She peered at him, her dark eyes wide. His skin tingled, and his heart thumped against his chest.

"Arthur—"

He cleared his throat and released her hand. "It has healed remarkably well."

She covered her injured hand with the other and pressed them against her stomach. "Yes, God answered my prayers. Have ... have you been in town long?"

A burn bit the pit of Arthur's stomach. She didn't appear happy to see him. "I've just arrived. I plan to stay at the aid company hotel tonight."

"I see." She studied his face.

"Have you finished school for the day?"

"No." She crossed her arms and watched the drunk man down the street. "The school has closed, at least for a time."

With the school closed, she would have time to talk with him, but she seemed cautious.

"Will you reopen it soon?"

Her chest swelled with a large breath and fell with a loud sigh. "I don't know. Parents won't send their children because it's not safe. Fights have erupted in the streets, and a rumor has spread that men will attack the town within the next two months."

He nodded. "Pro-slavery forces. I've read about the conflict in the territory, though not about this recent threat."

"Yes, ruffians come from Missouri, although we have a few of our own." She tipped her head toward the drunk, swearing at two men on the opposite side of the street.

"Ahh, I thought he was just full of liquor."

"No, full of *hate* and liquor." She licked her lips, her gaze sweeping the street in both directions before resting on him again. "Arthur, why are you here?"

"I wrote you two letters. Did you receive them?"

She brushed a strand of hair away from her cheek and tucked it under the bonnet. "I ... uh ... yes, I did."

His breath caught. "I never received your reply." His voice sounded as weak as his heart.

"I ... uh ... didn't read them."

"Oh." Her reluctance was a bad sign.

Kate's head tipped to the side, and her face softened. "You must understand. I came to Kansas, and you were in Boston. I thought you might ... propose ... and I didn't want to hurt you. I had to help defeat slavery, to fulfill my purpose."

Dryness scratched his throat. This was not what he'd planned, what he'd hoped. "May I tell you what I wrote?"

She glanced in the store window and shrugged. "I suppose since you came all this way, I should listen."

He swallowed despite his tight throat. "I implored you to return to Boston ... I love you. I asked if you would be my bride."

She gasped, her eyes wide, searching his face. "Arthur!" She darted a glance at a man inside the window with a dark mustache, her jaw trembling. She grabbed her skirt, turned, and ran back up the street.

The door opened, and the man with the mustache stepped out, a frown on his face. He turned and watched Kate. Arthur's heart sank. He had her answer.

Kate's heart pounded as she scurried up the street. Arthur wanted to marry her! She needed to think. The school building lay ahead, but she couldn't go there. She'd come from it earlier, and Dr. Robinson was in his office.

She couldn't look back as Arthur may still be in front of the store. She prayed he wouldn't speak to John. Where could she go to catch her breath, to think? *Elizabeth's*. She dashed across the street and turned onto the side street.

She didn't want to hurt Arthur. He was too good to be treated so rudely. Too good for her. Why hadn't he courted another woman after she left? Was he still pining for Dahlia so much that he traveled to Kansas to find a woman who reminded him of her?

She slowed to a stop and leaned her hands on her knees, drawing quick breaths. What would people think of her sprinting through the streets? Maybe they would think the Hungarian had started another fight. She straightened and smoothed her dress.

She strode the remaining blocks to Elizabeth's street. How long had it been since she'd visited her friend? The whitewashed house stood two stories tall, and the soddy had been removed. She mounted the two steps and knocked.

Elizabeth opened the door. "Kate, how nice—oh my! Something's wrong, isn't it? What's happened?" She took Kate's arm and drew her inside. "Are you hurt?" She pulled a chair away from the end of the dining room table. "Sit down, tell me what's happened."

Kate slumped into the chair. "I don't understand."

The room swayed as Elizabeth pulled another chair close and sat. "Kate, what is it?"

"Arthur's here."

"Your beau from Boston?"

She nodded. "He arrived this afternoon."

Elizabeth's mouth dropped open, and her eyebrows raised. "What did he say?"

"He proposed marriage to me. Right in front of the store. John was inside watching."

A squeal rose from Elizabeth. "You must be excited!"

Excited? Elizabeth didn't understand. "I'm terrified. I ran away like a little girl. They must think I'm a fool."

"What's to fear? This is wonderful! Didn't you accept his proposal?"

"How could I? Yesterday, a fight broke out in front of the store. I was knocked to the ground."

"Did they hurt you?" Elizabeth gripped her forearm, then cocked her head. "What does that have to do with his proposal?"

"Nothing. I got scraped hands and horse manure fouled my dress, but that's not all. John helped me away from the fight and said ... he was so tender as he brushed dung from my face. He said I should reconsider my decision not to marry."

Elizabeth sucked a quick breath.

"I ... I've started to think ... John didn't ask, but ..."

"Kate! He wants to propose too?" Elizabeth held her hands to her mouth, steepled like a prayer.

"That's what I think. I had planned to stop his courtship before he did, but I'm beginning to think maybe ..." She shook her head and tried to sort through her jumbled thoughts. "Mrs. Nichols—I met her at the post office—has done a great deal of good for the rights of women, even though she's married. I mean, I haven't talked about it with John, but I could continue to teach at least for a year or two. Maybe I could also, I don't know, speak for suffrage here in Kansas, maybe someday attend college."

"Two men want to marry you." Elizabeth slowly shook her head, her mouth open.

"I just don't know what to do. Maybe I was right all along and should stick to my decision to avoid marriage." A heaviness settled on her. Why had she even entertained the idea?

Elizabeth wrapped her hands around Kate's. "I've never understood you. Why would you avoid marrying Arthur or John?"

"I thought that was God's plan for my life. I want to stop slavery and lead other reforms. I didn't think marriage would work. A husband as a partner would be wonderful, but ..." She shrugged.

"Do you think only one path is God's will? Don't you think God can bless any righteous path?"

The idea made sense when her friend said it that way.

"God's plans also change or seem to. Have you read about Paul's mission journeys?"

Kate frowned. "Paul?"

"Yes, in the Bible. Paul wanted to go somewhere, Bith ... something, but God stopped him and made a way for him to go to another place."

"I don't understand. What does that have to do with me?"

"Your school is closed."

A chill settled on Kate's arms. "For a while, but as soon as I get enough parents willing to send their children, I'll teach again."

"*Or* maybe God's making a way for you to go in a different direction."

Could she be right? The snakebite had kept her in Lawrence long enough that she had become a teacher. But marriage? "You think God wants me to marry, don't you?"

Elizabeth laughed. "I don't know whether he does or not, but it is a righteous path, isn't it? Maybe he's offering you a choice to marry."

"He is?"

"Kate, two men love you!"

"They do?"

"Silly girl! Why do you think Arthur journeyed all this way? And John spends so much time with you. I see how he looks at you."

Kate's breath caught, and tears flooded her eyes. She buried her face in her hands. "Oh, Elizabeth, what have I done? I ran away."

Her friend slid from her chair and embraced her. "Nothing you can't change."

She'd known John was sweet on her, always spending time with her, his eyes seeking hers. But Arthur truly loved her? "What am I going to do?"

"Talk to them. You can choose one of them or choose to remain unmarried. Just trust God. He can bless more than one path."

Kate wrapped her arms around Elizabeth and let her tears flow. So much had happened—the school's closing, the fight, Arthur's proposal.

She lifted her head and wiped her eyes. "I should apologize to Arthur and talk to him first. He didn't just hint about marriage, he proposed. He's staying at the aid company's place."

"Would you like to stay for supper? It'd give you a chance to catch your breath and wash your face."

She sighed. "Yes, but only if you swear not to breathe a word of this to Samuel."

A smile spread across Elizabeth's face. "It'll be our secret."

39

The edge of the hard chair dug into Arthur's back, and he shifted his aching hips, turning to allow the breeze to wash across his face. Four wagons stood in front of the aid company guest tent, tongues on the ground and horses gone. They had no power to move, just like him.

Should he have waited to declare his love to Kate? She had run away. Is that why she left Boston shortly after he alluded to a future together? Did she choose Kansas to teach or to leave him? If teaching in Kansas was her dream, why hadn't she told him earlier?

"Arthur, may I speak with you?" Kate stood a few feet away, hands clasped in front of her.

He twisted and bolted to his feet. "Kate. Yes, of course. I would like very much to talk to you."

She looked at the ground. "I must apologize for the way I acted earlier. Seeing you ... you shocked me. I ...I hope your trip was good." She glanced up with a tentative smile.

He began to breathe again. "It was long enough, but no problems interrupted it. Would you like to sit here?" He gestured at the vacant chair beside his.

She glanced at the three men sitting in the other chairs. They watched them with straight faces. "No," she said. "Can we walk?"

"As you wish."

They turned and stepped past the wagons. Should he begin with his proposal or discuss something else to ease the way?

"Um ... perhaps you could show me the school where you teach."

She nodded. "I suppose that would work."

They strolled past the hotel construction, the street absent of horses and people. The evening had mellowed the temperature, and a few wisps of Kate's hair had escaped the bonnet and drifted in the wind.

He cleared his throat. "Your letter about leaving for Kansas surprised me. I thought I had offended you."

"No. Arthur, you have always been the perfect gentleman. I quite like you. It's just that I wanted to ... I needed to do something for abolition."

Warmth expanded in his chest. They had never discussed their feelings before, just the emotions of literary characters.

He drew a deep breath. "Lawrence is growing quickly."

She only nodded at his lame comment. Should he mention the book he had finished in Boston? He hadn't seen a library. Perhaps novels were not available here. She glanced at the storefront where he had proposed and bit her lip.

He remained silent, and they strolled until she stopped and gestured toward a building.

"This is where I teach. It's a public hall owned by the aid company. Perhaps a dedicated school will be built someday. Dr. Robinson—he's the aid company agent and a leader in the territory—has an office in the front corner."

"Is he the doctor who performed your surgery?"

"Yes."

"I'm so thankful you found a doctor here."

"We have more than one."

Her gaze swept the street, and he licked his lips. "Shall we continue walking?"

"Yes."

Why was he so tongue-tied? Thankfully, Frederic wasn't present. His friend would mock the awkward conversation. They walked past the remaining buildings and stopped overlooking the river flowing slowly around a sandbar.

"Kate, I'm sorry if I spoke abruptly earlier today. It has been so long, and I never heard ... I overstepped good manners. I may be doing so again, but I would like to talk about my proposal. Will you consider it?"

She crossed her arms and studied the river. "Arthur, I never thought I would marry. I want to address slavery and other evils, so I dedicated myself to abolition. I thought it was God's plan for my life."

"Is that why you left Boston so suddenly?"

She swallowed as her gaze fell to the ground. "It's part of the reason. As a woman, I can't become a politician or even vote, but I can help Kansas become a free state by teaching school. New England families want to educate their children, and my teaching helps make Kansas attractive to them."

Attractive? The wide-open country seemed hot and dry. Who would find it attractive? Yet people still flocked here to settle land to call their own. Bustling Kansas City proved that, as did the lines of wagons he had passed entering the territory.

"Couldn't you teach and work for abolition as a married woman? I know several women in Boston who support abolition. We could be a team, pulling together. I heartily approve of you teaching and working for the good of our country."

She searched his face, her lips slightly apart. "You wouldn't change your mind?"

"Never. We believe in the same things."

"Will you come to Kansas?"

He tried not to wince but couldn't stop it completely. "I left my apprenticeship to come here, but I want to return and complete it. Dr. Jackson has also encouraged me to join the staff at the hospital. He believes I will become an excellent doctor. I plan to accept his offer."

"I see." Her face fell, and she turned away.

"Kate, don't you think you could do more for abolition in Boston than in Kansas?"

Her lips tightened, but she remained silent.

"You teach a few children here, but your school has closed. People are talking about war, and violence has already started here. You mentioned a rumor that an attack on Lawrence is planned. What if they burn the school? What if they injure you? You could be safer, and you ... *we* could do more together in Boston. Marry me, and we'll make our dreams come true together."

"Oh, Arthur." A tear streaked down her cheek, and she grabbed his hands. "Your attention has delighted me, but I know the real reason I fascinate you."

Real reason?

Her face crumpled like he'd broken her heart. "You told me I remind you of her. I know you love her deeply."

His head jerked back. What was she talking about? "What did I say?"

"I remind you of Dahlia."

"You do, but—"

She choked back a sob, tears streaming down her face. "You don't love me. You love a memory." She pulled her hands from his.

He froze, his hands hanging suspended in front of him. He had loved Dahlia, but ...

He blinked away spots in his vision. "Kate, I love you. Yes, you remind me of Dahlia. You're intelligent and passionate about reform, as she was. Dahlia had been my best friend for years, but you mean more to me. I've spent the last six months thinking about you, worrying about you, missing you. I left my apprenticeship for *you*. I slept in rail cars, on steamboats, and rode a broken-down mare here because I love *you*."

She sniffed and swiped her nose with a handkerchief. "How can you love me?" She lifted her maimed hand. "I'm crippled, my face is flawed, and I'm ... I'm ... plain."

He took her hand and stroked his finger across her birthmark. "I find you beautiful."

She shivered, and her eyes widened.

"Your birthmark reminds me of a violet blossom. I like it, especially when you smile."

Her lips trembled, and he leaned forward, but stopped himself and kissed her hand. "I would be proud to have you as my wife. Will you marry me?"

Her gaze fell from his eyes, and she pulled her hand away. She turned to face the river. "I must think about it."

His stomach dropped. Didn't she understand his feelings? How long would she need? "Uh, I ... I see."

"I was anticipating ... I mean, another man has been courting me."

His mouth dried like sand. "Oh." *Another man.* His hope that she hadn't courted another had been in vain.

"John hasn't proposed as such, though he has hinted. I was considering whether I could work for abolition as a married woman before you arrived. Your proposal has ... has confronted me with that decision sooner. Since you came all this way, and you made a proposal, I wanted to talk to you first."

"When will I have your answer?"

She looked up at him. "Meet me at the school tomorrow morning at nine o'clock."

"I'll be there." He shifted his feet as she glanced back down the street, then squared his shoulders. "May I walk you home? Though you will need to show me the way." He tried to smile.

"No, I will stay here for a while. Please return to your lodging. I'll see myself home."

"Until tomorrow." He turned and walked down the street. He fought the urge to turn and wave, to see if she was watching him. But, no. It was best to continue walking.

Who was John? Did he love her, and she him? He forced his chin back to level. It could be a long ride back to Kansas City tomorrow.

40

John stood at the edge of the porch in the long shadow the morning sun cast from the house. At breakfast, Kate had asked to walk with him to the store. She'd barely spoken to him since he'd overheard the stranger propose. She missed supper and their normal evening stroll, disappearing on a long walk with Lydia, only to return at dark and head to her room.

Kate stepped through the door wearing a light blue dress printed with tiny white flowers—the one she saved for special occasions. Did she wear it for him or the other man? Maybe he could lighten her mood, and she would tell him her thoughts.

He doffed his hat and tipped his head. "An escort from such a beautiful woman makes this morning even more radiant."

A brief smile lit her face, but fine lines marked the corners of her eyes and the center of her brow. His stomach twisted. Had she asked to accompany him so she could tell him she'd accepted the stranger's proposal?

He had waited too long to propose. She had claimed she wouldn't marry, but her heart had seemed to warm toward him. Why had he waited so long?

They walked beyond earshot of the boardinghouse, and she drew a deep breath.

"John, I'm sorry that I ... I didn't speak to you last night. I assume you heard Arthur's proposal."

The back of his throat ached. "I didn't hear it all, but enough to know what he ... to know. His arrival and proposal distressed you, didn't it?"

Her cheeks colored, and she bit her lip. "Yes, seeing him shocked me."

If this other man's action had shocked her, maybe he still had a chance. "Is he the one who wrote the letter you burned?"

"Yes, Arthur courted me while I lived in Boston ... before I came to Kansas and met you."

The tightness gripping his chest eased. She had burned Arthur's letter. Had the man offended her?

John swallowed the lump in his throat and smiled. "I'm sure the last thing you expected was a proposal on the main street for all to see."

The man hadn't even knelt.

She shook her head. "His words took me by surprise. I mean, I knew he thought well of me, but ... but it happened so fast, and in the midst of everything else that has happened, I just ..."

John's heart floated. He still had a chance to win her. "You haven't decided what to tell him, have you?"

"No, I haven't. I had to ... to think about things last night and to speak with Lydia."

"I understand," he said, though he didn't. Why would she consult Lydia?

They turned down the cross street.

"Today, I want to speak to you," she said.

"To me? About his proposal?"

A smile broke across her face, almost a chuckle. "No, not his proposal. It's just that ... the other day, after the fight, you said I should reconsider my decision to remain unmarried."

"Oh." He couldn't breathe.

"I have."

His heart raced. Did that mean ... was she ... He halted and faced her as she gazed up at him with soft, brown eyes. This was his chance. He took her hand in his and knelt.

"Kate, you're the most fascinating, dedicated, and noble woman I've ever met. Will you marry me?"

Her eyes misted, and her lips trembled. "John, I enjoy your company very much. You are a kind and gentle man." A tear spilled down her cheek. "You make me smile every day. I'm honored by your proposal. Can you stand and tell me more?"

"More?" He stumbled to his feet. Did she want to hear how her brown eyes stirred his heart? About his thoughts of her cooking for him, lying next to her in bed?

She gestured down the street. "Shall we continue? We always have such pleasant conversations when we walk."

He nodded. Where was this leading?

"If I marry Arthur, we would return to Boston. What would my life be like if I married you?"

"Oh." His answer came out as a sigh. "I would cherish you every minute of every day. I want to build a life here in Lawrence and have a home, a family. I plan to own a store in the future."

"Not Ohio?"

He clasped his hands behind his back as they walked. "I'm sure I'd ... we'd visit, but I want to stay in Kansas."

"Would you allow me to continue teaching school?"

"Yes, at least for a while. I mean when ... *if* we have children—"

"I want to lead reform efforts like abolition."

He nodded. "I know, though I worry ruffians will attack you. They've done terrible things to some free-state men."

"What about suffrage? If I decide to speak out in support of a state constitution that allows women to vote ..."

"I haven't thought about that. If you want to ... I suppose you could."

She licked her lips and took a deep breath as they turned the corner onto the main street, the store only half a block away.

Arthur halted the mare and swung to the ground. He tugged the carpetbag hooked over the saddle horn, though the short ride up the main street shouldn't have loosened it. Sleep had eluded him during the night, but his every nerve tingled. He dug his watch out of his pocket—five minutes early. He hitched the horse to the rail in front of the school building and strode to the door.

He turned the cold doorknob and swung the door open, stepping into the building. On his right, a bearded man looked up from a desk in a side office and rose to his feet.

Arthur removed his top hat. "I'm here to see Miss Collins."

"I haven't seen her today. Since school is closed, I don't know whether she will be here today."

The brim of his hat crumpled in Arthur's grip. "She asked me to meet her here."

"You're welcome to wait in the hall."

"Thank you. I'll wait outside."

She wouldn't avoid him after promising to meet, would she? No, he was just early. He walked to the mare and checked the halter. The bulging carpetbag felt rough on his palm. Had he repacked everything? He could check, but he'd already done so three times.

If Kate rejected him, he would ride toward Kansas City. He might make it there by dark, or he could stop at the mission again. Would she deliver a firm decision, or would he get a chance to answer any concerns?

A block away, Kate and a man with a dark mustache wearing a bowler hat turned onto the street and strolled toward him. She wore a light blue dress. They stopped at the spot where he had proposed. The spot where she had *run* from his proposal. The man with her must be John, the man who had stepped out of the store yesterday.

Arthur watched as John gathered her hands into his and held them while she gazed up at him. John kissed her hands, then turned and entered the store. Arthur's mouth soured, and he struggled to breathe against a dead weight in his chest.

Kate held her breath as the door closed behind John. Thank God she had spoken to Lydia, who had agreed with Elizabeth—God could bless any righteous choice. When Kate had asked Lydia how to choose, she had embraced her and whispered one word, "Pray." Kate had paced her room half the night without a decision before collapsing in sleep.

But her morning walk with John had brought clarity like the sun in a clear sky. John and Arthur both loved her. Either could be a gentle, loving husband.

She turned and ambled toward the school.

Arthur stepped from behind a paint horse and waited by the school door, his top hat making him appear tall. A tingle jolted through her like lightning. She walked toward her future husband! She clasped her hands and held them against her stomach. If only she carried flowers.

Though both men loved her, Arthur was her choice. He shared a passion for literature and reform with her. He was right—she would accomplish more for abolition in Boston than waiting for peace in Kansas. She knew not how she would impact abolition, but she would find a way with Arthur.

He stood so stiff and serious. How would he react when she told him? She caught a quick breath. Why not surprise him? She clamped her lips tight and fought the smile tugging at her mouth, stopping in front of him. He gazed into her eyes, and a squeal almost escaped. She stared at his boots.

"Good morning, Kate."

He didn't ask for her decision, even though he must be dying to know. She cleared her throat. "Let's step inside."

He stepped to the door, opened it, and removed his hat. She stepped through, and he followed as she marched to Dr. Robinson's desk. The doctor rose.

"Good morning, Miss Collins. I see your acquaintance has found you."

Arthur stepped into the office beside her, and she gestured at him. "Dr. Robinson, I would like to introduce you to Arthur Eliot of

Boston." As they shook hands, she said, "I must resign as a teacher for the Lawrence school because I have accepted Arthur's proposal of marriage."

Arthur's mouth dropped open. "You have?"

Dr. Robinson's eyebrows arched, and she laughed. "Yes, Arthur, I have ... I do."

A grin burst across his face as he turned toward her, dropping his hat. His hands clasped her shoulders. "I thought ... I wasn't ... I'm so delighted!"

She wrapped her arms around him in a tight embrace and pressed her cheek over his heart. "I am too!"

She broke the hug, warmth flooding her face. Arthur shook his head and blinked. "Why did you choose me, Kate?"

"Because I love you. We're a perfect match."

"Congratulations!" Dr. Robinson beamed and offered his hand to Arthur, who pumped it several times.

Kate filled her lungs. "Dr. Robinson, I brought a few of my own books to Kansas. They're in the trunk in the hall. I want to donate them to the school. Hopefully, the school can continue at some point in the future."

"Thank you. I wish you and Mr. Eliot a long and happy marriage." He scooped up Arthur's hat, dusted it, and handed it to him. They all laughed.

As Arthur said goodbye to the doctor, her eyes filled with tears. When he took her elbow and guided her out of the building, her feet barely touched the ground.

"I guess we need to determine how to travel to Kansas City. I don't think this old nag will do." He chuckled and placed his hat on his head with a tap. "I'll find a wagon or a carriage here, though I don't know where. Will you be ready to travel tomorrow?"

"I'm sure we'll find something." She laughed and wiped her eyes as he unhitched the horse. "Arthur, may I ask you something?"

"Yes, of course."

"I know your family will expect a large wedding, and my mother will as well, but can we get married here in Lawrence ... now?"

His brow crinkled. "Today? You don't want to wait?"

She giggled. "Why not today? I have a good friend here, Elizabeth, and I want her to stand with me. Her husband, Samuel, could stand with you. A small wedding suits me fine."

How could she wait through weeks of uncertain travel and preparations? She couldn't risk anything ruining this dream. She wrapped her hands around Arthur's arm and pulled herself close.

"We could leave for Kansas City after our wedding. Our trip to Boston would be our honeymoon."

Color flushed his cheeks as his brown eyes gazed deep into hers. "Anything you want, my dear."

Her heartbeat sped, and a shiver ran across her shoulders. "Let's find that wagon."

John slumped into the porch chair as the sun dipped behind the houses across the street. The faint rap of hammers drifted from the south as someone worked into the evening. The town had grown over the summer as more people arrived and more houses were built. Everything had changed, not just Lawrence.

At the start of the year, he had been engaged to Susanna, but she had run off with another man. He had left Ohio for Kansas with a deep ache in his soul, but he had survived, even thrived. He shook his head. Knowing Kate had eased that ache for a while.

Should he have waited longer before courting her? He could have listened to her warning that she planned to avoid marriage. He huffed. She had avoided marriage to him, though not to Arthur. Had she loved the man all along? If so, why did she burn his letter?

At least she hadn't betrayed him like Susanna did. Still, if Arthur hadn't arrived, would she have married him? His shoulders drooped under a heaviness like a hundred-pound sack of seed. He'd seen her through the store window, riding beside Arthur in a wagon. They had left town by the time he had returned to the boardinghouse for supper.

Martha stepped onto the porch. "May I sit here?" She pointed at the chair beside him—the one where Kate used to sit.

He straightened in his chair. Martha had *asked* instead of taking the seat and starting to talk. This surely was a strange day.

"Yes, please do."

"I can't believe she left so suddenly. You must feel terrible." She gazed at him, her face soft, eyebrows drawn together.

"I do, but it could've been worse." The pain was not as deep as Susanna's betrayal.

"What will you do now?" Her big blue eyes searched his, her usual coy smile absent from her flawless face.

He drew a breath. "I wish them well." What else could he do? He'd never get answers to his questions. "Tomorrow, I'll go to the store like every other day."

"Perhaps we can walk together after our work tomorrow."

John looked into Martha's blue eyes. She seemed quieter now, more ... demure.

"Perhaps."

Follow Elmer Fuller's writing at: www.elmerfuller.com

The prequel to this book, *Dreams in Conflict*, is available as a free download in PDF or e-book format at the website.

Author's Notes

As a writer, I strive to craft stories of fictional characters amid the events and characters who shaped history. Kate Collins is a fictional character inspired by Kate Kellogg, a woman who arrived in the Kansas Territory in March of 1855 as a member of a party led by the New England Emigrant Aid Company.

Only a few facts are recorded about Kellogg. She was the second teacher in Lawrence, teaching for three months in the aid company building during the summer of 1855 before she returned to Massachusetts and married a physician.

These scant details about Kellogg provided the inspiration for this story, but the remainder of the events experienced by my character—the snakebite, surgery, job search, and romance—are figments of my imagination. So are John Whaley, Arthur Eliot, and Martha Groot.

However, many of the other characters in the book were inspired by actual people. The best known are Dr. Charles and Sara Robinson, who were critical to the early history of Kansas and are described in many sources. Sara's book *Kansas: Its Interior and Exterior Life* was valuable in understanding many of the events in Lawrence, including the July Fourth celebration and the violence in the streets during that summer. I did not exhaust the research available on the Robinsons and hope I have portrayed them well.

Clarissa Hurd, her sons, and Lydia Hall are based on names found in the sources I consulted. The Hurd and Hall boardinghouse existed, though I did not find descriptions of it. Lydia Hall did teach at a mission school for the Choctaw before coming to Lawrence. Other historical characters include Samuel Kimball, who leased the sawmill in 1855 with his brother, and Clarina Nichols, a reformer who settled in Kansas.

I hope that Kate's story entertained you with a young woman's desire to serve God by doing good amid the challenges and passions that stirred the early settlers of Kansas.

Acknowledgements

Crafting a novel and shepherding it to publication is a fun and glorious task, but it requires a tremendous amount of work. I would never have accomplished it without a supporting cast. I must recognize my friend, bestselling and award-winning author, Johnnie Alexander, who encouraged me and recommended resources when I asked her questions about writing a novel. She even critiqued the first five pages of my first effort (though not this story) and introduced me to the mantra that guides many authors: show, don't tell.

My writing has also improved thanks to my critique partners, Shannon Skaer and Gwen Gage, who read chapters each week and suggested improvements. The American Christian Fiction Writers (ACFW) online critique group also reviewed several early chapters. I also benefited from workshops and contests sponsored by the ACFW.

Every story needs a good editor. Sue Fairchild provided the substantive and line edits that smoothed this novel into its final form. The cover was designed by Diane Turpin. It was a pleasure to work with both of them.

The Kansas State Historical Society made my research much easier, thanks to their online archives. Many people have scanned and transcribed documents and photos over the years to create it. I've used it extensively and appreciate the people who have contributed to the archive.

Last, I must recognize the most important person—the woman who always cheers for me, my wife, Elaine. She allows me to disappear into my office for hours and walk around with my head lost in time. She proofreads manuscripts and newsletters, discusses story ideas, and blesses my world.

Discussion Questions

1. If you could travel back to 1855 and join Kate on her journey, what would you want to experience or ask her?

2. The story is set in 1855, a time of great change in America. How does the historical backdrop (e.g., abolition, women's rights, westward expansion) shape Kate's experiences and decisions?

3. Clarina Nichols talks about balancing activism, marriage, and motherhood. Do you think this is still a challenge for women today? How do you think society's expectations of women have—or haven't—changed since the 1850s?

4. Kate loves books and libraries. How do you think her love of reading influences her worldview? Do you think books play a similar role in shaping people's lives today?

5. Kate meets Clarina Nichols, a real-life advocate for women's rights. How does this encounter impact Kate? Do you think meeting someone like Clarina would have been life-changing for a young woman in that era?

6. Kate and Elizabeth seem to have a close friendship. What do you think draws them together? How does their relationship reflect the challenges and joys of female friendships in the 19th century?

7. Martha makes a veiled insult about Kate's birthmark. How do you think Kate handles this kind of criticism? Would you have reacted differently?

8. Lydia tells Kate, "That's what faith is—trusting God even though we don't understand everything." Do you agree with

this definition of faith? How do you think Kate's faith (or lack thereof) influences her decisions?

9. Kate debates whether to attend church, saying, "It is a day of rest after all." Do you think she's justified in skipping church, or is she avoiding something important? How do you balance rest and responsibility in your own life?

10. Elizabeth tells Kate, "Do you think only one path is God's will? Don't you think God can bless any righteous path?" Is it easier to make decisions with this belief or the belief that only one choice is God's will? Why or why not?

Selected Bibliography

"A Physician Putting Too Much Confidence in His Own Medicine." *The Kanzas News (Emporia, Kan.)*, October 31, 1857. https://www.loc.gov/resource/sn85030219/1857-10-31/ed-1/?sp=3

Barry, Louise. "The New England Emigrant Aid Company Parties of 1855." *Kansas Historical Quarterly*, 12, no. 3 (1943): 227-268. https://www.kansashistory.gov/p/the-new-england-emigrant-aid-company-parties-of-1855/16887

Cordley, Richard, D.D. *Pioneer Days in Kansas*. New York, Boston, Chicago: The Pilgrim Press, 1903. https://www.kancoll.org/books/cordley_pioneer/cordley.00.html

Cutler, William G. *History of the State of Kansas*. Chicago: A. T. Andreas, 1883. https://kancoll.org/books/cutler/

Encyclopedia.com. "The Birth-Mark." American History Through Literature 1820-1870. February 11, 2025. https://www.encyclopedia.com/arts/culture-magazines/birth-mark

Federal Writer's Project. "History of Education in Kansas." Kansas State History. Accessed July 3, 2024. https://www.kspatriot.org/index.php/articles/55-education/238-history-of-education-in-kansas.html

Gambone, Joseph G., editor. "The Forgotten Feminist of Kansas, 1: The Papers of Clarina I. H. Nichols, 1854-1855." *Kansas Historical Quarterly*, 39, no. 1 (1973): 12-57. https://www.kansashistory.gov/p/the-forgotten-feminist-of-kansas-1/13232

Harvard University. "Thirtieth Annual Report of the President of Harvard College to the Overseers, Exhibiting the State of the Institution for the Academic Year 1854-55." December 21, 1855. https://iiif.lib.harvard.edu/manifests/view/drs:427074891$37i

"How were rattlesnake bites treated in the 1800's?" Quora. Accessed July 3, 2024. https://www.quora.com/How-were-rattlesnake-bites-treated-in-the-1800s

Keating, Deborah. "Robinson, Sara Tappan Doolittle Lawrence." Kansas City Public Library: Civil War on the Western Border, The Missouri-Kansas Conflict, 1854-1865. Accessed July 23, 2024. https://civilwaronthewesternborder.org/encyclopedia/robinson-sara-tappan-doolittle-lawrence

Kansas Historical Society. "Sara Lawrence Robinson." Kansapedia. Last modified January 2016. https://www.kansashistory.gov/kansapedia/sara-lawrence-robinson/16901

Lowell Stories: Women's History. "Lydia Sears Hall (1816-1890)" University of Massachusetts Lowell Library. Last updated January 31, 2025. https://libguides.uml.edu/c.php?g=1127566&p=8964601

Mahr, Michael. "Medical Education in the 19th Century." National Museum of Civil War Medicine. Created December 18, 2023. https://www.civilwarmed.org/medical-education-in-the-19th-century/

Malin, James C. "Emergency Housing at Lawrence, 1854." *Kansas Historical Quarterly*, 21, no. 1 (1954): 34-49. https://www.kansashistory.gov/p/emergency-housing-at-lawrence-1854/13103

Malin, James C. "Housing Experiments in the Lawrence Community, 1855." *Kansas Historical Quarterly*, 21, no.

2 (1954): 95-121. https://www.kansashistory.gov/p/housing-experiments-in-the-lawrence-community-1855/13105

Matthews, Kellianne. "Discover the 4 Types of Rattlesnakes in Kansas." A-Z Animals. Last modified June 25, 2023. https://a-z-animals.com/blog/discover-the-4-types-of-rattlesnakes-in-kansas/

Harvard Medical School. "History of Harvard Medicine." Medical Education Student Handbook. Last updated July 30, 2018. https://medstudenthandbook.hms.harvard.edu/history-harvard-medicine

Nichols, H. "Lawrence Eating Salon." *The Herald of Freedom*, July 7, 1855. https://www.loc.gov/resource/sn82006863/1855-07-07/ed-1/?sp=1

Peterson, John M., editor. "Letters of Edward and Sarah Fitch, Lawrence Kansas, 1855-1863, Part I." *Kansas History: A Journal of the Central Plains*, 12, no. 1 (1989): 48-70. https://www.kshs.org/publicat/history/1989spring_peterson.pdf

Robinson, Sara T. L. *Kansas; Its Interior and Exterior Life.* Boston: Crosby, Nichols and Company; Cincinnati: G. S. Blanchard, 1857. https://archive.org/details/kansasitsinterio02robi/page/n7/mode/2up

Wikimedia Foundation. "Harvard Medical School." Wikipedia. Last updated February 15, 2025, at 15:00 (UTC). https://en.wikipedia.org/wiki/Harvard_Medical_School